EVERYDAY PEOPLE

Also by the author

FICTION
A Prayer for the Dying
A World Away
The Speed Queen
The Names of the Dead
Snow Angels
In the Walled City

NONFICTION
The Circus Fire

AS EDITOR
The Vietnam Reader
On Writers and Writing, by John Gardner

EVERYDAY PEOPLE

STEWART O'NAN

Grove Press
New York

"Good Morning, Heartache" appeared in slightly different form in *Glimmertrain*.

Published simultaneously in Canada
Printed in the United States of America

FIRST EDITION

Library of Congress Cataloging-in-Publication Data
O'Nan, Stewart, 1961–
 Everyday people / Stewart O'Nan.
  p. cm.
 ISBN 0-8021-1681-7
 1. East Liberty (Pittsburgh, Pa.)—Fiction. 2. Afro-American neighborhoods
—Fiction. 3. Afro-American teenage boys—Fiction. 4. Accident victims—
Fiction. 5. Pittsburgh (Pa.)—Fiction. 6. Afro-Americans—Fiction.
7. Paralytics—Fiction. I. Title.
PS3565.N316 E94 2001
813'.54—dc21   00-049052

Design by Laura Hammond Hough

Grove Press
841 Broadway
New York, NY 10003

01 02 03 04 10 9 8 7 6 5 4 3 2 1

For John Edgar Wideman

There is the sorrow of blackmen
Lost in cities. But who can conceive
Of cities lost in a blackman?

RAYMOND PATTERSON

Love me
love me love me
say you do.

NINA SIMONE

iNBOUND

EAST LIBERTY DOESN'T need the Martin Robinson Express Busway. It's for the commuters who come in every day from Penn Hills and sit in front, hiding behind their *Post-Gazette*s, their briefcases balanced across their knees. When you get on, their eyes brush up against you, then dart off like scared little fish. They might notice your suit is just as fine as theirs—probably even more styling—but then they look away, and you aren't there anymore. No one saying a mumbling word. Seats all taken like they got on in twos, driver switched them in like a herd of turkeys can't think a lick for themselves. Goddamn. 1998, and you're back in the back of the bus, seats underneath you hot from the big diesel, lump of nasty duct tape grabbing at your slacks.

What East Liberty wanted was a new community center with a clinic. The old one's small and falling apart and just lost its funding. What we need is a good clean place to take the babies, some after-school programs for the young people. But that got voted down in city council. The ballots

fell by color lines, paper said—not a surprise, especially the
way they said it. A Black thing, all your fault, like you were
asking for something no one else has. It was predictable,
that's the sad thing; even the good Jewish liberals in Squirrel Hill are pinching their pennies these days. Taxes this and
welfare that, like they gonna starve or something. Let's not
even talk about them simple crackers out past that.

There still had to be some way to get some money into
the community. That must have been what Martin Robinson
was thinking. You voted for him—have your whole life—
so who are you supposed to blame? And the money would
come in. Half the contracts were supposed to go to local
businesses, and Martin made sure that happened. That's the
good news.

The bad news is that the Martin Robinson Express
Busway basically stops all traffic—white and black and
otherwise—from coming through the business district. The
way the city council and their planners drew up the project,
the busway effectively cuts East Liberty off from the rest
of Pittsburgh. State money but they made a deal, took his
own bill out of Martin's hands. Two busy bridges had to go
(crowds gathered to count down the perfect explosions),
and South Highland had to be rerouted around the business district (meaning the dead Sears there, you understand). So if you ever wanted whitefolks to leave you alone,
you ought to be happy now.

Probably would be if it wasn't for the money. And the
services too, you know. It'll take that much longer for an
ambulance to get over here, and you think that's a mistake?

Fire engine, police when you need them, gas and electric in winter.

And then they name the thing after him. Good man, Martin Robinson, not one of those sorry-ass Al Sharpton, greasy-hair-wearing, no 'count jackleg preachers with five Cadillacs and ten rings on his fingers and twenty lawyers playing games. Martin's got thirty years in the state house, might be the best man to come out of East Liberty, definitely the one who's done the most for the people. Come up on Spofford, regular people, raised right. You ask Miss Fisk, she'll tell you. Old Mayor Barr who called out the Guard on us in '67, he got a tunnel named after him, and Dick Caligiuri, the poor man who died of that terrible disease, he got the county courthouse. Martin Robinson deserves the new stadium, or maybe that community center we need, something positive, not some raggedy-ass busway. It's plain disrespectful.

Thing has been bad luck from the jump. Martin passed this bill so they had to build walkways over top it so the kids can still get to the park. City council said they had to be covered so no one could throw nothing at the buses — concrete blocks or whatever. While they were building them, at night the kids would climb up there and spraypaint their names. It was a game with them. I'm not saying it's right, but kids will do that kind of mess, that's just the way they are. What happens is one night these two youngbloods get up there in the dark and everything half built and something goes wrong, way wrong, and it ends up they fall off, right smack down in the middle of the busway, and one of them dies. Miss Fisk's grandson, it was, so it hit everybody the way something like that does. Seventeen years old. Other child ends up in a wheelchair, for life they say. Another young black prince. Just a little blip in the paper, not even on TV.

And that's nobody's fault, I'm not saying that, but damn, it seems like that kind of thing happens around here all the time. Here's two kids who just needed a place to do their thing, and we don't get that, so there they go doing something foolish and it all turns out wrong.

I don't know, I just don't see the dedication of this busway as something to celebrate. I understand everyone wants to represent, you know, and show love for Martin. I got more love for Martin than anybody, but all this drama, I don't know. The thing's a month away. It's like those people get all excited about Christmas when it's not even Halloween.

I understand. It's a big day for East Liberty, all the TV stations will be here. Put a good face on. I'll be there, you know I will, cuz, but I'm just being straight with you, it's not all gravy, this thing. Everything comes with a price, and too many times that price is us. I'm getting real tired of paying it, know what I'm saying?

GOOD KiRK, EViL KiRK

GETS DARK, CREST unplugs his chair and heads outside. Been charging all day, both him *and* Brother Sony. Got to, you know? It's Wednesday, and everyone comes around for *Voyager.* Captain Janeway and shit. Got that voice like she always got a cold.

"Mr. Tupac," Bean used to say, "beam us out this motherfucker." Someone chasing them, Bean used to crack Crest up so bad it'd be killing him to run. Lungs busting like they're doing nitrous, dizzy whip-cream hits. Bunch of one-fifty-nine Krylons dinging in his pack, some Poindexter pocket-protector brother in a lumberyard apron chasing them cause they tagged the back of the fence by the busway. CREST in six-foot wildstyle, BEAN and his crazy Egyptian shit waking up the Bradys rolling in from Penn Hills. Look up from the *Post-Gazette* and get it right in their sleepy white eye before they can make downtown and pretend East Liberty doesn't exist. *Woo-hah, I got you all in check*. Yeah.

And speaking of sleeping, there's Pops crashed on the couch in front of some white-chick comedy on NBC—Suzie in the City or some shit, where they're all rich and skinny, which Pops definitely isn't—all the time smelling like a whole truckload of Ritz Bits and Chips Ahoy, like a time card and hard work over Nabisco, barn door open, hands in his pants like he's trying to hold down his pitiful old Jurassic Park jimmy in his sleep. Sure ain't *my* fucking problem, Crest thinks, and sees Vanessa getting dressed and leaving that last time, hauling on her bra, giving up on him, then can't stop Moms from breaking in, throwing the spoon from her ice cream at Pops the other night.

"Why are you here?" she's screaming. "Why don't you just go then?"

And Pops saying nothing, taking his paper out on the stoop, sitting there monking, smoking his stogie and going through the batting averages till she went to bed. Now she's out, working at Mellon Bank downtown in the checkroom, counting other people's money. The place is quiet but it's a quiet he doesn't like. It'll all change when she gets home at eleven. Pops will hang in for a while, then say he's taking a walk like he's afraid of her. Crest doesn't want to think what that means about him and Vanessa. The doctor says there's nothing physically wrong, that everything should work like before. Yeah, well you fucking try it then. He goes out in the hall and rolls sideways up to the elevator so he can reach the button. A lot of being in the chair is just waiting around.

The dude that chased them that time, skinny yellow buckethead dude, freckles all over his nose. Was it just bombing or were they on a mission, some interplanetary shit, putting up one of their boys? NOT FORGOTTEN. They did a big one with everyone from East Liberty: Baconman, T-Pop, Marcus. It's hard to tell now, Crest so mellow doing his two painkillers three times a day all week long, world without end amen. That's how the summer got past him so fast—laid back coasting with U's big fan going over him, Brother Sony bringing all of Hollywood, even free pay-per-view. September now, everyone back in school, the block quiet all day, fall coming on. Not many more nights like this, and he'll miss it.

That was some running. Old Poindexter boy musta run track at Peabody. Crest kept looking back thinking they were free but that orange apron just kept on coming. Cooking past the old Original Hot Dog with its dead windows soaped, number on it no one ever gonna call, all those famous pictures inside gone—dead John F. Kennedy, dead Martin Luther King eating black-and-white all-beef weenies, shaking hands with some Greek dude in a pussy hat like Smooth used to wear when he worked there. Booking past the post office with its barbwire and its rows of old Jeeps, good target practice on a Friday night behind a 40 of Eight-Ball, lobbing up chunks of old Simonton Street, falling out when metal went cronk or—Kordell looking deep!—glass smashed. Hit the fence where Fats broke out the wire cutters and it rings the way a chain net drains a swish, past the busted-up garages no one's stupid enough to use, and finally Mr. Stockboy from over Homewood can't keep up, doesn't know the back alleys, the yards and their dogs, sounding like they're hungry for some nice juicy booty. Back on the block Bean's capping on him. "Crest, you slower than dirt and uglier than Patrick Ewing." Crest just trying to get his breath, throat like a washboard. Never could run for shit — or bunt; no infield hits — thrown out at home so many times he can't remember. One hop and the catcher stick that mitt up your nose so you smell it all the way home. But Bean, now my boy could scoot.

Yeah, Bean.

Not forgotten. That's right, Crest thinks, ever get a chance I'ma do one for you.

Yeah, boy, right on the bridge. Right there, big as old BooBoo's up on the water tower — stupid big, somewhere everyone gonna peep it.

But just as he's dreaming this the elevator comes and goddamn if it's not one inch too high — fucking Mr. Linney, I'll kick his dumb ugly ass he don't fix this — and he has to try three times before he rolls over the bump, arms burning like when he's lifting in rehab, veins sticking out like highways. Makes him sweat, and he wanted to look good tonight. *Voyager*, everybody be there, maybe even Vanessa come back to say she's sorry, she's wrong. He'd like to see Rashaan. Why lie — he'd like to see Vanessa give him another try, let him forget about the chair a little bit, just for one minute. Be a man. When she put that bra on, there was nowhere to look but the floor, and he felt beaten, couldn't hardly breathe. He seriously thought right then about giving it up, going permanently on the injured reserve, just locking the bathroom door and scarfing down the whole bottle. He's still not sure.

But there's nothing wrong, the doctor says. In your head, that's where it's at.

Punches a button. Panel's all scratched up, spots of gum on the floor. Bean liked grape, used to blow bubbles so the whole bus smelled.

BEAN. Where would he throw it up? Kenny already did a piece on the bridge for both of them, like Crest is dead. Weak shit too, an easy hit, belt-high. He ought to get up there and cross that five-and-ten-cent clown out, slash that shit bigtime. *I'm alive,* that's what it'd say.

"Shit," Crest says, alone and going down, the cables singing like knives. "Fucking fly first."

He looks up at the light, round as an angel's halo, the halide sun above an operating table. Nothing wrong.

Yeah, Bean, beam me out this motherfucker.

Elevator hits bottom and the door rolls open, but there's no one to hold it. Never long enough, and he's got to fight it, rubber part banging against his wheel grip, door jumping back and then bumping him again, stupid fucking thing.

"Hold up," U says, "I got you," and stops it with one hand holding his Bible, all dog-eared and full of Post-it notes. He's got his hearing suit on cause he's just coming back from his meeting. Shoes with tassels like little leather flowers, handkerchief in his pocket making three sails, clipper ship. Since he's been out he wants everyone to call him Eugene, like he's different now. And he is, Crest thinks. He once saw U thump on Nene with an aluminum bat. Put a dent in it so it hit funny, and Nene was one of his boys, his partner even. It made Crest proud, U being crazy like that; all the way growing up, it kept him protected. When it was just letters, Crest could make fun of the Jesus stuff. Now that U's out,

Crest doesn't know how to talk to him. It's like they say, God will mess a brother up.

"U," Crest says, and thanks him with a nod.

"S'all right. Voyager tonight, right?" U says it like he's proud he remembered.

"You coming down?"

"Gotta hit it." He pats his Bible and gets in. "I'll come down round ten and check you out."

"Yeah, all right," Crest says, busting, cause he never does.

And it's like being transported, U pushes a button and he's gone, the motor going in the basement, all that grease covered with dust fuzz. Mr. Linney probably got his door locked, playing his 78s, pretending Mrs. Linney isn't dead. A couple years ago, he and Bean saw Mr. Linney dancing with himself, shuffling around, one hand in the air, singing Darling this, Baby that. Everyone's so fucked up around here.

"You oughta know," Crest says.

Outside a few earlybirds are parked on the stoop, couple of shorties riding their bikes under the streetlight. Across Spofford, two dudes are leaning against the fence, just hanging, splitting a Kool like a J the way he and Bean used to do. Used to, like U knocking Pops through the screen door that time, calling him a Tom. Crest shakes it off; all this memory shit isn't good for him. It's been six months, only two since he's been home. U's been out three, even got a job over Baierl Chevrolet, detailing. Puts on his jumpsuit every morning like he's in the Marines, makes a peanut butter sandwich for lunch, stocks up on the free Wheat

Thins Pops brings home Friday night. He's clean, he goes to his meetings. Done is done, Moms always says. Pick it up, clean it up, don't do it again.

A lighter sparks across Spofford and he can see it's just Little Nene and Cardell, probably waiting on him, blunting up before they blast off into space. Warp factor five, Mr. Sulu.

Yeah, it's a good crowd. He can see a clump of girls in front of Miss Fisk's, huddled so no one can scope them. Not Vanessa, none of them that tall yet. He gets up some speed and hits the door. At least Mr. Linney got the ramp right. Ones down Liberty Center so steep they shoot you out in the middle of traffic, bus run your ass down.

Everyone's waiting for him; even the girls turn.

"Showtime!" one of the shorties calls, doing a goofy Dick Vitale. They stick their bikes against the fence.

"Crest," they say, "c'mon, man, get that thing on!"

Little Nene and Cardell come wandering across the street like they don't care if they're late. Little knuckleheads fronting hard, want to build up some respect. Two years behind him at Peabody. Got to be sixteen now, both of them shaving every day. Crest used to kick their nappy asses once a week, not bad, just slap-boxing, give them a taste of what's waiting. Since the bridge, they still mess with him, but careful like. He used to groove on playing Little Nene, pop him hard and watch his eyes go psycho. Cardell's always been stronger, but he ain't half as crazy as Little Nene; Little Nene, he'll take his licks and give some back, but he'll never thump like his brother Nene. That's all used to, like eveything else. Now they think they're being respectful and take it easy on him. "Bring it on, suckas," Crest says, but it's just sissy taps, then they dance out of range and profile some styling footwork, show him their new moves. Not little dudes no more. Men.

What is *he* now?

Nothing.

Fucked up, that's what.

Crowd's waiting, and Crest backs into the corner so the door can't hit him. Hooks up Brother Sony to the juice and reaches under the ivy, spiderwebs grabbing at his hand—and there's the cable, spliced right off the box. He tips the set and plugs the jack in, clicks the knob where he wants it. Brother Sony has a plastic kickstand, and he flips it out and rests the set on top of the wall so everyone on the steps has a good seat. One last look at everyone looking up at him, and—ignition.

It's a golf course, late in the day, that Hennessy kind of light over a putting green. A bunch of old white people are shoving their clubs in the trunk of a huge Buick, all happy like they won something. "Aw, man," Cardell says, disgusted, "I don't want to have to see these old ghosts. I get enough of this shit in real life, you know what I'm saying?" Everyone agrees, an *mmm-hmmm* like church. There's a clubhouse behind the old folks, ivy-covered, and Crest thinks of when he used to do dishes at the University Club, the thick plates that held the heat from the machine so you had to wear cotton gloves to put them away. Used to cash his check Fridays and take Vanessa out to Isaly's, chip-chop ham and whitehouse ice cream. It looks like fall there, a few leaves on the green. It's a bank commercial, how rich you'll get if you give them your money. When Moms comes home from work she's got a dozen gumbands around her wrist, the rubber dirty with black streaks.

"Pump it up," Little Nene calls from the back, but Crest waits. Someone has a box of Better Cheddars—another father working day shift at Nabisco—and they break it out, pass it around, people filling their laps. The commercials are louder, and when *Voyager* comes on he adjusts it. They go right into the show, no credits, no nothing, and there's B'Elanna Torres with her old rhinoceros-looking head, and googly old white boy Tom Paris, phasers out, in some cave made of fake rocks; it's your basic away-team thing. Better believe someone's going to get fucked up.

This spirit thing appears, green and see-through, kind of a ghost, but the music lets you know it isn't. It circles around them like it's interested. The two of them don't move; it's like a *Star Trek* rule: Just stand there.

"Run!" Janelle French calls.

"Where they gonna run?" Cardell says.

"I don't know," Janelle says, "just run!"

"I'm not picking up any readings," B'Elanna says, and then—*whoosh*—the thing shoots into Tom Paris. His face changes like he ate something he's not too sure of, like he's going to throw up. The music gets loud, then goes soft, then ends. All of a sudden Tom's better.

"Tom!" B'Elanna calls, and runs over to him. She goes to touch him but doesn't. Everyone knows they're gonna make it one of these shows, girl just doesn't know what she wants. Crest always thinks it's like him and Vanessa, you know, just meant to be, no sense denying it. But V needs a man. She never says, but Crest understands. The doctor says it makes no sense, he should retain full feeling—that's the way he says it too, all official, like Crest can't do this. Fuck, he wanted to say, and make it plain: it doesn't fucking work. *He* doesn't fucking work. Vanessa tried twice. She cried the first time; the second time she just let go and looked at him all cold, like it was his fault.

"Are you okay?" B'Elanna asks.

"I think so," Tom Paris says, rubbing his head and looking googly as ever, like he doesn't even know the thing's in him. B'Elanna calls Captain Janeway to beam them up, and as they're being transported, you can see the green shape inside Tom's body.

"Aw, *man!*" Little Nene says. "Cuz is in for some serious shit."

"Thing went right down his mouth," Cardell says, and the two of them act it out, clowning, the girls laughing at them.

Crest has already seen this episode, it's a repeat. The new season doesn't start till next week, but no one complains, it's still fun. This might be the last nice night, and school's kicking in, homework, part-time jobs. Pretty soon he'll be back in his room, just him and Brother Sony. But not yet, not yet.

The green thing is the last of its species and won't leave Tom. The Prime Directive kicks in and The Doctor has to figure something out. Crest sits there watching, laughing when everyone else does, going quiet when The Doctor opens Tom's lips wide with this steel thing and shines a light. And then, of course, a commercial.

All day he's been waiting to be with someone, just lying in bed while the buses and rush hour went by, watching talk shows, then getting up and eating lunch with the noon news. Drive-by on The Hill, Pirates still three-and-a-half behind the Astros. All afternoon he let the set charge, listening as the school buses dropped the little kids off, and then the music of cartoons from the other apartments. Moms came home long enough to make supper, then left before Pops and U drove up, both of them too tired to give a shit. They ate at the table but it was just chowing down, pass this, pass that. No one asks, "What did you do today?"

I laid up in my crib and boomed the new Wu Tang, same jam over and over.

I drank all the red Kool-Aid and then emptied out my bag cause it was getting full.

I watched TV.

No one wants to hear that shit. Fuck, Crest thinks, *I* don't want to hear that shit.

"Going to your meeting?" Pops asked like every night, and like every night, U said, "If that's all right."

"It's fine with me."

"Me too," Crest said.

"You oughta come. You'd be surprised, some of the people you meet."

"z'at right?"

"'member Pooh Bear? He comes."

"That roly-poly bitch? I thought he got shot."

"He did. Now he's a deacon over St. James in Highland Park."

"Get on."

"Remember Guy Collins?"

"Now I know you frontin'. Guy Collins's name is Malik. I know cause his cousin Anthony told me."

"That's when he was inside. When he came out he changed back. He's married to that gal Florence now, they come twice a week. I'm telling you, you'd be surprised; it's not like Sister Payne's old-biddy prayer circle. It might be just what you need." He was really selling it, his eyes shining, his ham just lying there in its juice. "We got a ramp and everything."

"That's all right," Crest said.

"Door's always open." He said it like Reverend Skinner, like he owned the whole place, and all Crest could think of was the day U brought home Brother Sony, still in the box. He and Fats and Big Nene had busted into a truck over behind Sears. Used to be like that all the time—full of surprises.

After U went to put on his suit, Pops leaned across and said not to take it personal. "He's just a little excited right now. Remember, he was away a long time."

"I know," Crest said, thinking: What about me, how long was I gone?

Now The Doctor leans over Tom Paris's mouth again, this time with a steel test-tube thing, and one of the girls squeals, "Don't be doing that, fool!"

There's a blast of green light—"Here we go," Cardell says—and when the picture comes back, The Doctor's still looking, Tom's still got his mouth open.

The Doctor straightens up, stiff like always. "I think we've succeeded." He holds up the test tube, all smug. Inside it, a green light shines.

They're going to try to clone it, see if they can get it to reproduce so it won't go extinct.

"Now that's just a plain mistake," Janelle French says, shaking her head.

But then, in his quarters, Tom Paris gets this headache. It's killing him. He goes to the mirror, holding his head with both hands, and his eyes are completely green.

"Aw yeah," Little Nene says. "That's what happens you fuck with that green shit."

"Show you right," Crest says, punching the mute button.

A car cruises by, slides right through the stop sign, and they all watch it hard, thinking it might be B-Mo's crew from Brushton looking for some payback on Nene and his fellas, but it's just some old nutty-professor-looking white dude in a raggedy Oldsmobile, his windows rolled up. Must be lost—or on the pipe, looking to cop some rock. As he passes, Cardell walks out into Spofford to let him know he's being scoped, then comes back.

"Any those Cheddars left?"

In the middle of the next scene, Little Nene's beeper goes off, and he and Cardell gotta jet. "Later, C." Crest watches them down the block, thinking how tight he and Bean were. Boy always had his back, didn't matter if it was Morningside or North Braddock, Oakland or the North Side, and just like he didn't want to happen, he sees Bean on the bridge, going over, and he reaches for him and catches his sleeve and then both of them go, the hard white bed of the busway flying up at them like a blank page, a wall of snow. It was only twenty feet, that's the part he'll never understand.

No one knows Tom Paris is the alien. He spreads the
DNA like a vampire, biting people in the corridors. When
his eyes turn green, the test tube glows. Half the ship is
walking around like zombies, and now Crest can't remember how it ends—something with the Holodeck, or maybe
a special drug The Doctor cooks up. It doesn't matter; Bean
is here again, and the minutes Crest spent waking up in the
hospital, the light above the table, the operating room cold
and smelling like ammonia. When the doctor bent down he
could see a drop of blood caught in her blond eyebrow. Well
hello Miss Ann. There was a saw making the same screaming it did in shop. Wait, he wanted to say, hold up, but her
face came down, the drop of blood like a bug, a roach hidden in spaghetti. He tried to talk but the air was sweet, even
sugary, a licorice musk of rubber, and then there was nothing but space, floating, no stars, just a dark, bottomless night.
Welcome to the Delta Quadrant.

"Mute it," someone says, and Crest does. He's already
taken his pills; maybe that's it. This doesn't happen every
night, just some. He always looks for reasons but never finds
any, like he's being controlled by some alien force, like
googly old Tom Paris. Fuck.

It's just Bean.

The commercials go on too long, so they know it's the
end. When it comes back on, Crest remembers. It's not The
Doctor, it's B'Elanna who saves everyone. She kisses Tom
and his true personality comes back and kicks the alien's ass
right out of his mouth. The Doctor makes up some fancy
explanation that the other ones need Tom to keep living, so
they all get better, all at once. The green ghosts join up in a

blob and go out into space. The special effects are weak, and everyone laughs. Crest is wondering about Vanessa, if a kiss from her would make everything all right. Before, he would have said more than a kiss, but now he thinks: yes. He should call her tomorrow.

Some of the girls stick around for a preview of next week, the new season, then everyone leaves during the credits. It's a school night, but still he's disappointed. Janelle French waves. "Keep ya head up, baby."

The ten o'clock news comes on, the drive-by the top story. He knows the place, Aliquippa Terrace. There was a dance there years ago, in the spring. It's another Bean and me story, a fight over a stolen coat, and Crest doesn't even get into it, just squashes that mad stuff, shoves it back where it belongs. What the fuck. Even if he had someone to talk to he wouldn't say anything. What's there to say? In the paper they said he was the fourth teenager to die in East Liberty that week, like it was some drug shit. It made it sound like it was Bean's fault. And then nothing, just a little thing in the obituaries. Crest didn't even get to go to the funeral. Still hasn't been to see the stone Miss Fisk bought him. Hasn't even talked with Miss Fisk, said he's sorry. Soon. Got to, you know?

The door swings open, almost hitting him.

"Ay," U says, in some old street clothes, corduroy slippers.

"S'up."

"Where's all your little girlfriends?"

"Show's over," Crest says. "Pops go to bed yet?"

"He's out on the couch."

They sit there, Crest in his chair, U on the wall, watching the news. Pirates won; Kevin Young plants one in the stands.

"Go 'head, K.Y.," U says, and Crest smiles with him. He's so clean it's hard to believe. Quit everything, not even beer anymore. Back in the day they'd sit here and pound down Iron Citys. Had a fly rap with the ladies, decked-out Impala he used to cruise Highland in, stylin threads. That's all gone, and what's in its place is something Crest doesn't understand. And Crest in his chair; it's the same, he thinks. They've changed. Where they've been no one can go. It's like they've come back from different planets and they've got nothing to say to each other, or maybe they're speaking a completely different language. Maybe they're both fucked up. Maybe Bean got off easy. (No, that's cold.)

"U, man."

"Hunh?"

"What's up with Moms and Pops?"

"They're just fighting."

"Naw, man, it's different this time."

"You think so? Well, I'm praying for them anyway. I pray for you too, Chris. Every day."

"Thanks," Crest says, because there's nothing else to say.

"I pray for Bean too, you know? For all of us."

"A'ight, man," Crest says, and they shake, and it's almost like it used to be. But it's not. It's fine for U to pretend none of this shit happened, but Crest can't do that. Wouldn't want to neither.

The weather chick is on, and he looks at U—at this new Eugene—and thinks of Tom Paris, how no one could tell the alien was inside him. And he thinks it's like the real *Star Trek*, when there are two Captain Kirks, and one of them's good and one of them's evil. They look exactly the same, they talk exactly the same, they're even wearing the same clothes, just one of them's evil. You know they've got to fight it out, the two of them, and Spock has always got to choose which one is which. And every time—Crest is amazed by this— every single time he made the right choice. But what if, Crest thinks, what if one time Spock made the wrong choice? What if one time by mistake he picked the evil one? How would anyone ever know?

A REAL, LIVE PERSON

WHEN SISTER MARITA PAYNE hurt after listening to someone's troubles, it was a good sign. If, alone in her apartment, she broke into tears while feeding Nickels, or if on the bus to work she had to crush her hankie to her face, she knew she'd done some good.

They came to her about their husbands, their children, their money troubles. They came about their infidelities, their terrors, their failures, and in the basement of the East Liberty A.M.E. Zion, in the empty Sunday school room after choir practice, Sister Marita held their hands and listened, nodding in sympathy, trying not to interrupt.

"I'm not sure about Harold anymore," her cousin Jackie said, and though Sister Marita had never married, she knew precisely what Jackie was going through. How many countless husbands had strayed before him? And Harold, who'd always been quiet, a gentle man; she felt bad for him. She wouldn't have expected it from him, he seemed so steady, such a good provider. But their younger boy,

Chris, had had that accident, and now he was in a wheel-chair. A young man, it was a shame. And Eugene just out of jail. Sister Marita knew what a burden that could be on a father. How much hope folks had in their children.

"It must be hard," she said, "with Chris like that. And Eugene just back."

"Maybe that's part of it," Jackie admitted, "I don't know. He's changed. He doesn't talk. I haven't seen him all day and then when I get home he completely ignores me. He never used to be that way."

"It's all right, baby," Sister Marita said, and handed her a Kleenex. "Men get like that. And Harold's always been a quiet one, you know that."

"I just can't help thinking something's wrong."

"Then talk to him."

"I knew you'd say that."

"Well it just makes sense, doesn't it? See what's on the man's mind. If he won't tell you, then you *know* you're in trouble."

"You're right."

"I'm always right," Sister Marita joked, trying to get a smile from her. She got half of one, and a sad one at that. "Aw, come on, Jacks." She stood up and took her in a hug, rolling side to side, holding on. "You'll be all right. He got you this far, didn't He?" She pointed a finger up to the ceiling tiles. "Didn't He now?"

"Yes," Jackie agreed.

"All right then." And there was that smile that said everything would be fine. She could always get it from Jackie, from way back. She'd scrape her knee skating and her cousin Marita would be there to pick her up, brush the grit from her skin like her grandmother did and blow on the open cut. Nothing had changed.

But then, as she rode home on the 76 Hamilton, the tightness that struck Sister Marita's heart when her love went out to whoever needed it never came. Nothing but a tingling in her fingers she'd noticed lately, especially at choir, after clapping all practice, or sometimes walking Nickels, the leash squeezing off her circulation. It was like her fingers fell asleep, the way her legs did when she read something on the pot. She kneaded her hands in her lap, looking out the rain-spotted window at the stores pouring by, the shiny streets, the cars flipping their wipers. Real Pittsburgh weather, everything gray. She wondered how Jackie was, how her talk with Harold would come out, and if she'd really helped her. Maybe not.

At home, Nickels warned her not to open the door, barking long after he heard the key in the lock. He was slowly going blind, his dark eyes milky under the surface.

"It's me, dummy," she said, and bent down so he could lick her hand, his Scotty's beard tickling her. "All right, let's get you outside so you can do your business."

She put the mail on the counter, then opened the door and followed him out to the curb, holding the umbrella above him while he piddled. Across Spofford a shopping cart lay on its side in the high weeds. Nickels sniffed at the base of a sycamore; the street was covered with smashed seed balls.

"You got anything more, you better get it done now," she said.

He looked up at her.

"That all you got for me? That it?"

It was.

"Okay, but I better not find any surprises when I get home tomorrow."

At the door, she stopped and set the umbrella upside down on the porch to dry, setting him into a frenzy, his little tail motoring. Mr. Andre wasn't home yet, a dry-cleaning flyer sticking out of his box. It was the third night this week; maybe he was working a double shift. Sometimes they asked him to do that. Which was good, Sister Marita thought. He worked at Kaufman's downtown, selling suits, and he dressed well. Smart, a sharp talker. One of these days one of James French's girls would snap him up.

Nickels pointed at the door.

"Who wants a treat? Who wants a treaty-treat?"

She pushed the door open just a crack and he shouldered through and bolted for the kitchen, sliding on the linoleum.

"Okay, okay."

There were three kinds of treats, and she gave him the biggest, listened to him crunch it as she went through the mail. The chicken on the stovetop had thawed, and Nickels followed her around the kitchen as she made dinner. Carl's conch shell sat on the sill above the sink, the inside pink and shiny.

"And what did you do today?" she asked Nickels. "Lie around the house all day?"

He cocked his head as if he didn't understand.

"Lying on my couch, I bet."

She looked at the phone and thought of calling Jackie, but it was too soon, and if Harold was home he'd be suspicious. Who would it be, she thought. Someone from work. Not church, certainly.

So quiet you never knew what he was thinking. Some women liked that type.

"Harold, Harold, Harold," she said, shaking her head above the chicken, and she thought she hurt a little bit for them. So many years together and now this. And the children still at home.

When the chicken was ready, she filled Nickels's bowl with kibble, then washed her hands good. He waited for her to get to the table and say her blessing.

Lord Jesus, we ask in your name, please keep us ever mindful of your love and of the hearts of others. Amen.

"All right," she said, and he tucked in.

While she was eating, her hand began to tingle. She put down her fork and flexed her fingers like a pianist, rubbed them together. Pins and needles. The sensation wasn't quite painful, and in a minute it was gone.

"Peculiar," she said, holding her hands in front of her. She thought it must be the new keyboards at work. For months they'd heard rumors that they were changing over to the new ITT system, and finally they came to work one night to find new headsets, new keyboards, even new monitors, all in the same blinding off-white, beads of Styrofoam still clinging to the seams. Maybe the new keypads were springier, harder on her fingers. She hoped that was it.

She did the dishes, glancing at the conch Carl had given her so long ago. Another quiet man. Well, that was done with and no use crying over it. She watched the news. More fighting in Rwanda; God it was heartbreaking, all those babies. She couldn't stand to look. She brushed her teeth and got ready for work, put out a bowl of water and spread an island of newspapers by the back door for Nickels. Lately he'd been having trouble holding his water. It was age, plain and simple. For all her teasing, she didn't hold it against him.

"All right," she told him, and he stopped wagging his tail. He understood she was leaving, and she knelt down and petted him. "You be good now," she said, and locked the door behind her.

It was dark out, and raining the same, a drab, steady noise pimpling her umbrella. The bus was empty when she got on, a driver she'd never seen before. When the busway opened, the commute to East Hills would take ten minutes, but they still hadn't finished the ramps, so now the bus nudged through Homewood and Brushton and out Frankstown Road, stopping every few blocks to let people on, most of whom she recognized from work. When she'd started taking the 82, it was full every night, all the cleaning people for East Hills Village, the security guards; now the mall was shut down, sitting like a giant haunted house in the middle of the parking lots, and everyone on the bus worked for Bell Telephone. It made the ride like a church picnic, a lot of hollering and carrying on, but Sister Marita missed the old days too, the excitement of so many people headed in one direction. So what if it was work? They were glad to have it, and they were all together. That was how she met Carl, one night on the 82.

He was the night manager of the Thrift Drug in Brushton, and he was going home. He took the seat beside her, and all the women envied her, she could feel it. He didn't have to wear a uniform like the pharmacist; he had a jacket and tie. When she talked to him, he let her go on and on, looking right into her eyes, nodding, getting every word. A wise man, his father told him, says little and listens much, and Carl had taken that advice to heart. Every night she kept an empty seat for him, and every night he walked past everyone else and sat beside her, his valise balanced on his knees. It took him a week to get up the courage to ask her out, and then he barely said a word over dinner. He'd been to Morehead, graduated fifth in his class. He'd spent three years in Ghana working for a relief organization, finally coming down with malaria. The government had to ship him home on an army transport, strapped to a cot, moaning incoherently. He'd been in Pittsburgh six months, and this was the only job he could find. His father was disappointed in him.

"No," Sister Marita said. How could that be?

"He's a judge," Carl said. "He wants me to go to law school."

That was all she could get out of him about his family. When she took him to meet her family, her grandmother asked where he was from, and he paused as if it were a difficult question, then said, "Richmond. Also Baltimore."

At dinner, he ate everything on his plate and two slices of her potato pie, but never commented on it, just folded his napkin and smiled, satisfied. In the sitting room, she could see her grandparents were hoping for him to make some great declaration, but all Carl could talk about was his job, his responsibilities. They felt sorry for her, she thought, but only because they loved her. She was thirty-seven and had never been pretty, never would be. She knew they worried; she couldn't ask them to stop.

"He's a strange one," her grandmother said when he was gone, "isn't he?"

"But nice," her grandfather said. "Very well mannered. You can see he's from the right kind of people."

She never got to meet them. A few months into their courtship, Thrift Drug shut down the Brushton store and transferred him to Waxahachie, Texas. He wasn't a letter writer, and on the phone his listening lost its intensity, became just silence, inattention, and after a while she dreaded his calls, the groping for something to talk about other than their mutual absence.

They decided to take a vacation together—a last chance, a last time or good-bye. A last fling, she didn't kid herself. Florida in February. Her grandmother didn't tell her it was a sin, going down there unmarried. It was a time in her life when she thought hard about happiness and what it meant to her, what she would do to get it. Carl made love to her when they came in from the beach, the sand itchy between them. They ate dinner late, walking far out along the pier, taking a table by the rail, the water sweeping in beneath them, slapping the pilings. He found the conch on a long walk far into a bird preserve, brought it to her dripping and brilliant from the shallows. She looked both ways up and down the white line of beach and couldn't see anybody, then pulled the straps of her top off her shoulders and

together they gently folded to the sand, knees and feet mixed
up. After, they tried to blow the conch like a horn, but neither of them could get even the smallest fart out of it.

He never said he loved her. He never said it was forever. At least in his silence he was honest, and she was smart
enough not to test him. He called her a few times after that,
but each time Waxahachie seemed farther and farther away.
He wouldn't say they were over, he was that close-mouthed,
that kind of man, and so she had to.

"I guess we are then," he said.

"Like you didn't know."

"Well," he said, and then didn't finish.

"Well good-bye," she said, and that was it.

Nine years ago, and since then she hadn't been with
another man, as if she were waiting for him to return from
somewhere. She knew what people said, knew the children
who called her the widow Payne really thought it was true.
In a way it was; sometimes she felt as if a death had been involved—besides her parents', that ancient history of smashed
glass and bad luck she refused to look at too closely, not
wanting to blame her loneliness on them, no matter how
obvious it seemed to everyone else. Sister Marita did not
want to be a child again. She was a woman, and had been
for more than thirty years. And a strong one, she thought.
It took strength to live with disappointment.

She'd wanted children and she would never have
them.

She'd wanted a husband.

And still, she made an offering of her days to God. She
tried to help others with her listening (yes, that was Carl's

gift to her), and in the choir she raised her voice in praise. She was thankful. She was grateful. But Lord, sometimes she was so tired. Give me strength, she said then. Give me the grace to think of others rather than myself.

The bus cut through East Hills, rain thumping the roof, and Sister Marita looked out at the dark night, the news-stands and pharmacies closed, their steel shutters rolled down like garage doors. She flexed her hand, nails digging into her palm. Arthritis maybe. Not a heart attack. Her grandfather had lived to eighty-six, her grandmother to ninety-three. She had a ways to go yet.

At work she punched in before she got her coffee, then waited behind Serena until it was time. At eleven the dinger went off—like an elevator reaching the right floor—and Serena finished her last call and gave her the headset.

"Busy?" Sister Marita said.

"Not too."

Her seat was warm, and the mouthpiece smelled like the menthol cigarettes Serena smoked. Sister Marita cleared the screen of the last number before taking a call.

"Bell Atlantic assistance," she said. "What city, please."

They wanted Butler and Beaver Falls and Kittanning. They wanted McKeesport and East McKeesport and McKees Rocks. But mostly they wanted Pittsburgh. Pittsburgh, Pittsburgh, Pittsburgh.

"What is the name of your party, sir?"

The mumbled names, the arcane spellings. The impatient callers and the ones who talked to her as if she couldn't spell at all. She punched it into the new computer, careful of her fingertips. No listings came up.

"Do you have a street address for that party?" she asked.

They were actually looking for an address for them.

"I'm afraid I can't give you that information," she said.

They swore at her, called her this and that. There was a game the girls played, shouting it out when they got a good one.

"Completely useless piece of shit!" Annette said in a nerdy white-guy voice, and everyone laughed and tried to top it as fast as they could.

It wasn't a hard job, and it wasn't dull. There was always someone who needed help, and you were there to help them, to put them in touch with someone they loved, someone they had to talk to. "Please wait for your number," you said when you found it on-screen, and then waited on the line, silent, while the computer spliced together the ten prerecorded digits. In case they missed it or had a question. It was a strange time then, Sister Marita thought, waiting for them to hang up. Your mind wandered all over the place, and then the line clicked and the dial tone came on, and you went on to the next call. Otherwise the job kept you busy enough so you didn't think about yourself. Not like the bus.

In the morning when she got home, the newspapers in the kitchen were wrinkled and tinted pink.

"What's this?" she asked Nickels.

He peered back at her.

"You feeling all right?"

She took him outside and watched as he went against the street-cleaning sign. His pee was the color of iced tea.

It was blood, the vet said. Internal bleeding. It would be best if they took a look. As soon as possible.

"Right now's fine," Sister Marita said, not even worrying about what it would cost yet.

"We're a little backed up, I'm afraid." Dr. Thomas walked them out front and had the receptionist pull a schedule up. "I can give you Friday, and I'll need him overnight tomorrow."

"Why can't we do it today?"

He had to calm her down, tell her it was probably minor, that this happened with older dogs — and cats. It was probably just an inflammation or infection of the bladder. They just needed to be sure. If she was still worried, he could do an emergency procedure right now, but at this point, in his opinion, it would be better to wait for Friday when they had the full surgical staff there.

"In the meantime what am I supposed to do?"

"Do what you normally do. Keep him comfortable, make sure he doesn't overexert himself."

"All right," she said doubtfully, and led Nickels out onto Penn Avenue, where traffic whizzed by, ignoring her. She picked him up to cross the street, and when she reached the other side she didn't set him down again but kept him in her arms. She walked him all the way home like that.

He didn't act sick. The minute she put him down, he scooted into the kitchen, lobbying for a treat. She gave him one and watched him crunch it up and swallow it down. She never knew where he put all that food.

"How you feeling? You feeling all right?"

He just looked at her like he always did. Why did she always expect more from him?

She got to bed late, but there was no choir practice today, and she slept till six, getting up just as night settled outside. It was windy. She took a flashlight from her nightstand to see what color his pee was.

It was hard to tell.

She was reaching for the paper towels to lay some down on top of the newspaper when suddenly her one hand went numb. The whole thing.

"Mercy," she said, and bent over, squeezing it with her other hand. She opened and closed it, and the feeling slowly drained back. Tingly, like spiders, or when you came inside after being out in the snow and held your hands over the radiator. She should see Dr. Williams. She'd call him tomorrow.

Her and Nickels. "Falling apart, we are."

She heard Mr. Andre thump upstairs, then his door close, his footsteps moving across the ceiling. Another late night. And then, before she could say good-bye to Nickels, Mr. Andre came rushing down the stairs and out again. Well, a young man, she thought. How unlike Carl he was. But pretty the same way, those big eyes. She was surprised there weren't women hanging around, ringing her doorbell at night by mistake.

She knelt down and held Nickels in her arms. "You be good now. You go on the paper."

The bus filled up, and Sister Marita wondered what she'd say to Jackie tomorrow. They were practicing for the dedication of the busway next month, a whole program.

Martin Robinson was flying in from Harrisburg. She'd heard so many stories about him and how he grew up on Spofford, right next door to Miss Fisk. She'd always wanted to meet him, just to shake his hand and tell him how proud he made them all feel. It wasn't fair that it was just a busway they were naming after him, everybody knew that.

But what could she say to Jackie? Maybe everything was fine now between them. Still, a false alarm on that account was almost as bad as a real one. With Carl she didn't know when it started, the feeling that something was wrong. She didn't know what exactly, but that feeling was there, and while she knew what it meant, she never told him or anybody. She just let things go along, hoping it wasn't so. But it was.

She was glad for her work; it kept her mind off things. It was only at break that she thought about Nickels in the apartment, probably on the couch, watching the TV she'd left on for him with the sound down.

In the morning the paper towels and the newspapers were completely dry, untouched. She searched through the apartment, inspecting the carpet until, in her bedroom, on the far side of the bed, she found a brown stain the size of a pie.

It was darker than coffee, and when she came back into the kitchen for some paper towels, Nickels slunk away, eyeing her sideways.

"It's all right," she said. "Just try and hit the paper next time."

He let her pick him up, and they watched TV, Sister Marita stroking him slowly. His fur was a dirty silver the color of a nickel; that's how he got his name. Now his muzzle around the rubber nub of his nose was pure white.

"Listen," she said, during a commercial. "Tonight I'm going to take you to Dr. Thomas's and you're going to stay there, okay?"

He looked up at her, his eyes dark and cloudy. It was always hard to tell just what he understood. "It'll be all right," she promised him.

She thought of calling Dr. Williams about her hand. She would, as soon as this business was over.

They slept the day away, the alarm startling her. She had to get Nickels down there before Dr. Thomas closed, and she was short-tempered with him, and then, leaving him, regretted it.

"I'll be back tomorrow," she said, squatting, and she knew it was wrong to just leave him. The doctor's assistant had him on a leash. Watching her go, he strained against it, his claws scrabbling on the hard floor.

Outside she had to stop for a minute on the sidewalk, a hand over her nose as the cars whistled past. I'm sorry, she wanted to say.

And then, getting ready for practice, she thought she was being silly. He'd be fine. If Dr. Thomas said he needed the operation, then he needed it, and that was that. It was stupid to cry.

She remembered the nights as a girl when she cried into her pillow, just then understanding the terrible loss of her parents, though they'd been dead seven, eight years. "You go ahead and cry, baby," her grandmother said, rubbing her back through her flannel nightie. But that wasn't what Sister Marita wanted. It was better when no one came and she could cry as much and as hard as she wanted, picturing the faces on her grandmother's mantel alive, riding in the big fifties Buick that would always crash, the police car coming through the intersection too fast, its lights on but not its siren, the two of them dressed for the movies. What were they talking about in that last minute? She wanted her father to laugh, appreciating the wit of her mother. To keep it hers, she waited till everyone was out of the house, and then indulged herself, or, at night, crushed the pillow to her face so it caught her sobs.

At practice she tried not to think of Nickels, letting her eyes wander across the stained-glass windows above the organ loft. She was a soprano with a deep reach, but had trouble hitting some of the higher notes, and for several measures she merely stood there next to Jackie, listening to the solid, perfect wall of voices around her, then, when the melody fell back into her range, joined in again.

Jackie said everything was fine and thanked her for listening the other day. "It's work, I think," she said. "And the boys. Chris mostly."

"Eugene seems to be doing fine for himself," Sister Marita said, because she'd seen him in church and not on the street the way he used to be.

"Yeah, he's going to be fine. It's Chris we're a little worried about right now."

She seemed sure. She didn't want to talk, didn't need to, and Sister Marita thought that was a bad sign. Things didn't change that fast, especially big things, if she was any judge. Maybe it was her job, or how good a listener Carl had taught her to be, but she knew how people talked, and at home she didn't hurt for her, not even the littlest twinge.

The apartment was quiet, and she turned on the TV, heated up some chicken from the other night. Taking it from the microwave, wouldn't you know she slopped some sauce on the floor and he wasn't there to clean it up. There was water in his water bowl, his Porky Pig chew toy in the middle of the rug. It was only tomorrow, she thought. Tomorrow night he'd be back, all better. She'd do something special for him, and they'd spend the weekend together, maybe go to the park. She wondered if he'd have to rest. Probably.

Cleaning up, she couldn't stop looking at the conch. Why had she kept it so long? It was like her grief over her mother and father, she thought, something she couldn't let go of. She turned off the water and dried her hands and lifted the shell. It was chalky on the outside and smooth within. She held it to her ear, and there was the distant swell of the ocean, a far-off trembling caught and echoed forever inside the spiral, like white noise, even though there was nothing there. It was like Carl that way. She should throw it away, she thought, even as she gently replaced it on the sill.

She was getting dressed for work when she heard Mr. Andre upstairs. He was yelling something, angry. She stopped, one arm half in a sleeve, and cocked her head, waiting for another voice.

"What?" Mr. Andre shouted. "What did you just say to me?"

There was a crash, something heavy falling over, and Sister Marita fitted her wrist through the cuff. She wished Nickels were there.

A door slammed. Thunder on the stairs. He was going out, or maybe it was the person he was arguing with. Maybe they'd fought and the one had knocked the other down, maybe hit him with something.

She hurried to the front door in time to see Mr. Andre walking to his car, a little sporty Japanese thing. He was wearing an undershirt and shorts, rubber beach thongs. He got in and flipped the lights on and peeled out like he was after someone.

"My gracious," she said, and went back to buttoning. It wasn't like Mr. Andre at all, it was like someone else completely. She was glad she was going to work. She wouldn't have to be here alone, and the time would go quickly.

She had her bag on her shoulder and her key in her hand when she heard someone on the porch. Mr. Andre coming back, she figured. She flattened herself against the wall so he couldn't see her silhouette and peeked out from behind the blind.

It was Harold Tolbert with his cigar. He leaned close to the buzzers and thumbed one, and upstairs Mr. Andre's bell rang. Twice, three times. She waited for him to go away.

Maybe it was something about money. A loan maybe.

Harold opened the stair door and clumped up. She watched his progress as if she could see through the wall, then stood there frozen as he made the landing and rapped on Mr. Andre's door. She couldn't leave, and she waited for him to come back down, watching the clock above the sink, blaming him in advance for making her late.

And then he came downstairs again and across the porch without a glance in her direction and off down Spofford, not looking back.

"Oh, Jackie," she said. "Girl, we need to talk."

On the bus, everything churned in her head. The Thrift Drug was still there in Brushton, boarded up, only holes where the neon had been, a huge mortar and pestle above the door. Had she really asked for that much? A mother, a father, someone to love her. You go ahead and cry, her grandmother said, and she did, but it wasn't the same. Mr. Andre and Harold doing who knows what. Why did he come? He knew she lived there. The only man she had any respect for was Reverend Skinner. Of course her grandfather when he was alive. Carl, yes. Did she really love him? It was too late for all of these questions, she thought. The tingling had gone away, that was a good thing. It could always come back though.

No. She believed in God. She had Nickels, and tomorrow she would bring him home. She had work tonight. Fine.

"Busy?" she asked Serena.

"Not too."

She sat down and fit the headset on, smelled the menthol on it. She cleared the screen and punched up a caller.

"Oh, thank God," a woman said, "a real, live person. I've been dealing with nothing but recordings."

"What is the name of your party, ma'am?"

"Walter Clemmons, or Clements, I'm not sure how you spell it. I only met the man once, on a plane, and he just happened to mention that he lived in Pittsburgh, and I'm not even sure I know what I'm doing calling him. I'm an older woman as you can probably tell, but he seemed so nice and there are so few nice ones out there that I thought, well, you know."

"Yes, ma'am."

"You must think I'm crazy."

"No, ma'am. You wouldn't have an address for this party?"

"Clemmons," the woman said. "Walter Clemmons, that's all I have. I've never done anything like this before."

"Please hold," Sister Marita said.

She punched the name in. There was a gap while the machine processed it. In the silence she could hear the woman on the other end of the line, breathing, waiting. It seemed a perfect time to speak. But what could she say to her? And would the woman listen? She didn't dare. The procedure was clear, and in all the years she'd worked for the phone company she'd never broken the rules, not once. The name came up on her screen, and an address, a street she knew, a nice place in Shadyside. She listened to the hiss of her headset, waited for the prerecorded voice to kick in.

She wanted to say she was happy for her, that she hoped the two of them would get together. She wanted to say she was tired of living alone and having no one, that she was frightened about tomorrow and the surgery. Of all people, surely this woman would understand her. She wanted to say that her life wasn't over yet, that there was still time, that maybe Carl was out there somewhere thinking of her. Inside the machine, the numbers were being linked together. Sister Marita wanted to talk, to tell her everything, but she knew she couldn't. She knew what she was supposed to do. There was a procedure. She'd had practice at it, she'd done it a million times, her entire life really. She was supposed to be quiet, like she wasn't even there.

AFRICAN AMERICAN HISTORY

THE FIRST THING was the professor was white. A white woman. Very white. Like 90210 white. Vanessa didn't have a big problem with it, but the rest of the class wasn't happy. It was Vanessa's first college course ever, and she didn't know if she should join in with the grumbling, the low, class-wide groan of disappointment, the muttered curses of disbelief.

"Excuse me," one big guy right behind her said. "Do you think this is appropriate?"

"Actually I don't," Professor Muller said. She was tall and blond and young, and wore a chiffon scarf around her neck like Barbie. Like the women behind the perfume counter who asked if they could help you, all the time checking out your pockets. "Professor Shelby asked me to fill in for him while he's in the hospital, and I couldn't turn him down. I think you'll find I know the material."

"That's not the point," the guy said.

"I understand," Professor Muller said. "It's only going to be for this first week, I promise."

The guy shook his head bitterly, as if he'd been cheated.

She waited for someone else to challenge her, then started in on Professor Shelby's syllabus. There was a lot of reading. Vanessa knew the authors but had never actually read them. W.E.B. Du Bois, Claude McKay, Ralph Ellison, Malcolm X, Toni Morrison. It looked like a good class. The professor didn't really matter to her.

In fact, the class didn't matter; she was only here because her mother expected her to be. Whenever they argued about it, she reminded Vanessa that she was the first person in two generations who even had the *chance* to go to college, and dammit she was going to take advantage of it. Pitt was cheap, they could afford a class, maybe even two. Vanessa thought she could use the money for something else, that they should just save it. She'd never liked school, she'd always been a C student. But she had to agree. Her grandparents had sacrificed, her mother had struggled, her father had even died for the privileges she seemed to take for granted. "I don't know what's wrong with you," her mother accused. "You ought to be grateful." It wasn't enough to just say, "I don't want to."

"Personally," Professor Muller was saying, "I'd like to see more women on this list, and more contemporary writers. More gay and lesbian writers as well. To remedy this, I've created a list of my own."

She passed out a stack. The list was three pages long. There was Terry McMillan and Alice Walker, but the rest of these people Vanessa had never heard of. Yusef Komunyakaa, Patricia Smith. She could tell which ones were women, but which were gay and lesbian? She thought it was important to know. She hoped someone would ask about it.

"I'd like each of you to read at least one book from this list this semester. History isn't something that's done with, it's what's happening right now. The purpose of studying history is to influence history. To *make* history. Every person in this room is going to make her or his own history."

Vanessa wrote this down, even though it seemed obvious. She wrote down everything Professor Muller put on the board, which wasn't much. Mostly the professor leaned back against the desk and went on and on in these long, perfect sentences about oral traditions in different African cultures and how it was important to take these into account before looking at decidedly American texts.

"American in what sense?" the big guy behind Vanessa said, and she turned to look at him. He was fat and kind of Sinbad-looking and had a leather jacket and a Black Power pick in his hair like Ice Cube. He glared at the professor like he was debating her.

"In that their authors resided here and were influenced by the dominant culture, whether they were of this country or merely in it."

"In it," he insisted.

"That's what we'll discuss next time."

She assigned the Du Bois, and then it was time; everyone started putting their backpacks together. "And I want you to have arguments for both sides," she ordered, "not just the one you agree with."

In the hall, waiting for the elevator, Vanessa overheard Sinbad saying, "Thesis-antithesis. Completely European concept. It's another form of brainwashing."

It was true, Vanessa thought on the bus, but what other way was there to think? How did you even think at all, all the different factors that went into it? It seemed too huge a concept to grasp, and she shook it off and studied the plastic ads above the windows. Be All You Can Be. Learn Computers at Triangle Tech. Like her mother would ever let her. Outside it was nice, the light still lingering, pretty. And it was just her first day. It was only going to get worse.

Rashaan was in the living room, gnawing on his plastic snap-together blocks in front of the TV. She picked him up and nuzzled him—pudgy and so smooth. Those big cheeks. He giggled and then hiccupped. "Did you miss me? Did you miss your mama?" He smelled of fabric softener and curdled milk, and she set him on her hip.

Her mother had kept her supper in the oven. Vanessa thanked her, and her mother just said, "Uh-huh," meaning she'd have to thank her again later, at length. She looked tired; she still had her nametag on and the white Nikes all the nurses wore. Vanessa sat Rashaan on her lap and picked at her chicken.

"Everything go okay?" Vanessa asked, meaning with Miss Fisk. She watched Rashaan, and they were lucky— she always did a good job, it was good for her after Bean— but the other day she'd left a cake in too long and the fire department ended up coming.

"She's fine. How was class?"

"Good," Vanessa said.

"I hope you had fun, because I wasn't having any fun here, let me tell you. First thing I did when I came home was make supper. I'm still not done cleaning up and I haven't even started the laundry."

"I can do that."

"You've got to eat, and then you're taking care of him. He's been a little devil since I picked him up. Oh, and his father called. Twice. He wants you to call him."

"Thanks." She kept eating.

"Are you going to call him?" her mother asked.

It was none of her business. All she knew was that they'd broken up a month before the accident, and Vanessa wanted to keep it that way. *His father* — she was the only one who called him that. Vanessa looked up from her string beans, and her mother looked away, all salty, like she'd done something to her. Why did it always have to be like this?

"Maybe," she said.

"Suit yourself," her mother said, and went to change.

Vanessa sat there chewing, staring at the sampler on the wall. *Bless this house.* What was she supposed to say to Chris? After Rashaan, he hardly came around. He still loved her, he said, but the way he said it made it clear he hadn't planned on being a real father, that he thought it was a trap. It was a mistake, and she would have to pay for it, simply because she was a woman. How many times had her mother warned her. "You are not going to be like those Coleman girls dropping babies when they're sixteen and living sorry lives. You're not from that kind of people." Vanessa never brought up her father, the fact that he left when she was just a baby, went off to Grenada and got killed, one of only three Americans. The odds were ridiculous. A stray bullet, a ricochet. The Marines called, and the Pentagon. Her mother kept his picture on her dresser, and one Veterans Day took her to plant a little flag at the cemetery. She wanted Vanessa to have what she'd lost—a man to help raise her baby, a real family, college, a chance to get ahead. It seemed she'd thrown everything away by keeping Rashaan. Like her mother said, it was too late to put him back now.

Her mother returned in a powder-blue housedress and slippers, the belt knotted floppily at the waist. "Don't you have homework?"

"Just some reading."

"You need me to watch him?"

"It's all right."

"Because I will. I'm just going to be watching TV."

"That's all right."

"Okay, baby. Don't stay up too late."

"I won't."

Her mother said this every night, even though she knew Rashaan wouldn't be down till eleven. Half the time he was up again at two, needing to be rocked. She didn't even have to turn the light on anymore, knew the exact number of steps to his crib, already had a clean spitcloth draped over the arm of the rocker. Sometimes that was the best time, there in the dark with the streetlight in the window, his lips tugging at her little finger, and sometimes it was the worst. She'd think of Chris alone in his room, stretched on the bed where they made love those cold mornings, cutting school, and she'd picture his legs beneath the sheets, growing thinner, the muscle leaving him. "My pearl," he used to sing after they made love, "my precious little girl," coming on just too smooth so she'd laugh at him. It was good then, what he'd bring out in her. And then she'd think of Bean and of Miss Fisk not even crying at the funeral, how she didn't let anyone help her back to the limo, slapping at Mr. Spinks the director's hands when he tried to take her arm. All of that was history.

Rashaan grabbed one of her string beans and crammed it in his mouth.

"Why you little crumbsnatcher," she said, and swooped in and kissed him on the ear so he giggled.

She finished her plate and rinsed it in the sink, the water calling her mother out of her room. "You do your homework and don't worry about this mess," she said, and Vanessa knew better than to argue, just thanked her again and unzipped her backpack.

She'd found the Du Bois used at the campus store, a yellow sticker on the spine accusing her of being cheap, announcing it to the world. It was a cracked softback copy from the sixties. *The Souls of Black Folk: A Negro Classic*, the cover said. She gave Rashaan his blocks and opened her notebook on the kitchen table, but when she turned to the introduction she saw the pages were covered with highlighter, whole paragraphs double-underlined, the margins busy with scribble. Beside one line, the previous owner had written: *Bourgeois elitist garbage.* It looked like a woman's writing, curly, the *e*'s nearly circles. Some revolutionary sister, she thought, and wondered how long ago she'd written it.

There was a name inside the front cover—Mary Durham—but no date. It could have been this spring or 1969. Maybe there were clues.

The introduction said the book was an argument against segregation, against Booker T. Washington's accommodationist position. Black men needed to assert their rights as citizens and demand the government honor the constitution. The very best men would form the Talented Tenth of the population and lead the rest of the people forward.

It was all underlined and highlighted, the yellow going dingy with age. *No women in the struggle?* Mary Durham had written. *Forward into what?*

Good questions, Vanessa thought.

The book itself was actually pretty boring, Du Bois going on and on in this stiff official voice, but Mary kept things interesting. *White patriarchal / Black matriarchal stereotypes,* she wrote. *Reality a combination.*

Rashaan scratched at her ankles, trying to climb her shin. Ten-thirty and she'd only read twenty pages. She wanted to watch TV. She remembered Professor Muller's question. Was Du Bois *of* this country or just *in* it? She thought she should choose a side and start collecting evidence, but with every new idea he seemed to switch. He wanted the people to *become* part of the nation, to be respected and accepted as men. So were his dreams *of* the country even if *he* wasn't? But didn't he know that?

She quit around midnight, getting Rashaan down, then going through the apartment, shutting the lights. Her mother's light was on, and the TV, but her mother was asleep on top of the covers, the clicker in her hand. Vanessa slid it out of her fingers and turned off David Letterman.

"Bedtime, Mama."

"What?" her mother grunted, "I'm watching," and sank back again. Vanessa helped her get under the covers, then went to the dresser to make sure her alarm was set. Beside it leaned the picture of her father in his dress blues, the Marine flag in the background. He looked older than twenty-three, but only because she knew he really wasn't. She used to stare at his picture after school when her mother wasn't around, as if by concentrating harder she might get to know him better. She tilted the frame to the light, hoping she'd find some hint of her own face in his, but she never could. High cheeks, even teeth. He'd come from Youngstown, his father a shop foreman for U.S. Steel until the Southside closed down. Good, solid people. She knew his birthday and the day he was killed. She knew her mother was ashamed they'd never married, which Vanessa thought was sad. Now she set the picture down again, the white-gloved young man smiling grimly back at her, a warrior. In five years she'd be twenty-three.

Rashaan was already asleep, and she slipped her cold pajamas on and got in, then lay there listening to him breathe. *Of this country or just in it.* In her cedar chest her mother had a flag neatly folded in a triangle, a box of medals lined with red crushed velvet. She turned on her side and looked out at the streetlight, starlike behind the gauzy curtains, and wondered if Chris was awake. Probably watching his little TV, smoking up some of Nene's weed. He loved the Sci Fi Channel, and MonsterVision on TNT. Their one

year together they must have seen every horror movie that
came out, every trip to the theater a test of her nerves. When
she jumped or sucked in her breath, he just laughed and held
her closer. He and Bean knew all the directors and their
movies, the history behind everything.

It would be easier if he was straight shiftless, she
thought. She knew him better. He was so proud of his art —
his writing, he called it. You could see it in everything he
put up, in the colors and all the details, the way it jumped
off a wall. He was the one who should be going to college.
So what if it was his own fault, it didn't make it any easier
on him, stuck in that chair.

You're afraid of him, she thought. Of the chair.

Maybe.

The same way he's afraid of you and Rashaan.

No, it's different.

How?

Because he didn't want us to start with. It's only now,
after everything.

It's only now that you *don't* want him.

That's not true.

You're still afraid of him.

"Maybe," she said, and Rashaan stirred. When she
looked, the curtains seemed to move, just like in one of
Chris's movies.

Then she *was* afraid of him.

In the morning she didn't remember how she'd figured
it out, or exactly what it meant. She took Rashaan over to
Miss Fisk, holding on to that one thought, and at work it
made her forget her orders. As usual, the Pancake House

was crowded with students. The entire breakfast rush she threaded her way through the tables, apologizing, the coffeepot heavy as a bowling ball. She always wondered where these kids got their money from; was it all their parents or did they have jobs? Some of the other girls were students, but they never lasted; Vanessa didn't consider what they did real work. They had a choice. She didn't.

She didn't recognize any of her new classmates, which was good. The orders kept pouring in; Lainie was keeping her tables full. Her top was spotted with drips of syrup, and every few minutes her hand caught on one and she had to dab at her shirt with a wet napkin. She was supposed to be thinking about Du Bois, she'd even brought the book to look at during break, but instead she found a chair back in the little dead end by the coat rack and sat there with her feet up and her eyes closed, listening to the other servers push through the swinging doors, the jingle of the silver in their bus boxes. If college would get her out of here, then it was worth it.

And how long would that take, one course at a time? It was stupid; her mother had to know that.

Her mother had a double shift, and Chris was on the answering machine, saying he'd try later. Miss Fisk said Rashaan wouldn't eat his strained peas. "He was just fussing all day long," she said. "Could be he's coming down with something."

"He's not allowed," Vanessa joked, and when they got home, took his temperature. It was over a hundred, but there was no way she could take tomorrow off. She found some children's Tylenol in the bathroom; it was only a month past the expiration date. She figured that meant when you bought it.

She was cleaning up from dinner when the phone rang.

It was her mother, checking in. "We've got a head-on coming in from the Parkway," she said. "I wouldn't expect me before midnight."

"You be careful," Vanessa said, thinking of the dark parking lot behind West Penn. When she hung up she realized she'd forgotten to ask her to pick up some more Tylenol. She was relieved when the phone rang again, thinking it was her mother.

"Nessie," Chris said, all happy. "I finally caught you."

She crossed her arms, cocked a hip—instant attitude, and she knew it. "Why do you keep calling like this?"

"Because I miss you. You know that."

"Why now?" she said. "Why didn't you miss me before?"

"Before."

"Yeah, Chris—before. Remember?"

There was silence, and she let it ride, shaking her head. Outside, Tony the candyman's truck jingled by, enticing some Colemans. Sometimes she wondered if Chris would ever grow up. Rashaan held on to her leg so she couldn't pace.

"I remember," he finally said.

"So?"

"So I'm sorry, all right? What do you want me to do, take it all back, make everything the way it used to be?"

No, she thought, that's what *you* want.

"Look," he said, "I just want to see you and Rashaan, all right?"

"Why?"

"Because I miss you—I already said that."

"Wouldn't be because you're feeling sorry for yourself."

"A little, maybe. I don't know. I'd just like to see you."

"How's U doing? I saw him in church the other day."

"Oh yeah, he's saved now. He's okay though. I don't know, there's a lot of things that don't make sense lately."

"Yeah," she said.

"So like, you think we can get together or what?"

"I'm working all week. I've got night class now too."

"Miss Fisk told my Moms. She said it was like nursing school."

"It's one class at Pitt."

"How you like it?"

"It's okay. It's only one class."

"But shit, you're in college. That's all right."

"Yeah," she said, almost believing it, and she found she wasn't angry with him. She jiggled her leg to give Rashaan a ride.

"So maybe Saturday, you know. We could do whatever, doesn't matter. Take Rashaan to the park or something."

"Will you stop calling all the time?"

"'f I can see you."

"Promise," she said, and laughed, but then after she hung up she was sure it was a mistake.

She didn't touch the Du Bois until she got Rashaan down, giving him the last of the medicine. She had to finish the first six sections by tomorrow night. A lot of it was about education. He sounded like she imagined Professor Shelby did. *The function of the university is, above all, to be the organ of that fine adjustment between real life and the growing knowledge of life, an adjustment which forms the secret of civilization.* She had her notebook open to a clean page, her pen lying across it. When she woke up it was still there, her mother just closing the door.

She tried to skim it at work and then on the way in to class, finding a bench on the lawn outside the Cathedral of Learning. It was a huge Gothic tower, fifty stories straight up, a black stone rocket. Inside were rooms dedicated to all the nationalities that made up Pittsburgh, even a new African room. She bent her face to the page, learning about the education of the race, the early teachers in the South and the rise from enforced illiteracy, then Tuskegee and Atlanta. It had to do with her being here, at Pitt, as if all those years of history ended with her sitting on this bench, reading this book, and it was her job to carry on the tradition. For a minute it all made sense, it all seemed possible. For a minute she understood why her mother made her go.

Professor Muller was there again. This time Sinbad sat in the front row, getting in his comments on Du Bois. Vanessa sat near the back, afraid of being called on. The discussion was good. The professor and Sinbad had a lot to say that Vanessa hadn't even seen in the reading. And the professor seemed to agree with him: Du Bois was *in* this country, he only wanted to be *of* it, something the Africanist movement would later criticize him for. For most of the class they talked about the reconstruction of the South and the role of state governments in denying the freedmen their voting rights. She should have taken more notes, she thought. She should have read it slower.

"Okay," Professor Muller said, "your assignment for next time is," and wrote *ORAL HISTORY* on the board. She wanted them to interview someone about their experience as an African American. Tape-record it, then edit it down.

Someone raised a hand. "What if they don't consider themself African American? What if they consider themself Black?"

"That's fine," the professor said. "The whole idea of oral history is self-definition."

It was past time, and people started getting up, the room filling with the noise of chairs.

"One more thing," the professor hollered, so everyone stopped. "*Who* you interview. This is important. I want you to interview the oldest person you know." She scrawled it across the board, part of the chalk breaking off and falling to the floor. "Again—the oldest person you know. Any questions?"

Immediately Vanessa thought of Miss Fisk. It was a good assignment. It was way easier than reading.

In the elevator Sinbad had nothing to say, and she realized she hadn't thought of Chris in hours, or even Rashaan, his fever.

Miss Fisk said it would be fine. She didn't have any plans tomorrow afternoon, if that was all right. She promised she'd try to remember. It was hard when you got to be her age, but she'd try. Some days were better than others, she said, and Vanessa didn't have to say she wouldn't ask anything about Bean.

"How was class?" her mother asked.

"Good," she said, and told her about the assignment.

"What are you going to ask her?"

"I don't know," Vanessa said.

"I'd ask about her family, the people she came from."

"That's good."

"And maybe how they made it through the Depression."

"Let me get a piece of paper," Vanessa said.

Rashaan's fever was gone; he was eating again. After dinner she was working on the list when she heard the electric bells of Tony's truck. She thought it was almost fall and that she wouldn't have many more chances to see him, and she patted her pocket for some money and scooped Rashaan up and ran down the stairs and outside.

Tony's old truck was parked across the street, Tony around back of it, hunched and reaching into the freezer. The truck was from the thirties, its fenders curved, its grille a fence of chrome. The visor above the front window was red, white and blue, the rest of the truck white, with faded stickers of all the different treats. When she was a little girl, the Bomb-pops were just a quarter, and you couldn't finish one before the juice melted down your arm; now they were eighty-five and half the size.

There wasn't much of a crowd, just some Colemans. Tony had a white shirt and pants on, his white apron over top of it, white gloves. His eyebrows were bushy and gray, his ears furry nests of hair, and his lips always looked wet, as if he licked them. Vanessa was surprised to find she was taller than he was, his hunch more pronounced now, painful to look at. He seemed to have gotten old while his truck had stayed the same. He dipped his arm in and pulled out an ice-cream sandwich for the Coleman in front of her.

"Vanessa Bopessa," he said, "and Rashaan Manon. What can old Tony get for you today? Bomb-pop? Cap'n Crunch bar? Strawberry, your favorite."

"They still make those?" she asked.

"No, I'm just kidding."

She ordered a Creamsicle and a Tootsie push-pop for Rashaan, then stood on the sidewalk with a hip cocked, helping him eat it. The Colemans sat on the steps of their building, ranking on each other, dripping sticky dots on the stone. She remembered those summers when every day ended like this—her and Taniquah and Bean and Chris hanging around on parked cars while the locusts droned. Tony would run a Dove bar over to Miss Fisk sitting on her porch. When it got dark they played flashlight tag and Terminator. It wasn't that long ago, she thought. Where had it all gone?

Tony served everyone, making change from his apron, then came over to socialize. Was everything all right? Everyone all set? He was like a bad magician, someone's nutty grandfather, so goofy you had to like him.

"How's Renée?" Vanessa asked.

"Good, good. She's at the William Penn now. She likes it. You?"

"Still at the Pancake House. And going to Pitt part-time."

"Good school. I took a lifesaving class there, long time ago."

"Oh yeah?" Vanessa said, and he started telling her
about it—the pool and the other students and the smell of
chlorine, and suddenly Vanessa wondered if he was older
than Miss Fisk. He was white, so it didn't matter, but she
wondered. She couldn't imagine him swimming, leaving the
gym in winter with his hair still wet. He had this whole life
behind him she knew nothing about. A family, a history. She
would never know it, she thought, and now she wanted to.
He was sharper than Miss Fisk, who sometimes forgot what
she was saying. Vanessa would have to ask her just the right
questions.

"Well," Tony said, "I got a lot more stops," and waved
good-bye to Rashaan. "Study hard."

"I will," Vanessa said.

She did that night, staying up with the news to cut
down her list of questions. At work she added some of the
old ones in again, and came up with some new ones, so that
when she sat down with Miss Fisk late that afternoon she
had more than when she started.

Miss Fisk was ready for her, a leather-bound photo
album laid out on the coffee table. She'd made a pitcher of
lemonade and a plate of gingersnaps. The lemonade was fine,
but when Vanessa bit into one of the cookies she realized
that some ingredient was missing. She covered her surprise
by taking a big sip.

"Let me make sure this is working," she said, and
turned on the recorder. "All right, the first question I'd like
to ask you is about your family."

"Mm-hmm."

"Your mother, what was she like?"

Miss Fisk rocked back like she was thinking. She closed her eyes and then opened them again, smiling as if proud that she'd remembered the answer. "My mother was from Carolina. Columbia, South Carolina. Her grandmother on her mother's side was a slave and her grandfather was a sharecropper. After the Surrender they set up their own place outside Decatur, Georgia. That's where one of the big slave markets was, in Decatur. That's where they met."

Vanessa checked to make sure the tape was running. Once Miss Fisk got going, she tried not to interrupt. Miss Fisk was saying exactly what they'd been talking about in class—how her great-grandparents had been burned out by the Klan and headed north, chopping cotton for traveling money, how her grandfather was the first man in the family who could read. Everything they did seemed heroic, an endless struggle, and Vanessa thought of how exhausted she was, how she counted on the fact that there was just one more day till the weekend. In a way it didn't seem real to Vanessa, all this history. It was strange what you didn't know about a person, like last night with Tony—all the things behind them.

"Now my father," Miss Fisk was saying, "was just like your daddy. Talk? He could talk a cat into a bath. I have never heard a one of those so-called preachers spill it the way those two could. Didn't they know it too. They'd go on for hours right there on that porch. You could come in and cook dinner and go out and they'd still be bumping their gums."

It couldn't be right, Vanessa thought. Her father was just a boy when Mr. Fisk died. Miss Fisk noticed her reaction and paused, just a second, as if trying to figure out what she'd said. She shook it off, leaning back and remembering again.

"Yes indeed. And talk about handsome. My Lord that man was sharp. When he dressed for church, the whole street would turn out just to look at him."

Vanessa wanted to stop her, to ask her if it was a mistake, but she was off in another direction. She didn't mention him again, and she didn't say anything about Bean, but Vanessa expected that. Maybe the older history was, the easier it was to talk about.

She mentioned it to her mother that night while she was working on her report. She brought the recorder into her bedroom where she was watching TV. "Listen to this," she said, and played the tape.

"Now my father," Miss Fisk said, "was just like your daddy."

Her mother listened, squinting, trying to make sense of it. She looked up at her like Vanessa might have an answer.

"I'm getting worried about her," Vanessa said. "I don't know if I want to leave Rashaan with her."

"She *is* slipping a little."

"But she knew Daddy, didn't she?"

"Not well," her mother said. "She met him a few times." Vanessa filed it like a clue. It was the most she'd said about her father in years. She wanted to sit down on the edge of the bed and turn on the recorder and ask her mother what she meant: not well, a few times. When? Where? Why only a few? Instead she went back to her room and sat at her mother's ancient Apple II, typing with two fingers while Rashaan watched her, clinging to the side of the playpen, every once in a while calling out, reaching for her. It was three when she finished, Rashaan whistling under his quilt.

The next night Professor Muller was late. The class muttered and buzzed. In the front row Sinbad fumed, shaking his head like it was typical. Vanessa was ready to defend her; she'd been on time both times before. Maybe she had babies to take care of. It was five after, seven after, but no one moved. Maybe it's a test, Vanessa thought, how long they'd wait.

At ten after, the door opened and in walked a short orange man with a gray goatee and a briefcase fixed with duct tape—Professor Shelby. There was a smattering of applause, led by Sinbad, which the professor quieted with a wave of a hand. He was almost bald and wore a deep green suit, its lapels cut in the wide style of the seventies. He popped the locks of his briefcase and opened a notebook, went to the board and wrote *EVOLUTION*.

"What does this mean?" he asked, and though five or six hands went up, he answered it himself, going on about white biological theories of inferiority, filling the board with dates and definitions. Vanessa didn't follow all of it, thought maybe another book had been assigned. Everyone else seemed to understand, nodding along, laughing at his bad jokes.

He added an *R* to *EVOLUTION* and went on for the rest of the class, rambling about active versus passive resistance, about Touissaint and Nat Turner, Angela Davis and George Jackson, chalking names and philosophies and linking them with a confusion of arrows that Vanessa tried to duplicate in her notebook. She was still writing when the bell rang.

"You should have the James Weldon Johnson read for next time," he said, and started shoving things into his briefcase.

Nobody moved, and he looked up, puzzled.

"Professor Shelby," Sinbad said, "what should we do with our oral histories?"

The professor looked at him like he'd never heard of them. "Just hold on to them for now. We'll go over them Monday if we have time. We've got a lot of catching up to do."

Then why did I bother, Vanessa thought, but in the elevator no one complained.

"How'd it go?" her mother asked.

"It didn't," Vanessa said, and told her the whole story.

She had reading to do, but she didn't feel like it, not after class, and she watched TV with her mother and Rashaan until it was time for bed.

"You said you're taking him to see his father tomorrow," her mother asked, and now Vanessa was sorry she'd agreed to.

"We're just going to the park."

"Give him my best."

"I will," Vanessa said, knowing Chris would ask after her. He was like that, polite; it was another thing her mother liked about him. Vanessa had liked it too; she wasn't sure why she found it tiresome now. From the dresser her father smiled down, and she thought she was a coward.

She got ready for bed and then lay there trying to sleep. It wasn't that she was afraid of him, that wasn't it. She didn't know what it was.

In his crib Rashaan hiccupped and woke up and called out for her, not quite a cry. She lay there a minute, hoping he'd go back to sleep. When it was clear he wouldn't, she got up and picked him up and sat down in the rocker.

"Hush now," she said, "hush," and rocked him against her.

Outside, the streetlight burned in the trees, the shadows of leaves shifting on the wall. Rashaan was quiet, only the swishing of the wind. She thought of tomorrow and the park, of her father sitting on the porch in Miss Fisk's memory. She thought of how little she knew about anyone. What could she honestly tell Rashaan about the people he'd come from? That was the lesson class had taught her. Which professor didn't matter. Tony, Miss Fisk. She would have to learn her own history first, she thought, ask questions, find the truth out for herself.

She caught herself rocking and stopped, but in a minute she was doing it again. She put Rashaan down and got in bed and listened to her heart throb in her ears. She wasn't going to sleep, she decided, and clicked on her bedside light. She found her backpack and the book inside it and sat there tailorseat on her bed reading, leaning in to circle an idea, to underline a sentence, to puzzle over a word. Suddenly she needed to know everything.

THE HAWK

ON THE SIDEWALK in front of Miss Fisk's, Harold Tolbert stopped and took the cigar out of his mouth and looked up at the moon, then stood there a while as if searching its face for answers. "Hunh," he said, remarking on a crater round and sharp as a smallpox scar. The moon itself was nearly full, just a lip missing. It seemed too close to Harold, a fat gold coin in the cold night air, peeking over the row of town houses across the street, painting the leaves of Miss Fisk's hedges silver, throwing his shadow halfway to her porch. Hunter's moon, his father would have said. He'd have to wait a day to wish on it proper.

And what would he wish for, for Chris to get his legs back? For Eugene to stop acting all God-struck? For that mouthy little fool Bean to come back from the dead? Or — honest now — would he betray all of them just to be with Dre again?

He wasn't sure. He wasn't sure of anything anymore. For now he was relieved to be alone, out of the house. He was even glad, for the moment, not to be there yet, faced with Dre.

He breathed out a blue cloud. Around him, Spofford was dark and quiet, a few upstairs windows filled with a cozy yellow light. He liked the night, and finally being away from the brightness of the living room, the stupidity of the TV. He'd waited till Jackie left for choir practice, Eugene for his meeting, then told Chris he was going for a walk. Stretch his legs, he said, maybe pump an Iron at the Liberty. Now ain't that a bitch, a grown man needing an excuse to leave his own home. He was like a prisoner, he'd have said, if his own son hadn't just been released. No, it was like Dre was always saying—he was a free man, no one was forcing him to stay.

And what could he say to that? They both knew Dre was right, that it was up to him to pick up and leave, and they both knew he wouldn't do it. After the thrill of finding each other, after the stolen days off spent in Dre's bed, everything came down to the one decision he didn't want to make.

Not, as Dre accused him, because he was afraid of admitting what he was. No, Harold Tolbert had always loved men. He thought it was from his mother, her harshness, and from boxing, all those winters spent in steamy gyms admiring the courage and physiques of other boys and then young men like himself. The sleek, hard muscle. The agility and will. Behind the locker-room ass grabbing and towel snapping, there was something deeper—the comfort of brotherhood, he supposed. The possibility of being fully understood. And physically too. After a fight he always wanted some, his blood still jumped-up, filling him. He remembered making love in the stalls and showers with Mason, who won too, usually, his lip cut from knuckles and the gloves' laces, the anger and triumph still in his eyes. Only when you conquered could you surrender so completely, totally give up control. No woman would ever know that with him, only Mason. In all his years, Harold had never been loved so well, and now, nearing fifty, he feared he never would be again.

He wouldn't leave though. Dre could make him feel cowardly for staying, but he couldn't make the reasons go away. It had nothing to do with Jackie. Chris needed him, and Eugene. If he wasn't much of a husband, he was still trying to be a father. He had an obligation to them.

"An obligation not to be a faggot," Dre would say.

And again, what could Harold say? Yes. Maybe so. How could he explain: His life wasn't just his.

"You can at least be a man and tell her," Dre said. "You can at least do that."

A train called in the distance, its trucks clattering high in the sky. A fast freight off to Cincy, Cleveland, Toledo. He knew he should get moving. Friday choir practice was only two hours long and he'd already wasted ten minutes wandering around thinking. He wished it was like at the beginning, when they hardly talked. First thing in the door, they kissed and whisked each other's shirts off, tumbled into bed. There was talk afterward, a necessary sharing of histories. Dre had discovered himself late. The first time he made love with another man he couldn't stop laughing. "I was so happy. Finally, after all the awful times with girls my own age. I didn't know it could be like that."

Harold laughed, recalling his own astonishment, the sweetness of giving everything. Then why was he disappointed it had been an older man, a janitor at that? Did he see himself as part of a rough trend? Dre thought it was funny that Harold was a grandfather. He and Mason had come to each other as innocents, twins, their secret shared, their fumbling unsure. It was a kind of miracle it worked at all. This was different, and both he and Dre knew it. Their need wasn't equal.

They talked until they were ready again, and then talked after that, but that first month it was lovetalk, not this constant arguing over why they were together, whose fault it was, what they were supposed to do about it now.

"Do you love me?" Dre would say, and Harold would honestly say yes. It made Dre curse and slap his pillow. "How can you lie there and say that and then leave me by myself? Every night you leave me. Do you know how that feels?"

It feels terrible, Harold said. It feels terrible knowing I have to leave you. Should I just not come over then? Should we just stop?

He'd offered this before, a way out, a retreat. After a while, Dre accused him of really wanting it to be over, as if Harold had gotten what he wanted, had only come for the one thing. His youth. His beauty. Now he was bored with him, was shucking him off like a spent condom. Was it true? At times, straining against Dre, feeling as if his very skin would split, he remembered Mason, the mildewed, cob-webby stalls and lime-crusted pipes. Blood in his mouth, ears open, terrified someone might come.

"I don't understand why you're here," Dre said. "What do you want from this?"

Harold wasn't sure. The question silenced him, and his silence frustrated Dre. Love? Sometimes it seemed an hon-est answer.

"You're asking me to love you but then I can't rely on you. Like last Saturday. When I need you, where are you?"

Exactly, Harold thought, walking under the moon. "Nowhere," he said, and turned the corner onto Allegheny. Across the street, Dre's windows were lit.

They'd agreed not to see each other. Dre laid out his logic bitterly, making it seem inevitable. "How long?" Harold asked, thinking a week would be good, just a test to see if they could stay apart that long. "What's the point then?" Dre said, and Harold came up with some excuse even he didn't believe. He couldn't process the thought of not seeing him again. It seemed a waste, an opportunity squan-dered. Wasn't there some other way? "No," Dre said. "We keep going in circles. Don't come back unless you're ready to do something."

All week he'd thought about it at work, mulled it over as the rows of crackers vibrated by, the noise of the con-veyor just a pinprick of sound inside his earphones, the steady buzzing of a gnat. Why was it all or nothing? After such intimacy, how could Dre be so cold? It seemed unfor-giving to him, rigid. It reminded Harold of his mother, the way she expected his father to take care of everything that went wrong with the Mercury and then blamed him when, twenty years old, it finally died on the turnpike. And his father, resigned to his life, patiently bearing her insults in front of the trooper as if they were casual, not really caring. That wasn't love, it was a form of punishment.

He watched the curtains, hoping to catch a shadow crossing the room, then took a last puff of his cigar, knelt down to the sidewalk and gently stubbed the hot ash off. He unzipped his jacket and fished in his shirt for the pack of gum he'd bought special from the machine at work, thinking of just this moment. Friday used to be the worst day, the long weekend apart stretching in front of him. The night air slipped in with his hand, chilling him. Nearly autumn, the Hawk almost on them. Winter it would be harder to get out of the house; there would be fewer excuses.

Walking across Allegheny he chewed the juice out of his gum and spit it in the gutter. The moon doubled the bars on the windows. Sister Payne's little dog yapped as he climbed the porch stairs and then up to the second floor, the steps creaking under his feet, giving him away. The landing smelled of moldy carpet and plaster dust; a muddy pair of Converse sat beside the door on a crinkly sheet of the *Courier*. He knocked and stood on the bristly mat, waiting.

No answer.

Outside a bus ground by, and a panic came over him. Friday night was their time. Was he out at some club? All he could see was Dre laughing in some other man's arms, lighting his cigarette from the vanilla candle he kept by his bed.

He rapped harder and stood back.

Nothing, just the wind. He really wasn't home.

What a waste. It had been a risk, stealing the time —
and for what? The whole week had been a waste. It was clear
now: Dre had never loved him, had always thought he was
pathetic, a flabby old chickenhawk. For a moment, standing there in the cold, musty hall, Harold agreed. He should
be stronger, he thought. He didn't belong here. It wasn't
love, only vanity, a last shot at some ideal of romance. He
was too old, too meek, too married.

He thought he should leave a note but didn't have a
pen on him. He looked around the landing, then took the
Converse and set them on the mat in front of the door, leaning the toes of the two shoes up against each other like praying hands, trusting Dre would figure out who it was.

And what would he think, standing there with the guy
he'd picked up, the one he'd invited to stay the night, something Harold had never been able to do?

There was a gray boy, a flight attendant he'd been seeing off and on named Michel. Thin, educated, hip. They
could talk about all the books Harold had never read, the
places he'd never been.

He bent down and picked up the Converse and set
them back on the newspaper. Fuck him, play me that way,
the little shit.

He trudged down the stairs, out of energy now, the dog
barking away. He didn't bother to peek outside to see if
anyone was coming, just pushed through the door and
headed across the street. Dre's car was gone; he should have
realized it earlier. It seemed colder out now, too cold for
September, and he stopped to light his cigar, dipping his

head to the cupped match. It filled his lungs and he looked back at the house, at Dre's lit windows, and couldn't stop himself from picturing the two of them together, how just months ago he would have given up everything for him. How did that change? Had it, really? Because here he was, standing on the sidewalk in the wind. He looked up at the moon—still there, huge and inscrutable. The dog wouldn't stop barking.

"Shut up," he said. "Goddamn little rat."

He walked down Allegheny toward Moreland, the moon over his shoulder, smoke curling up. The trees rustled above him. Crazy how fast the weather changed this time of year. He dug his hands in his pockets for warmth, squinted into the wind.

He didn't want to go home, and he didn't want to go to the Liberty. He thought of Chris in his room, watching his little TV, his chair sitting there empty beside the bed, the way he covered his legs with the blankets. He wanted to say something to him, to let him know they all knew what he was going through, that they would all do whatever they could. But didn't Chris know that already? Hadn't Jackie already said that a million times until Chris was so sick of it Harold told her to stop? It was something they argued about with the door closed. She had to understand, he didn't need pity. It wasn't enough to acknowledge what he'd lost. Okay, Jackie said, then what were they supposed to do?

And Eugene at his meeting, thumping his Bible like a drum, spouting slogans like old Reverend Skinner. Attitude of gratitude. He didn't know his boys anymore. All those years he was working, putting money in the bank, they'd

gotten away from him, gone off to school, fallen in with the
wrong friends—the same thing he'd done as a boy. Nothing they'd done was that bad, and look at the price they paid.
It was the way things were set up, always had been. If Eugene could have gotten a decent job after he graduated, none
of this would have happened. Same with Chris and Bean.
There was nothing for them to do but get in trouble.

The house at the corner of Allegheny and Moreland
had burned down Memorial Day weekend. It was still sitting there, plywood filling its windows, sooty streaks licking the melted vinyl siding. Catty-corner, some youngbloods
wearing camouflaged army jackets over their hooded sweat-
shirts were hanging, one riding a bike far too small for him
in tight circles. Harold recognized him as one of Eugene's
old hoodlum friends. Lopsided old-school 'fro. Twenty-five
and nothing better to do on a night like this. Seen him out
here twenty years and couldn't remember his name to save
his life. Punks. He made sure they all saw him before he
turned the corner.

Was he looking for a fight, was that it? He was ready
for Dre now, and where was he?

He supposed he should go home and be with Chris,
wait for everyone else to get back. There was no point now,
with Dre out. Maybe it was a sign; maybe this was the way
things were meant to be. He would just have to live with
that. It made sense anyway. Dre didn't really need him. It
was just trouble all the way around.

Moreland was deserted, trash piled by the curb even
though the next pickup wasn't till Monday. A rusty baby
buggy, a legless table. On both sides of the street, people

were watching TV, the same station in different windows. One family was just sitting down to dinner, but he couldn't smell anything. Ahead, a streetlight bathed the corner of Taine in a weird orange glow. He tapped the ash off his cigar and laughed. All these months he'd been telling them he was taking a walk around the block. Now he really was.

How did it come to this—being surprised by the truth?

He was a fool, that much was plain, and only a fool would claim the rest of it was just bad luck. He would end it with Dre. It would be easy; it was over already. All he had to do was keep himself from going over there. He would do it for Chris and for Eugene, for all of them, even Jackie. It wasn't that he didn't love her, only that he didn't love her enough. And that could change, he thought. He could work on that.

Across Taine the Liberty Grill was doing a booming business, the neon blazing away. Bass thumped from the door, the staticky rhythm of cymbals, and he could see the Christmas lights inside, blinking in the mirror over the bar. A few people stood on the sidewalk, smoking and leaning against the parked cars. It was where he and Dre had met, a night like this, an aimless conversation over a double of Imperial. Dre thought he was straight, didn't think he'd catch the way Dre moved his glass closer to his. He was shocked when Harold laid a hand on his shoulder as they were playing darts. Later, his legs over Harold's shoulders, he was still amazed, laughing at his good luck, this unexpected gift. He joked about leaving bite marks for his wife to find.

That was at the beginning, so long ago that Harold could only bring it back like a fondly remembered dream.

It was over, and to think like this wouldn't do him any good. A drink wouldn't help either, and besides, he had a bottle of Johnny Walker at home. He hit his cigar hard and kept moving, trying to feel righteous about not giving in to the Liberty.

By the corner of Spofford he'd convinced himself it was true, that he would be a better man. It wasn't like he had much choice. Dre had been right all along; he'd never leave Jackie, he wouldn't do that to his boys. It seemed simple now, his love for Dre wishful, unreal, just lust. Why deny it, now that it was over?

He checked his watch, pressing the button so the face lit up. He'd been gone long enough to pretend he'd had a draft at the Grill.

Why lie? He didn't have to this time.

He was climbing the steps of their building, proud of himself, when he heard a car coming down Spofford. It didn't sound like Dre's Eclipse, but he turned anyway. It took him a minute to find the car because its lights were off and it was going slow—inching along, as if searching for a parking spot. There were tons of them. The car glided like a shark, its windows open.

He realized what it meant and ducked into the vestibule, already fishing for his keys.

A dark Pontiac, it crept down the block and past Miss Fisk's. By the stop sign at Allegheny its taillights flared an instant before crossing, and in the glow of the streetlight he could see the backseat was full.

"Fucking punks," he said, and let himself in. He took the stairs rather than wait for the elevator, thinking they might double back. If Jesus kept Eugene out of that mess then it was fine with him.

Chris was still in bed, watching *Millennium* and drawing something on his sketchpad, dipping into a box of colored pencils. Harold stopped at the door, in back of the imaginary line. The room smelled like sleep and stale dope smoke. Jackie had been on him to talk with Chris about it, and now he thought he really would have to soon. Chris was getting heavy in the face. Since the weather turned, all he did was sit in his room and watch TV all day, maybe play Nintendo with Eugene after dinner. He ate raw Pop-Tarts for lunch; the garbage was full of silver wrappers, white rings of milk dried at the bottom of the glasses he left in the sink. He was the one they thought would go to college; the money was sitting in the bank, every month the hospital taking another chunk. He'd always been their funny one, they used to call him Smiley. Now he came back from therapy on the van and sat in his room with the light off, playing the same tape over and over.

Chris glanced up at him, as if surprised he was still there. "That was fast."

"Too cold out. Hawk's coming on."

Chris didn't stop drawing. The TV was on just for company, he supposed. He hadn't seen Chris cry or swear or shout about what had happened, just this dull calm, this silence. He'd always been a nice kid, not like Eugene, who'd gone wrong somewhere, turned crazy on them, pulling that gangster bullshit. For a few years he wasn't their son anymore. Suddenly he was back, born again and working steady, and then this happened to Chris.

I'm sorry, Harold wanted to say. He already had, crying by his bedside, watching the IVs drip, angry with the
hospital for not calling in a better specialist. He'd said it so
much that he was afraid Chris resented it, was hurt by it,
but this time he wanted to take his son in his arms and finally mean it with a pure heart. It would be different. Somehow it would change everything.

From outside came a blast that shivered the window,
a cannon answered by the rattle of another gun—smaller.
Shotgun, must have been. Sure as hell wasn't a backfire. For
a second nothing, then a third opened up, finally silenced
by a blast that echoed over the rooftops.

It had only been a few seconds but it seemed the noise
held him there in the doorway, released him only when it
stopped altogether. Tires bit with a screech, and a car roared
up Moreland, the engine rabbiting. He rushed to Chris's
window. Nothing but the dark backyards and garages, the
few slices of street empty, just parked cars, hedges. A porch
light went on. People were coming out of their houses, standing in their driveways.

"Wanna bet it was B-Mo's crew," Chris said. He'd
pushed himself to the edge and shifted his butt into his
chair.

"Who's that?" Harold asked.

Chris told him as he rolled over to the window. A crazy
dude from Brushton and his clique. It was the same when
he was a kid—turf.

They waited at the window for a siren but nothing
came.

"I think they might have been gunning for some of your brother's old homies. I saw them hanging out down Allegheny."

"Was Nene with them?"

That was his name. Harold even knew his real one—Nehemiah Sykes. He'd known his mother, years ago, used to drive him and Eugene to their Little League games. "I think so."

"Word is B-Mo's been looking for him."

"Why's that?"

Chris shrugged. "Stuff, you know."

"Stuff," Harold said, but Chris didn't have to elaborate. They all knew what went down out there, even the police. He couldn't remember how long it had been like this. His entire life, it seemed. "You're not into all that mess."

"No."

"I know you smoke a little reefer but you're not dumb enough to do that other stuff."

"That's right," Chris said, but hard, as if he'd insulted him, called him an idiot. He was rolling away, the conversation was over.

Outside, a siren wound up, approaching, growing louder, and then a red light strobed over the houses. Chris was getting back in bed. He dragged the blanket across his legs and started on the sketch again, the light from the TV shading his face. A show about ritual killings. Chris switched pencils, bit his lip. Harold wanted to say something to him, but what? He thought of his own father coming home exhausted from another day at the mill, his hands and face swollen from the heat, as if he'd been beaten. What had he ever said to the boy he'd been? He honestly could not recall. And yet his father had loved him. It was obvious in the way he shared the evening paper with him, trading the front page for the sports, in the way he taught him to read the sky like a hunter. "That's Roy Eldridge blowing that horn," he'd let mention. "Never eat eggs twice in the same day." It was not one great proclamation but a quiet abiding, years of coming home from work and saying grace at dinner, asking what he'd done that day. It seemed simple, and he prayed it was not too late for him to do the same. Chris needed him way more than Dre.

"What are you drawing?" he asked.

"Nothing."

"Let's see."

"It's not ready yet."

"Come on."

Chris sat up and turned it to him, and Harold saw why he hadn't wanted him to see it.

It was a picture of Bean and Chris—a cartoon of the two of them spraypainting a wall with graffiti. They were dressed like commandos, in Rambo headbands. Their muscles bulged, bandoliers of aerosol cans across their chests. Above them the letters MDP shone like gold.

"What's that?"

"Our tag. Million Dollar Posse."

"Great name."

"It was."

Chris took the pad back and started sketching again, filling in a section with red, pretending to concentrate hard, and Harold knew he was supposed to leave.

He wanted to ask if Chris was okay, if he wanted to talk, but that chance was gone, lost. It was all his fault.

I'm here, he'd say. Everything's going to be fine.

He went into the living room and turned on the TV — the same thing Chris was watching — then lay down on the couch. He could talk with Dre for hours, waste whole days slinging it, but with his own son he came up empty. Again, he thought of his father's silence, his patience with his mother that could sometimes seem like suffering, or, worse, in a child's eyes, cowardice.

What was there to be afraid of now?

The truth. How could he explain Dre to him, or Mason, all the other men he'd wanted and then given himself to. And why?

On TV there was a serial killer loose, like every Friday, a new set of clues to figure out. A white guy usually, into religion. There were only twenty minutes left in the show. He lay there not watching it, picturing Dre stepping out of the shower, the water caught like diamonds in his hair. Choir practice ended at ten, so did Eugene's meeting. The van would drop them off at a quarter after.

So it was over.

Good. One less thing to worry about.

Outside, another siren joined the chorus. He thought of Nene — if it really was him — and what kind of love Chris felt for Bean, how long it would take him to get over it. He thought of his father and the cop pushing the Mercury to the berm, his mother steering, himself strapped in the backseat like a precious package. Maybe never. But that was all right. Was there another choice?

He could do it. He would have to.

The killer walked the dark neighborhood, keeping to the shadows, peeking in at his unsuspecting victims. He had to choose the most innocent one, pretty, her back to him. The wind sent leaves tumbling across the lawn. The music turned strange, the beat slowed and speeded up, and then there was just his breathing, faster and faster, as if he was going to come. No, Harold thought, they'd gotten it all wrong. That was not at all what it felt like.

GHOSTBUSTING

THEY HELD THE funeral Tuesday morning, not at Spinks Bros. but out in East Hills because they were afraid B-Mo's crew might try to bum-rush it, flip Nene's casket over and trash the place. Eugene knew Fats and the other old heads were strapping, ready for some of that getback. Leon and Smooth were there too, all of them G'd up, the last of the Spofford Rolling Treys. Legally Eugene wasn't supposed to be seeing any of his old associates, but naturally they came together on the sidewalk, a solid wall of security. It was cold, the sky gritty. Rush-hour traffic bombed past. Eugene felt defenseless in just his suit and his good shoes, his shirt too thin to stop anything.

"Damn, U man," Fats said. "Ain't peeped you in a while." In his gray pinstripe and gators, he seemed smaller than Eugene remembered, not at all fat, barely even stocky. He gave Eugene the Trey handshake and took him in his arms.

It was like a reflex. It made Eugene feel like he was lying, like he was being spied on. He could feel the steel under one of Fats's arms.

"Long's it been," Fats asked, "like two years and shit."

Nineteen months, eight days.

"Too long," Eugene agreed.

"Serious," Leon said. "I couln't believe you got rolled up like that."

"Heard you was working," Smooth said.

"S'right," Eugene said. "You know, s'one of the conditions." It was strange; ten seconds with them and he was back on the corner talking shit like nothing happened, like he hadn't been avoiding them. He noticed he was easing into his old homeboy slouch and straightened up.

"How's Chris doin'?" Fats asked. "You know we're all sorry about that."

"That shit was hectic," Leon said.

"He's all right, he's just layin' up."

An older couple came hobbling across the street, and Smooth went over to help them with the curb. Trash blew around the parked cars—sheets of newspaper, fast-food wrappers—and Eugene wanted to run and catch it, start cleaning up the whole city. Nene. He couldn't believe it.

"So what's up with all this?" he asked.

They looked to Fats.

"Shit's fucked up," Fats said. "You know I got mad love for Nene, but he was just gettin' outta hand."

"Straight cluckhead," Leon said. "Boy was gone."

"All the way lost," Fats said. "You know he was slangin' the shit. Afterwhile I guess it just got good to him. You were gone, he started smokin' up all his product. Got so he was stealin' shit from his Granmoms."

"Dude was wired up nonstop," Smooth said. "Crazy as a bag of angel dust."

"He was into his people for some green, so he started rippin' people off, sellin' nem wax, inside of Lemonheads, whatever. He got in a beef with this dude from B-Mo's crew and went for the steel."

"Threw it right up in his face," Smooth said.

It was an old story, and Eugene didn't need to hear the rest of it. In group, they did situations where someone pulled a gat. You were supposed to come up with a peaceful solution. The class went around and around, arguing over whether you had to use it once it was out. Darrin, their leader, wanted them to say no, but they all knew the answer was yes. Nene didn't, so someone else did, cold smoked his ass.

And they didn't need to tell Eugene what Nene had turned into; he knew. Every day on his way to work he'd see him on the corner of Moreland, riding his bike in little circles, crew of shorties running for him. Stone jitterbug. Didn't matter how cold it was. Sometimes he just stood there in the street, looking around and talking to himself, dancing, laughing at nothing like a crazy motherfucker. Pickup truck would slow down and he'd slide up to the window. "Any happ'nins here?" "Yo, what you need, man?" Nine in the morning or half past midnight. Raining, snowing. Big old nutroll of dollars in his pocket, wearing the same holey old sweatpants all week, that stupid 'fro half flat on one side cause he didn't remember to look in the mirror, maybe hadn't slept in a while. "Else you need, man? Got some crazy-ass Indo, ain't no janky weed neither. Jim Jones too, only three of them left. What you want, I got it. Crazy ill sherm, that nice ice, some of that Karachi. Buddha, moon-rock, whatever you need. You know it's *all* good." Eugene knew the smell of money on his palms, the way when you were fiending your brain kept reminding you it was time to smoke up before it really was time, the way that belly habit ate away at you, made you hold yourself like someone gut-shot in the movies. It was the life he was trying to forget, to clean out of his own head, so he didn't go over to see Nene, just kept walking, thinking about work and the hours piling up on his time card, maybe church later. He didn't have time for that shit anymore, the same way he didn't have time for Fats and his old homies, and fuck them if they didn't under-stand. He couldn't afford it. Like Darrin said, he was mak-ing a concentrated effort. He wasn't that person anymore.

The rented limousine with Nene's Granmoms pulled up, and they all stood at attention, an honor guard. The driver opened the back door and helped her out. She had gloves on, and a veil over her thick glasses. She was a big woman all around, gap-toothed, down-home. Nene did an impression of her looking for her glasses after a shower that used to make Fats fall out laughing. "Godzilla titty one way," Nene said, and knocked the TV over. They were drinking Eight-ball in the park, sitting on a picnic table and passing a blunt, Nene just buck whylin. "Godzilla titty the other way," and —*boosh*—there went the lamp. Fats cackled and dropped off the table. "Turn around—oh Lord, run for the border, here come that nasty Godzilla butt." He stuck his own out, and Fats slapped the grass like Mr. Fuji surrendering to Andre the Giant, tears squeezing down his chubby cheeks.

Now he bowed, their ambassador. "Mrs. Jenkins."

The look she gave the four of them was half thanks and half warning; today, please, she wasn't putting up with any trouble.

Fats nodded; they'd make sure.

Little Nene was with her, in a suit Eugene recognized as Nene's, the cuffs at his wrists. He wasn't a shortie anymore. Sixteen? Seventeen? And stone crazy, always had been. Eugene had forgotten how much he looked like his brother. What was his real name? Eugene didn't even remember, and he'd known it like his own. That would be hard—he'd always be Little Nene.

That's what Fats called him, solemnly offering his hand.

Little Nene threw the Trey sign, three fingers jabbed at his heart, and glared at Fats as if he'd killed his brother, as if he'd let him down.

Fats flashed the sign back, and they shook hands, Fats patting his shoulder.

"You see that little critter?" Leon said when the party had gone inside.

"He better chill that shit right the fuck out," Smooth said.

"I don't know," Fats said, looking up at the white sky, and Eugene could see he was thinking. He came to a decision and measured them one by one, throwing the same hard face Little Nene had, letting each of them know. "We got to handle our business. Square business, know what I'm sayin'?"

Eugene didn't say he wasn't down with that, that legally he couldn't afford to be around any kind of drama. He didn't remind them that none of them had come to see him, only his Moms and Pops. He couldn't say, "But I'm doing so good." In group Darrin made it sound easy, like all you had to do was make your case and the life would just stop and let you off. Put that negativity behind you. Give yourself an alternative. It was easy when you weren't in it, when it wasn't where you'd come from, who you were.

It didn't get easier when he went up to see Nene in his casket. It had been a shotgun, and he'd taken some pellets in the face. The holes were plugged with something and painted over with makeup, but the light was bright and you could see everything. The organ was going on and on, wandering through some tune. His Granmoms had bought him a new suit, with cuff links even. Little Nene had laid his black belt across his hands. Eugene remembered playing Bruce Lee with him, seeing how high they could leave a sneaker print on his bedroom wall. He had a poster signed by Willie Stargell and a model of Battlestar Galactica hanging from the ceiling on nylon fishing line. Long summer days they walked the train tracks, peeking in boxcars, pretending they were riding the rails, heading down south, home. That's where he'd be now, Eugene thought, a better place. He bowed his head and said a prayer and went back to the pew.

Fats and Leon and Smooth were bored, folding their programs, scratching the back of their necks, looking toward the door. Didn't look like B-Mo was going to show. Eugene settled himself and looked back at the casket. It was a small chapel and there was hardly anyone there. Above the minister, Jesus gazed down sorrowfully from his cross, and he thought of his mother dragging him to church as a boy, how when his attention wandered he'd flip through the prayer book, searching for the good parts. The Burial of the Dead was a favorite, and the Psalms. Lately he'd found them again, all the complaints to God by the lost, the trials and tribulations of faith. Maybe he was supposed to find them as a child so he could appreciate them now, try to live his life by them.

He looked over at Fats leafing through his program, Smooth picking his nails. They hadn't mentioned his getting religion, but he knew what they thought—that he'd gone crazy, that he'd been brainwashed. It was what Chris thought, and Pops. Only Moms thought it was a good thing, and even she wanted to know what happened, how he'd changed so completely.

Had he?

Yes, for the better.

He remembered the last time he and Nene were together, a late night at his crib when he still had a crib, beamin'. They'd smoked up everything and didn't have enough to get any more. They'd been chopping the rock on the coffee table. First they scraped the top with a razor blade, then they got down on their knees and leaned in over it to see if they'd missed a piece. They licked their fingers and then their palms, trying to swab up some dust. They got down on all fours, pushing the furniture out of the way, their fingers going over the carpet, reading it like a blind man, feeling for any little bump, any crumb, rooting around the room like hound dogs—total ghostbusting.

He shook his head, smiling, trying not to laugh. But it
wasn't funny, it wasn't funny at all. Not then and not now,
and if no one understood the changes he was going through,
that was fine with him. He knew.

The organist switched tunes, James Cleveland's "Peace
Be Still," one of his mother's favorites. Little Nene and his
Granmoms went up to see Nene, to say good-bye one last
time. He gave her his arm, and she leaned into him for support, every step an effort. Like Fats, she seemed smaller to
Eugene, as if she'd withered. She had to be in her seventies, her hair one of those superglue jobs, stiff as a wig under
her bonnet. Still with that big old Godzilla butt. Used to take
the back of a hairbrush to Nene's behind, make the two of
them fresh blackberry cobbler. She'd buried Nene's grandfather before Eugene was born, and then her daughter,
Nene's Moms, when he and Nene were in first grade. Now
she was burying Nene.

He'd pictured his own Moms leaning over him, imagined her tears, her screaming. Oh Lord, don't take him now.
Throwing herself on the coffin so all those biddies from the
choir would have something to chew on at coffee hour. It
wouldn't be like Miss Fisk standing pinch-faced over Bean
for just a second, stunned, still in shock from the news. He
was ready for Nene's Granmoms to go off, to fill the empty
chapel with her beseeching. It wouldn't embarrass him the
way it would Fats or Smooth or Leon. No, Eugene thought,
she'd earned it.

Nene's Granmoms leaned down — to kiss him, maybe —
then straightened up again. Eugene thought he heard her
crying. Little Nene released her arm and bent down and held

his brother, pressed his head against the new suit. He stayed there, his Granmoms's hand on his shoulder. What would he be saying, Eugene wondered. What would Chris have said to him?

Finally Little Nene let go and the two of them turned arm in arm and walked back to the pew. Little Nene wiped his eyes, his face shining, lip quivering. His Granmoms helped him in.

"Aw, man," Fats said, and looked down at his gators.

"On the real," Smooth said.

In the receiving line, Fats hugged Little Nene like a brother, held him close for too long, whispering in his ear.

"I told him we'd take care of the situation," he said in the parking lot. Smooth had a pint of Imperial in his glove compartment and they were passing it around, remembering Nene. Eugene hadn't had a drink since he'd been in, but out of respect, every time the bottle came around he took a sip, and now he wished he'd eaten breakfast. They were telling stories about the time Nene stole the box of instant lottery tickets from the state store. The five of them sat around his crib scratching off the cards, their thumbs turning silver like the Tinman's, the losers piling up on the floor. It was still a gyp; they only won a few hundred dollars.

"But you know that shit di'n't stop Nene from buying them every week," Leon said.

"Then be crying 'bout how he's losing all the time," Smooth said. "Dude never had *no* sense."

"Ay," Fats said. "Squash that shit 'fore I have to smack you."

Eugene appreciated him defending Nene; he knew how tight the two of them had been. Strange, he thought, woozy and looking around the circle, how he didn't feel tight with any of the fellas now. He had their backs if any serious, for-real funk went down, that wasn't it; he just felt cut loose, floating out there. It would be different, he thought, if Nene was here.

Well no shit.

He took the bottle from Leon and tipped it up. The whiskey went down easy but stung his tongue like pepper, left it hot and thick in his mouth.

"I just remember how funny the motherfucker was," Fats said. "That's what I'm gonna miss about him."

"And that stupid hair on him," Leon said.

"Yeah, that hair," Eugene agreed.

They stood there in the lot, knowing they had to go. Smooth was due back at work, they only gave him a half day. Leon was plastering a bathroom. Eugene thought of his job—all the cars in the lot he'd have to wash and wax until someone bought them—and wondered what they thought of him. It didn't matter, really, but the more he thought of it, the worse it seemed. It was just the whiskey, he shouldn't have had any.

Smooth gave him a ride home. He had a Regal, all paid off, with tinted windows and serious gangster walls. He worked at the airport, bucking luggage. The pay was good, and the benefits.

"It's loud," he said. "That's the only bad part." He said he might be able to get him in if he was interested.

"Sure," Eugene said, and wondered if he'd been wrong not to see them. It wasn't like he had another set of friends. Besides Pooh Bear and Guy Collins, he didn't know the people at his prayer meetings. It wasn't like inside, in group, where he knew what everyone's story was, and some nights he didn't speak, just begged off, sipping his coffee, eating the free doughnuts. Some nights he wasn't sure he belonged there. But where else was there to go?

"Smooth," he said.

"Yeah."

"What you think Fats is gonna do?"

"He'll find someone to take care of it. You know."

"Yeah," Eugene said.

They were on Spofford, and Smooth swerved to miss the big pothole. "You got some other plan?"

He didn't. He hadn't forgotten Nene, the holes in his cheeks. Fats would make it stick. It's like that, that's all. Motherfuckers, do his partner like that, what did they expect?

Smooth let him out in front of his building, asking again if he was interested in the job. Eugene thanked him, then watched him off. The street was empty, just some squirrels playing tag on the wires. He stood there and watched them chase each other down a telly pole, thinking absolutely nothing. Just Nene, the wasted day. He climbed the stairs slowly, took his time getting his keys out, then dropped them on the floor. "Fucked up," he said, and picked them up.

"Hey," he called inside.

"Hey," Chris said from his room. "How was it?"

"All right. You eat lunch yet?"

"No."

"I'm 'onna make some soup. You want some?"

"Okay."

First he ran himself a glass of water. Mushroom, to-mato, chicken noodle. He opened the chicken noodle and turned on the stove, then stood there gulping the water and stirring. He had a twenty in his pocket. In fifteen minutes he could be in the park, tipping his own pint of Imperial, trading sips for a hit of cheese. He pictured Nene the last time he'd seen him, staggering across the street, his eyelids drooping like he was about to fall asleep, twitching like a zombie and shit. Eugene had put the freeze on him, breezed right by like he'd never met him.

"Fuck," he said, and turned up the burner.

Chris rolled in in his chair. Eugene still wasn't used to seeing him like this; he kept thinking he'd stand up, fold the thing up and lean it against the wall. There was lint in his hair, and he had on the same jeans and sweatshirt as yesterday. "How was Nene's Granmoms, she all right?"

"Yeah, it was Little Nene who was all broke up."

"Straight," Chris said.

He poured the soup out and took the bowls over to the table, then wiped the counter with a paper towel. When he sat down, Chris had already started in. They ate for a while, saying nothing.

"So what's up with B-Mo and them?" Chris asked.

"What do you think?"

"When?"

"I don't know when. It's not my beef."

"Oh, it's not?"

"What'd I just say?" He put a look on him, but Chris didn't back down. "Oh, now you're coming on all hard, is that it?"

"It's not your beef—right."

"Fuck you, think you know something."

"Oh, okay then."

"That's right," Eugene said.

When Chris had left, he cleaned up, wondering why they fought. He wasn't angry with Chris.

He found him on his bed, drawing something with the TV on.

"Hey," he said. "Sorry I went off on you."

"That's all right."

"Naw, I'm just fucked up about Nene."

"It's okay," Chris said. He flipped the big sheets of the sketchpad and showed him what he'd done this morning— a portrait of Nene. Nene was around twelve in the drawing, dressed in his Lynn Swann shirt. He was the way Eugene remembered him: that goofy smile and that Gumby-looking hair. He recognized the pose; it was from a picture his father had taken. Chris had it out, and handed it to him. In the picture it was the two of them, their arms over each other's shoulders. Eugene was Joe Gilliam, Number 17. Each of them had a hand on the ball, Nene's under, Eugene's over, teammates.

"That's nice," Eugene said. "That's real nice."

"I thought his Granmoms might like it, you know."

No, Eugene thought, *I* want it, but said, "That's a good idea."

"I'm going to put him up on the bridge," Chris said. "I'm going to put everyone up."

And Eugene didn't ask how, didn't bother figuring out the ropes and pulleys they'd need. He just said, "I'll help you."

That night Fats called. Pops held the phone out for him, already watching TV again.

"Yo, U," Fats said, "you're all set. Much love, my brother." That was it, the phone went dead.

A few hours later it was on the news. Two unidentified teens in Brushton, the anchorwoman said — late-model car, senseless violence, the usual deal. Even the pictures were stock: a police car, yellow tape knotted to a fence, looped around a telly pole. A neighbor holding a baby said she heard shots and looked out and saw them on the ground. "A shame" was all the anchorwoman could say; the man agreed with her. It was amazing how little they knew about anything.

He couldn't sleep, thinking about it. He clicked his light on and took his Bible from the nightstand, leafing through it, trying to find a passage that was meant for him, but there was nothing, just wedding feasts and easy miracles. He closed it and tried to reconnect with his group, think of the circle of them in the dayroom, poring over their dog-eared Bibles like a team with a new playbook. The intensity of belief, that's what he missed. The certainty of a new direction. You've paid the wages, Darrin said, now stay focused on your choices. Understand that you're not in control of the situation, you can only control yourself. Be responsible for your actions. Get yourself to a place where you can help others.

Had he even tried to do that?

He saw Nene's Granmoms walking back from the casket, dry-eyed behind her glasses, tired, as if she'd been waiting for it, as if it was natural. And he wondered about his own Moms, if she'd had the same vision he had, except instead of him looking up at her, she was looking down at him. She must have. That would be harder, he thought. To see what was going on and not be able to do anything—like him and Nene.

In the morning the story was in the paper, back by the obituaries. It gave their names and ages. Bryan Tolliver, 15. Jamal White, 17. There was nothing else about them or their families, only that the police suspected it was drug-related. The ad for the Wilkinsburg funeral home was bigger than the whole article. He tore the story out and stuck it in his shirt pocket, and at lunch he took it out and read it again, remembering his own worst sins, a boy that age he was responsible for, a night he didn't like to think about. He saw the two of them standing on the sidewalk, kicking it in their Timbs, joning and vibing off each other, waiting for someone to pull up. Someone did. Fucking little knuckleheads.

That afternoon he was rubbing down a new Lumina, still turning the pictures over in his head. Folks were getting shot on the corner when he was a little shortie. It just didn't stop. It was like no one ever learned. He'd had to. It was like Darrin said the first day: Either you smarten up or you die, one or the other, your choice. It took him a while to get to it, but Eugene knew it was true. He knew Nene was headed that way, everyone did. Only Little Nene was surprised by it.

The Lumina was navy blue, and he could see his face in the quarterpanel, stretched like at Kennywood, the crazy mirrors the one free thing in the penny arcade. He had his Baierl Chevrolet jumpsuit on, and a white rag in his hand. He could still be in the slam, working motor pool.

But you're not, he thought. You're out. You've got a job. You've got some direction. Don't fall back into that old trap. You need to focus on what you need to do for yourself, then start thinking about the community. Don't forget, Darrin always said, you've got a chance to be a leader.

A leader of what? He stared at the man in the quarterpanel. He didn't look like a leader of anything, just some fool with a rinky-dink eight-hour slave.

He walked home along the sunken busway. The road was done except for the exit ramps, and those were laid out, plotted off with string. Graders sat abandoned like dinosaurs. Eugene walked up the middle of the road, looking at the walls on both sides, the graffiti he knew was Bean's and Chris's. MDP IN EFFECT, one big piece said, ten feet tall, a fierce-looking hawk spreading its wings. He didn't stop to appreciate the yellow highlights on every feather, the fresh, wet shine Chris gave the letters. As he crossed under the footbridge, he turned and looked up, and there, beneath the tribute Kenny did for them, was their last, unfinished piece.

Eugene couldn't tell what it was supposed to be. It was a blue outline, kind of square, just the beginning of something. A word? MDP again? It wasn't even that big. He pictured the two of them working above him, a rainy night, laughing, the hiss and rattle of cans, and then it was just him and Nene playing Chinese checkers or some dumb game in his room, lying on that zebra shag, wondering if his Granmoms had any frozen burritos in the fridge.

He looked around for evidence of the accident—a spraycan flattened by the dump trucks, a single blue Puma, a smudged rag but there was nothing, only the unfinished piece. BEAN & CREST, Kenny's said, with clouds around it, sun just breaking through. Not even their real names, Eugene thought. Ben and Chris. Why did he think he could have done something?

He was crossing Allegheny when he saw Little Nene on the corner of Moreland. He was riding Nene's ten-speed, bumping it over the curb and into the street, then back on the sidewalk again, circling a bunch of little critters Eugene didn't recognize. Little wannabes straight perpetratin'. Would have made him laugh back in the day. Not now.

A van pulled up and one of the shorties ran around the driver's side, his back to Eugene. He reached a hand through the window.

"Motherfucker," Eugene said, and started running down Moreland toward them. "Yo!" he hollered. "Yo, hold up!" waving his arms like a cop.

The dude in the van saw him and hit it, peeling away, nearly running over the kid.

Everyone else bounced, split like roaches, threw their sweetest ghost move, Little Nene booking down a walkway between two houses. By the time Eugene reached the corner, he was alone. Around him Moreland was deserted, the gutter matted with glassine envelopes and spent Bics. He scowled at the houses and their empty windows, searching for a single concerned face. The place across the street had burnt down months ago, the windows boarded up, the yard overgrown, going yellow. Why did he expect anyone to give a shit?

After supper he put on his good suit and helped Chris into the elevator and down the front steps. The city was supposed to put in a lift for him but so far only a surveyor had come by. He had Nene's picture in his lap, in a frame they bought. Moms had wrapped it for them, and it looked sharp. On the sidewalk Chris used his motor, and Eugene had to slow down to stay beside him. Still, it was good; Chris didn't get out enough.

The corner of Moreland was empty, the streetlight burnt out—no, broken. He helped Chris over the curb. It was like a mission; the two of them didn't say anything. A car headed up Moreland toward them, its headlights searching beneath the trees, and Eugene imagined B-Mo's boys riding down on Nene, weapons ready, windows rolled down.

It was harder getting Chris up the stairs at Nene's Granmoms'. His back hurt from work, and he had to stretch after.

"Sorry," Chris said.

"S'all right, I got ya."

Nene's Granmoms asked them into the living room. That gap-toothed smile, those old glasses—it was like she never changed. "Now don't go away, I've got something for you," she said, patting Eugene on the shoulder, and vanished into the kitchen.

Chris looked around the walls, covered with framed paintings. Above the fireplace hung an Oriental rug with an intricate pattern. In the corner stood a black laquered piano. The sofa was black leather, with a heavy glass end table, a fern in a crystal planter. Nene's Granmoms always kept a good-looking house. It made the jump from Moreland even stranger, like the two didn't fit.

She came back with a tray of cheese and crackers and water for all of them, taking the end of the couch by Chris's chair. "Eugene," she said, "I wanted to thank you for coming the other day." She looked at Chris sympathetically. "I know you would have been there if you could."

"I'm sorry about Nene," Chris said.

"Thank you," she said, and touched his knee.

Chris held the package out. "We brought something for you."

"That's sweet, you didn't have to," she said, making a face, then took it. She peeled the wrapping paper away and turned it over to see Nene. She sat like that a minute, looking at him. "Oh," she said, "it's beautiful."

"Chris did it."

"Chris, oh," she said, "thank you," and stood up to take him in a hug, still holding the picture, and all Eugene could think of was Nene doing his Godzilla routine. She came over to him and he held her, breathing in a whiff of baby powder and Dixie Peach, a smell he remembered from church and birthdays.

She looked for a place to put it. "There's not enough room on these walls. I'll have to move something."

She seemed happy, and Eugene thought he'd at least done something constructive today. Darrin would be proud of him. They ate the cheese and crackers and drank their water, answered her questions about their parents. He didn't ask if Little Nene was home until they had their coats on.

"Who—Leonard? I'm lucky he came to see his brother. He's another one, out all hours, gallivanting around town."

Eugene didn't ask why she couldn't stop him. He'd run the same game on his Moms when he was sixteen, then served Pops when he tried to get in his business. He just said to let Leonard know that he'd asked after him.

"Leonard," Chris said when they were outside again. "What's up with that?"

"She really liked your picture."

"I just thought, you know."

The corner was still empty, and they rolled up Allegheny to Spofford under the one streetlight. Chris's chair made a whir like a remote-control car.

"Those steps are gonna be a bitch," Chris said.

"I'll handle it," Eugene said, and he did, pulling him up backwards, one at a time.

Moms was waiting for them. She wanted to know how it went, and they told her. "Good," she said. "That woman, what she's been through."

Chris looked up at him. Neither of them had to remind her of what she'd been through with them; they just nodded.

Chris whirred into his room. Pops was watching TV with a beer, Moms reading the paper at the kitchen table.

Eugene used the bathroom, unloading some of that water, then announced he was going out.

"Where?" Moms asked.

"Church. I told Reverend Skinner I'd help set up for practice."

"How late, you think?"

"Not late. Maybe ten."

"You be careful," she said.

"You stay out of trouble," Pops threw in, but he was gone, already on the stairs.

He started with Spofford, circling the block, checking out the crowd hanging in front of the Liberty Grill. Too old, and the cops always cruised through. He swept the four corners at Taine and Moreland, then headed back toward Nene's Granmoms'. There was a crew working Allegheny under the busted light, a punk Little Nene's size in a Hornets jacket and a Marlins cap, but when Eugene got close he could see it wasn't him.

"Whassup?" the boy challenged him.

"S'up wit chu?" Eugene said, coming on hard, putting on that yard face. One of his toy-ass partners was giving him the red eye. "I'm looking for my boy Little Nene."

The Marlins cap flashed the Trey sign.

Eugene laughed and returned it. "A'ight, but I don't play that no more. I'm too old for that shit."

"You sposed to be some kinda O.G. or something," the boy said, looking his suit up and down.

"Big Nene and me were partners."

"I'm real sorry. I ain't seen Little Nene round tonight. He might be down Lenora."

"A'ight," Eugene said, and traded the handshake. "Tell him I was looking for him."

He walked on down Moreland, sure of himself now, on a mission, square business. It was clear, the streetlights throwing shadows into parked cars. There was no one at Lenora, only a cat slipping across the street. He kept going, past Larimer and Thompson and Paulson, thinking of what he'd say to him. Nothing about God or anything big, just the facts of the matter, like Darrin laying it out in group.

Lowell was empty, and Mayflower, but he kept on, block by block, checking every possible spot. He remembered Nene and him searching the carpet on their hands and knees, running their fingernails over it like a comb. That last night they were so fucked up it didn't occur to them to stop. It was a good thing too. After like half an hour, Nene pulled a chunk out of the couch. He pinched it between his fingers like a diamond, smiled like he knew it was there all along. And he did, they both did. That was the lesson of ghost-busting. You had to have faith. You had to believe that if you just kept looking hard enough, eventually you'd find what you needed.

GOOD MORNING, HEARTACHE

HE CAME TO her because his mother was going through some hard times moneywise. Of course it was not money really; there was a man who'd almost married her, a lost job, a car stolen from their parking lot. The schools, the neighborhood, even the weather seemed to play into the decision. Milwaukee was a city with no jobs, Yvonne said, and cold in winter, ice reaching into the gray lake. Maybe it was time to try Chicago (Miss Fisk didn't say it was the same lake, the same cold, the same city finally). Yvonne called her night after night, sometimes swearing bitterly, sometimes crying, and Miss Fisk could not say no.

He was ten when he came, a wick-thin boy with a high forehead and tiny ears. He had turn, a brisk way of saying "Ma'am" and "You're welcome" that she recognized as her own—a gift her daughter had passed on to him. He was a bright child, talkative, and quick to pick up on what she needed. He didn't cry when his mother got in the dented Chevy and drove away. At supper he ate everything on his plate and then asked if he could watch TV if he did the dishes. He wanted the bedroom next to hers, he said, and that first night how could she deny him?

Nothing changed. Maybe it was because she was a grandmother, ready to give everything, nothing left to save up for. She flattered herself that he favored her; wasn't it plain in the slope of his forehead, the just-enough-to-whistle gap in his big front teeth? He knew when she needed to be alone and when she needed a little sugar. He could always get what he wanted from her, not like Yvonne. She wanted to think it wasn't weakness on her part, that she didn't give in to him just because he was a child. But didn't she secretly smile to herself in the kitchen, making cornbread for him, thinking she'd been blessed? He was a gift she hadn't known she'd needed. He was hers.

He was her good boy. That's what she wanted to say when the police came and then the one reporter from the *Courier.* Smart as day in school too. She didn't know how he got mixed up in all that nonsense. But it wasn't completely true, no, not by that time—she'd found things in his closet, tucked deep in the toes of his winter boots—and so she told the reporter it was a shame, that just last week he'd started a program at the Vo-Tech, he and Chris (the other boy, she said, so he'd know), the two of them together. Graphic design. He wanted to be an artist, she said, wondering if that really was true.

Yes, it was true, an artist. Why did she have to question everything now, as if his life with her had been false, had never happened?

There were people who needed his liver. The doctor said there was nothing else they could do, so if she would just please go ahead and sign the papers they could begin the procedure. She needed to call her daughter, she said, and then there was no answer, the phone ringing in Milwaukee, in the new apartment she'd visited just once, marveling at the plush, just-vacuumed carpet, the frost-free refrigerator, the view of the freezing lake — marveling at Yvonne's hard-won success, after all her troubles. Benny only had another year in school, and he was on the honor roll again. It didn't make sense to take him away from his friends.

"Legally you *are* his guardian," the lady in the office reminded her, and turned the form so Miss Fisk could write on the line. It wasn't like he was alive and she was saying take him off the machine; he was already dead, the blood stopped, his body cooling. There was someone who would die if she didn't sign this, that's what it came down to. She was not a selfish woman, Lord knows. She would do anything to save another mother this pain. Then why did she have to call Yvonne again?

The woman turned her phone to Miss Fisk, and she punched in the number, then waited. She pictured the empty apartment and wondered where Yvonne had gone off to. The corner store with its Miller sign and its high-priced milk. She thought of her walking the dark streets, smoking her cigarettes one after another like when she was angry. Was it raining there too? The phone rang five, six times. She put the receiver down and looked at the woman. "You say we need to do this now."

He was ten when he came and seventeen when he was taken from her, but there was another time before that when he was a baby, her first grandchild. She'd flown to Minnesota to be with Yvonne when the time came. She wasn't in the room, but she was right outside, waiting with her third awful cup of coffee, reading the classified ads from a discarded *Star-Tribune* as Herman stared out over the city. He was her boyfriend, and Miss Fisk knew he wouldn't be around to see this child raised right, but there was nothing she could do about it and every time she said something, Yvonne would stop calling. And he did leave, eventually. He was still in St. Paul, still doing something in radio (she never knew quite what it was that he did). He came to the funeral, bending to her, accepting her arms as he never had before, saying, "Bertice," sadly, as if there were no words.

And where were you, she wanted to say. Call yourself a father. You have no right to grieve over him—no right. Benny never liked you because he knew what you are, and that is a no 'count man who will never come to nothing.

Instead, she held on to him, told him to take care of Yvonne, something he'd never done, and never would.

They laid him to rest beside her Sherman, in the plot they'd bought for Yvonne. It seemed strange, standing there as the motor lowered the box; it was the first time Sherman had met Benny. They were neighbors now, and she liked the idea. Sherman would have liked him, mostly. In fact, if Sherman had been around, none of this would have happened.

But it did, it had. She had to remind herself sometimes, warming Rashaan's formula, that Benny was not going to be home in a few hours. When Vanessa came by after work and thanked her and took Rashaan home, cooing to him, tickling his chin, the house went quiet, only the clinking of the radiators, and she remembered everything. She had to turn the radio on to stop it.

"Yes, ma'am," the woman said, "it's no good after twelve hours," and still Miss Fisk hesitated, didn't pick up the pen. There didn't seem to be anything wrong with him, just the bump on his head, a few scrapes. How many hours had it been—two, three?

Some days she escaped completely, reading to Rashaan on the sofa, fixing his strained peas, but then he left and the night spread endlessly in front of her, the rotation of the earth—the entire universe—her enemy. After Sherman, after Yvonne left for college, she thought she'd learned how to be alone. Then Benny came and changed that, dragged her back into the world of the living. Now the opposite was happening. Dusk congealed in the trees, crows flew over. She walked from window to window, stood with a hand gathering back the drapes, peering out over Spofford as if expecting him to come home for supper, his boots muddy from the new busway. Once, suddenly waking up in the present, she saw some of the Coleman children eating ice cream on the sidewalk, pointing up at her; when she waved, they scattered as if she was a witch.

"The tissue is what's important," the doctor said when they called him in. "The individual cells can live for a time by themselves, but eventually without nourishment from the blood, they die."

Yes, Miss Fisk wanted to say, I understand, but can't I just call one more time?

Supper was the hardest. Rashaan was with Vanessa again, and she could hear the clock above the sink tick off the minutes. The news was always the same. Sometimes she didn't make anything, just reached into the fridge, lifted the tinfoil and picked at a cold chicken, a butt of ham. She'd found a frozen macaroni she liked, and two or three times a week she preheated the oven and slid the little pan in, actually thankful for such convenience. It was thick, the crust on top brown and crunchy, the cheese inside steaming and heavy, burning the roof of her mouth. She ate until it was all gone, and then, disgusted with herself (remembering the velvet bite of her mother's, the pride she took in her own), she scrubbed the little tin and stacked it with the rest under the sink, thinking she could use them for something. For what?

And then there was the TV, the book from the library, a long biography of Mrs. Roosevelt. Now that her life was almost over, Miss Fisk was interested in history, as if to appreciate what she'd been through. Vanessa was taking a course; she always wanted her to read about people like Ralph Bunche and Adam Clayton Powell. Miss Fisk couldn't explain: Mrs. Roosevelt meant more to her, especially back then. Adam Clayton Powell she didn't particularly care for, though she couldn't remember why.

It was her Sherman, he must have suspicioned him of using the people for his own good. Sherman didn't trust a one of them baby kissers, not even Martin Robinson, and he'd been a friend. Oh, he'd listen to them talk, he wasn't closed-minded, but the smoother they were, the less he heard.

It had been hard for her after Sherman died, but she had come through that. When Yvonne asked if she thought of him every day, automatically she said yes. It was so long ago, but she couldn't say that. People forget. And she had. It was natural. But now she found herself thinking of both Benny *and* him, the two of them over in Homewood Cemetery, lying there while the grass knotted its roots around their boxes.

He would have a long scar where they plucked it out with their instruments. No, not a scar, the skin wouldn't heal. Under the suit Yvonne bought for him would be a zipper of stitches. But how could she say this to the lady without seeming crazy?

Outside a siren boloed over the housetops, a car ripped past. Last month she'd been broken into, someone kicked out the basement window and stole her mother's silver. The screen was bent, glass all over the washing machine. She knew Yvonne was afraid for her, living in such a big house all by herself, but Miss Fisk was used to it. The only thing that scared her was the furnace. She'd get into bed and listen for it clicking in, the radiators knocking. When it didn't, she wondered if a gust had knocked out the pilot light, the basement slowly filling with sweet-smelling gas. Her greatest fear was going to investigate, flipping on the light at the top of the stairs and suddenly being engulfed by a fireball. For that reason she kept a flashlight slung over the doorknob, and when she went down to do laundry, even in the summer she clicked it on and picked her way through the cool, mildewy darkness like a burglar, sniffing.

Now the furnace kicked in, the radiator next to her bed gurgled. She closed Mrs. Roosevelt and set her on the night table and cut off the light, fixed her pillows just the way she wanted them. She could sleep, it wasn't like she stayed awake all night, but there were a few minutes at the end of the day, in the dark, when it seemed there was nothing to do but think about Benny, and then Sherman, and these were the hardest times for her. Sleep would be merciful. And it was, it was, just not quickly enough.

Rashaan was a help. He was something to look forward to. In the morning Vanessa would ring the bell and then come right in, carrying his diaper bag, the big red dinosaur he slept with, and Miss Fisk would be fine again. But now, here in the dark, she remembered Benny eating cereal at the sink before running off to school, or in his room with his headphones on, doing his homework, and she closed her eyes tightly, wishing it away. Not him, no, she never wanted him to leave her — just as she would always have Sherman — but she was tired, so tired, didn't he understand?

In the morning it all began again. Five, five-thirty, rising with the sun. Tuesday, then Wednesday. August, September. Making her poached egg and toast, she noticed she'd forgotten to change the calendar. She ate with the radio, and still it didn't stop her from falling.

"We'll need your consent before we can do anything," the lady said, like she'd forgotten, and Miss Fisk picked up the pen and angled the paper so she could write her name. "Press hard," the lady said, "you're making three copies," and then when Miss Fisk sank back in the chair, the one gesture exhausting her, she had more forms. Miss Fisk signed these without reading them, her perfect signature — practiced diligently, a source of pride to her as a girl — degenerating into scribble, huge loops and slashes. What was the date again?

June he did her hedges for her, him and Chris, working without their shirts to impress the girls, red bandannas rolled into headbands to stop the sweat. He cut the lawn with the old push mower, oiling it from the same little can Sherman did, replacing it in the same spot in the garage. She made lemonade for them because he didn't like ice tea (another part of Yvonne in him), and they drank it on the porch, watching the Colemans playing whatever crazy game they'd made up. A week after the accident, Harold Tolbert came to the door and said he thought he might trim her bushes out front if that was all right. She didn't have to ask, just showed him where the clippers were, rolled open the garage door. She made lemonade, and he was kind enough to sit on the porch with her, sipping it slow.

"Chris says hello," he told her. "He really wanted to be there."

"Well," she said, "it's not like he had a choice in the matter," and she asked after him. A wheelchair — for life, the doctors said. She couldn't imagine it, a young man, and so she said she was sorry and to please send him her regards. They didn't get into Chris and Vanessa breaking up, or Rashaan, though it hung in the air a minute. They didn't talk about how Harold never much cared for Benny, thought it was all his fault, a bad influence on Chris. It was just mischief, neither of them was wild like Harold's older one, though folks said he'd gotten Jesus in prison.

The ice in Harold's glass rattled, and they both stood up.

"If there's anything we can do," he said.

There was and there wasn't. He could come and rake the leaves and shovel her walk and dig the garden in spring, but really there wasn't a thing he could do. It was exactly like after Sherman, she thought. She'd been so selfish. She'd thought that Benny would last her the rest of her life.

The one question she had for the lady was selfish, in a way: Who would get his liver?

The lady shuffled through a file to one side.

Miss Fisk expected her to say it was privileged information. She was ready to tear up the papers. Give you my only grandson's liver and you tell me it's none of my business?

"A Richard Skoda," the lady said. "Age sixteen."

White boy, she thought. Figures.

The lady went on to tell Miss Fisk about the condition he was born with and how he'd been waiting since he was eight, but Miss Fisk was picturing the doctors lifting it out of Benny and fitting it into Richard Skoda, the white boy all better, laughing with his family, and Benny being rolled away under a sheet.

Was it wrong to think this way?

She knew she would get past it eventually. She knew it was just grief, a temporary weakness, a susceptibility to all the things that had gone wrong in her life. And she knew just as strongly that she would return to her life, just as she had after Sherman. It would take time, that was all. Vanessa helped, and Rashaan. Sometimes she thought it was unhealthy how much she loved to hold him in her arms, that it would spoil him later. "You know your Auntie Bertie loves you, you know that, little boy, don't you?" she said, and tickled him the way she'd tickled Benny so long ago, the way she'd cooed to Yvonne, wrapped safe in her arms. Her sorrow now made those times seem that much sweeter, and she was grateful, yes, truly she was. This hurt of hers would pass, become a memory, join with all of her other ones, and those were mostly, oh, overwhelmingly happy. In time she would be fine.

But until then she was powerless in the grip of this, paralyzed, and knowing it was little help and no real comfort. She made lunch for the two of them, turned on the noon news while she spooned up Rashaan's diced turkey and potatoes, his whipped beets. There was weather and then sports and then it was his nap time. She did the few dishes they used, draped the dishrag neatly over the faucet. In the living room, Mrs. Roosevelt waited, no longer the first lady, gallivanting around the world now, an ambassador of goodwill. One son had been killed in the war. They mentioned it just once, and Miss Fisk thought that was wrong. Did it really go away so easily? Wouldn't she—like herself—look up from some book she was reading and think of him? Wherever she was, wouldn't her son be with her?

She had called Yvonne twice that night, hoping she would be home so she could make the decision. She was Benny's mother. But she wasn't home, and Miss Fisk had signed, and they'd taken his liver and given it to Richard Skoda. She was afraid of explaining this to Yvonne, and when she finally did get through, she waited until there was a lull and she could hear Yvonne clicking her nails the way she did when she was distracted and trying to think.

"Baby," she said, "they asked me if Benny would want to help some other people."

She waited but Yvonne just clicked, went mmm-hmm.

"They said his insides were fine."

"They wanted him to donate his organs," Yvonne said, making it plain.

"I said I'd have to talk to you."

"I think he'd want to help other people."

"Oh, good," Miss Fisk said. "Oh thank goodness."

"What?" she came back fast. "*What?* You didn't say they could, did you?"

"Now wait a minute," Miss Fisk said, but it was too late for that, and she knew this would stand between them for the rest of her life, would live in Yvonne long after she was laid to rest next to her Sherman. But hadn't she done the right thing?

Yes, she would answer herself, those steamy afternoons when the fan only pushed the hot air around the living room. She folded her clothes, fresh from the line, the TV on low so as not to wake Rashaan. Outside, the Coleman children were running up and down the sidewalk with their dog, a big German shepherd named Joey. One of the boys had a ball, and every time he threw it, she was ready to hear the squeal of brakes, the thump of the dog's heavy head against the bumper.

There was nothing, just the shrieks of children playing, the occasional car. Calm, bright. Shadows on the lawn. A day like today he'd be playing baseball down at the park with Chris, the two of them dragging back when it got too dark, grass stains on their ashy knees. He'd apologize for missing supper, then gobble down seconds and go out again with a new shirt and hang out on Chris's stoop and smooth-talk the girls.

She finished the laundry and put it away, then checked on Rashaan, still sleeping, curled around his dinosaur. She stood there looking at him in the heat, a bright square of sun on the carpet. Soon he'd be grown too, off to a life she'd never see, and that was good. Time kept them moving on, that was the way of the world.

It was when she had nothing to do that she got in trouble. Like a child. Like a willful boy. In this house she'd lived in so many years, she could not help but have memories. But why couldn't she choose the ones she wanted to visit with?

It was the phone there in the front hall she answered, maybe a week after it happened. The funeral was done with, the expensive stone in place, Yvonne back in Milwaukee, Herman in Minnesota, Chris still in the hospital. When the phone rang it could have been anyone. Those phone people were always trying to sell her windows that saved energy.

"Hello," a white woman said, overly polite, "is this Mrs. Bertice Fisk?"

"This is she."

"This is Maxine Skoda, Richard Skoda's mother. I just wanted to call and thank you and express our condolences about your grandson. I just wanted you to know how much your Benjamin's gift means . . ." Her voice wavered, broke and she began to cry. "What this means," she tried, but she couldn't stop.

"That's all right," Miss Fisk said. "I understand."

"I'm sorry, I know it must be so hard for you."

"It is." But you don't see me crying, do you? she wanted to say. And *my* boy's dead.

It was a brief conversation, and pleasant, but while Miss Fisk said she was glad she called, in truth it meant little to her. She did not know these people at all. Yes, she was pleased they'd taken the time to acknowledge her loss, and she was genuinely relieved that her son would live because of Benny, that the operation had been a success, but she could not let the woman's happiness and grief touch her. She *would* not let it. There was so little left she could call her own.

This house. Yvonne's calls every Sunday. Vanessa returning from work to pick up Rashaan. It was enough, along with her memories, to fill the seasons. Fall was almost on them, then winter. She'd have to get Harold to come over and turn her garden, hang the storm windows. Have to have him look at the furnace, clean the burners.

There was always something that needed taken care of. The fuzzy rug in the upstairs bath sorely needed a wash. Those old Ebonys in the cellar she'd been meaning to get rid of, and the green duffel bag with the stain. They could wait till spring, she supposed.

That was the kind of thing she needed to keep her eye on, not all this mooning over what was already done with. Drive you to distraction, sure.

She had everything she needed right here. *Oprah* was on in fifteen minutes, and she had to wake up Rashaan, get him dressed and looking good for Vanessa. She had to start thinking about supper.

Changing Rashaan, she found herself thinking of what his life would be like, how she wished she could see how he turned out. She thought of Richard Skoda. His mother never called back, and since Miss Fisk hadn't seen his name in the obituaries (she read them every day, still shocked to see people she knew), she supposed he was fine, that he would grow to be a man and marry and have children to carry on his blood. Not like her and Sherman. Benny was the end.

Was that why he was so precious?

No. It was those tiny ears, and the way he couldn't stop asking questions at supper. The birthday presents he drew for her. The birdhouse he made in woodshop. It was because he favored her so, because for all those years she had raised him like he was her own, and he was, despite anything Yvonne might say. It was not a lie: He was her good boy.

"Who's my good boy?" she asked Rashaan, lowering her nose to his. "Who's my bestest, goodest little boy?"

Later, when Vanessa had come and gone, she went back into the living room. *Oprah* was over. It was suppertime. She looked in the fridge, then searched the freezer for a tin of macaroni and cheese. She struggled with the plastic wrap, lifted off the cardboard instructions, preheated the oven to 400. It would be dark in another hour, the world shrunk to a room, a light, the book she was reading.

Outside, the Coleman children were squealing, running Joey into a lather. She stood at the window, a hand gathering back the drapes. The dog knocked one of the littler girls over, and she sat on the sidewalk, bawling and cradling her hand. Miss Fisk thought she should go out and help, but in a minute the girl's brother came by and knelt down, examining her like a doctor.

And then Miss Fisk was on the porch — oh, years ago, when Benny had just come from Milwaukee. He'd been riding some other boy's bike and lost control, and his palms were torn raw. The scrapes were filled with grit and she had to take him in to the sink and scrub them with hot, soapy water. He screamed and wrenched back and she had to pin him against the counter with her body, grip his wrists hard under the running water as he struggled. "It's the only way," she said, trying not to be angry with him. When she was done, he looked up at her, trembling, tears leaking out his eyes as if he didn't understand how she could be so mean. "Oh, baby," she said, "I'm sorry. Come here." She went to her knees and held him then, saying she was sorry, that she loved him. Didn't he know that? He had to know that.

"Benny," she said. "Baby, please."

"I know that," he said, and she crushed him against her, grateful — oh yes, blessed — vowing that as long as he was with her, she would never let anything hurt him ever again.

ANY WOMAN'S BLUES

DID HE THINK she didn't know everything? Did he honestly think that? She knew. She knew everything from the beginning and even before that. There are things a man does when he's in love, her mother taught her, ways he makes it known before he even knows it himself. Shaving every day, taking special care of his hair. Trimming his eyebrows with her scissors and then leaving the evidence right there by the sink. Smelling different. Did he really think she was that stupid?

The sheer disrespect of it made Jackie work faster. She killed the last one in the stack and waved to Sandy, standing by with the cart.

"Ready over here," she said.

"Go 'head, Jacks," Sandy said, and passed her another bundle of checks from the metal basket. She whipped the rubber band from it and dug in, punching up the numbers, double-checking them against the deposit number of the other bank or sometimes Mellon Bank's own familiar green ink stamp. The room was bright and filled with the clicking of keys and the constant hum of the printer. They weren't allowed to have the radio on—too many mistakes. Around her wrist Jackie had three rubber bands, meaning she'd done three bundles tonight, each worth thirty dollars. It was the beginning of the month, a busy time for them. Rent, electric, credit cards, car policies; they all came due at the same time. She wondered where people got the money.

Sometimes it was plain by the address on their checks. You had to know the city zip codes, the streets. People from Sewickley came from money, or people from Squirrel Hill. You didn't see a seventy-five-dollar cable bill from someone in East Liberty. But there were always surprises. Last month Jackie had entered one for sixty thousand dollars to Rohrich Cadillac by a man from Garfield. Paid in full. Walked right in, signed his name and drove it away. How many times in her life had Jackie heard their song on WAMO—*Sit back, relax, in a Rohrich Cadillac*—thinking how ridiculous buying a new one would be. Yet here was proof that people did just that, cash money—and someone from Garfield.

Tonight's weren't half as glamorous, a steady succession of water bills and magazine renewals. A speeding ticket, the signature a vicious squiggle, the pen digging into the paper, nearly tearing it.

How would she put it to Harold? Part of her wanted to just pack her bags while he was at work and leave a note, but another part of her craved the satisfaction of saying it to his face, telling him this was her house, that he could leave right now. Think you're slick, think you're all that. So you want to give up this good thing for some little tramp—after all the good years I gave you? Then you go right ahead but you had best know it's gonna cost you. I will get everything I can, cause I do not deserve this, do you understand? Every red cent, you can bet on it.

Who was she kidding? All they had was bills, and with Chris it was just going to get worse.

The money wasn't the point. Maybe she wasn't the girl she once was, but look at him, gone gray and slack years ago, never could dance a lick, all herky-jerky. Had to teach him everything about loving, even how to kiss, and then he went and quit on her. Only thing he did anymore was lie on the couch and watch TV, say he was taking a walk and come back late from the Liberty stinking of whiskey and cigarettes, Lord knows who he was with. Then he'd drop off to sleep like an old dog, twitching, mumbling things she couldn't make out, and she'd lie there silent, wide awake now, untouched and unwanted, like she wasn't good enough anymore, like she'd gone bad some-time, spoiled on him.

Goddamn that man. After she'd had his babies. How could he do this to Chris? Forget about her—didn't he know that Chris needed both of them now?

It was because of Chris that he'd stayed this long, she thought. Eugene too. Probably got tired of looking for a good time to leave, realized there was no such thing. But it was true: He was leaving them as much as he was leaving her. It made her hate him even more. Nothing lower than a man, her mother used to say, and Jackie had to admit she was right again.

She punched in a check from some woman to Kroger's and thought about how she needed to go shopping, how she needed to plan her meals for next week. Heaven knew no one else was going to do it.

She should go on strike, she thought, just stop doing what she did for him.

Think he'd notice? Ha.

Maybe after his clothes started piling up and smelling all funky and there was nothing to eat in the house.

The thought of it made her smile wickedly, but would it really change anything?

No, nothing would. He did not want her. He made that clear to her every second they were together. They didn't talk in bed anymore the way they used to, going over the day and its little pleasures, their worries and dreams for the boys. When she talked about her work she could see he wasn't listening. It was boring, she knew that, a roomful of canceled checks, but how many Nabisco stories had she sat through? It was rude, and she told him so, but then all he did was nod along, waiting for her to be done.

"Forget it," she said.

"No," he said, "finish telling it."

What's the difference, she wanted to say. You're not interested.

Aw baby, of course I am, he'd say, and then he would roll over to face her and take her warm in his arms and make love to her like a good man should. I was just tired, he'd say. I was just thinking how pretty you looked.

No. He slept and she lay awake, night after night.

She concentrated on the pile, dipped the orange rubber thimble in the little tin of Tacky-Finger for a better grip. Someone was buying antiques, someone else was paying off a car loan. Here was a check with a lighthouse background, here was a tabby cat licking its paw. Downstairs they would be sorted and shipped back to the people who wrote them so at the end of the month they could balance their checkbooks or just toss them in the garbage. Planes full of them took off every night, headed west to Chicago and Denver, the big Treasury banks, while she lay there listening for the frosty rush of their engines.

It could not go on like this. Her mother didn't raise a fool. She just needed to decide on the right way to go about it. The funny thing was it helped her work. The last few weeks she'd been the fastest, the rubber bands piling up on her wrist.

Sandy saw she was almost done and rolled the cart over. "'nother one?"

"No," Jackie said. "Four's enough for me," though she could have fit another one in. There was twenty minutes left. She'd get home early, have it out with him now. It made sense. She'd put it off too long already.

She peeled off her thimble, capped her Tacky-Finger, and tidied her work station of stray paper. In the bathroom, washing her hands, she peered at herself in the mirror. In the cold light, she could see she was too old, her skin pouchy and lined beneath the eyes. She didn't try a smile, knowing what thirty years of coffee drinking had done to her teeth. Even her eyes seemed yellow tonight, a dot of blood in one of them, chocolate syrup dropped in milk. She backed away and the water went off automatically.

How she looked was not the problem, she thought at the bus stop, watching the clouds cross the stars. She'd looked like this the last ten years and she didn't hear any complaints then. It was that she was being compared to someone else now, that he'd gone shopping behind her back. He wouldn't look so good against Denzel either, now would he?

Young, that's what he'd want, just like her father. Some little hoochie at work, probably on the same line with him. Thin and pretty, not a thought in her head. Low-class trash. If that's what he wanted, he could have it. Girl would turn around and leave him like he deserved. Then he'd come crawling back, and guess what, she wouldn't listen to a word of it, hunh-unh. Change the locks on him so he'd holler at the door till Mr. Linney called the cops. Whyn't you go back to your nasty little bitch? I thought that's what you wanted, cause you *sure* weren't interested in what I got.

The bus rolled up and she climbed on, flashing her pass. It was mostly empty, so she took a seat up front, close by the driver, her bag in her lap. Across from her sat an older couple, dressed for a night on the town. The woman was her mother's age, with a wig and big pearl earrings that had to be fake. She was sleeping against her husband, her lips brushing his pink carnation. The man had a long scarf, a walking stick and gleaming patent-leather shoes. He smiled at Jackie with perfect dentures, and she nodded back, but secretly she was jealous, as if their happiness were rightfully hers.

It was Harold's fault, not theirs, just as it was not her mother's fault her father had left them. Don't you ever be surprised, her mother said. A man will do anything anytime for any reason at all. A dog'll eat anything, doesn't matter if it's hungry.

She was tired, and so she silently agreed, sat there looking over their heads as the bus rocked along, stopping at the stops. They passed through the Hill, the bright lights of downtown giving way to dark blocks of row houses, vacant lots and chain-link fence, a stripped car under an overpass. Why did people have to be like that, she thought. No more sense than to go messing up their own homes. Least they can be is clean.

At Negley, the dressed-up couple got off, tottering arm in arm. A number of the old hotels were apartment buildings now, some of them fancy nursing homes. She was glad the two of them had their own place, that they could still get around with their senior-citizen passes. Her mother had stopped going out after a while, and her sister Daphne had to go over every day to check on her, make sure she was eating. Had the Meals on Wheels for a little bit but she didn't like it, said it was always cold. Finally Daphne had to take her in. It was only Indiana, but they never seemed to visit her. Harold had work, the kids had school, there was always something. They made it for Christmas and Easter, all four of them crammed into the guest bedroom. Jackie flew out herself when her mother was dying, then Harold drove the boys in for the funeral. A month later, Daphne sent Jackie a list of furniture and jewelry to choose from; she could have first pick, Daphne said, and this shamed her more than anything. She took just the love seat from the parlor and her jade bracelet, neither of which she really looked at anymore.

Her father was gone, possibly dead. Her mother had lost track of him. The last they'd heard, in the mid-eighties, he was in Europe—doing what, no one was sure.

Her mother would say: Don't treat a man too good, he'll only get used to it. She said: You need to keep him on his toes all the time.

Well, she had experience, didn't she? Nothing teaches like it, Jackie thought. No sir, no ma'am.

But her mother always liked Harold, that was the thing. She always talked like Melvin would be catting around on Daphne because he was a salesman, a fast talker driving all over the Midwest in his shiny Chrysler. Harold she liked because he was quiet and modest, tender with the children. He called her Mrs. Maynard, and for some reason she thought that was the most charming thing.

They turned onto Penn Circle, the bus leaning into the endless curve, the big diesel growling. Outside, trapped inside the ring, East Liberty flew by in the night, glowing under a halo of streetlights—the steeple of the old Presbyterian Church and the closed Sears towering above the other buildings. Again she thought of the shopping she needed to do, what to have for supper tomorrow.

Ham and cheesy potatoes. Lima beans, except Chris hated them. Biscuits and alaga syrup.

She wouldn't do it. She'd go on strike. She'd treated him too good for too long, that was a fact. This time she'd finally listen to her mother.

She wouldn't even tell him. Think she didn't know everything from the jump. Two could play that game. See how long it took him to figure it out. Then when he said something, she'd just let it drop on the floor between them, let him try and pick it up. It's your mess, she'd say. I got nothing to do with it.

Her stop was next. The bus slowed, and she shouldered her purse and clutched the pole, shifted sideways and let the momentum lift her to her feet and swing her toward the door. She was the only one getting off. Spofford was deserted, the parked cars throwing shadows, the ceiling of trees above the sidewalk menacing. She held her bag tight and walked softly, thinking any decent man would be waiting for her at the stop.

Any decent man wouldn't have her out working till eleven at night to pay the bills.

She didn't have to marry Harold, that was the terrible thing. There was Alvin Reese, who played the trombone in his own band and had a Nash Rambler. He'd asked her first, and the only reason she didn't say yes was because her mother didn't like his family. Too down-home, his father a farmhand. Now he was a car dealer in Bloomington and donated vans to the university. Then there was Gregory Mattison, whose father owned the butcher shop, but he wasn't after her to marry him. Her mother couldn't keep track of him either. There were more, though she couldn't name any particular ones right now. There could have been more, that was the point; she wasn't forced into marrying Harold. Then why had she? What had she seen in him? How had it led to this?

She didn't have to think long on it. He was nice, that was the thing about him. Polite. Her mother thought he was responsible. Jackie had too. Luckily her mother died before he could prove them both wrong.

So what do you think of your favorite son-in-law now, she wanted to ask, as if it were her fault, her choice, and suddenly Jackie wondered if all those years ago she'd sensed something of Daddy in him, if that was why she'd picked him in the first place.

She could only blame herself for believing in him, for believing everything was all right all along. That part of it was her fault, she was willing to admit that. Maybe she was stupid for doing it, but she'd wanted to keep some kind of hope too. It was beyond that now.

As she crossed Spofford she dug in her bag for her keys, getting them ready before she opened the door to the vestibule, turning just that much to make sure no one followed her in. Inside, it was quiet, a burst of curry coming from the back of the first floor. On the stairs her heels sounded loud.

She would start by not doing the dishes. She knew they'd be waiting for her, piled up all greasy in the sink since supper, barely room enough to run a glass of water. Maybe she could excuse Chris, but there was no reason she should have to come home from work and do them when Harold had been there all night. What, she'd say, are your arms broken?

She wouldn't give him a kiss (not that he'd notice). She'd ignore the grease on the stovetop, the newspaper strewn about the living room, the boys' hampers overflowing. She'd run a hot bath and soak in it, put on a robe and go to bed, and if he wanted anything he could just get it himself.

But wasn't that what he wanted, for her to leave him alone?

This would be different. Everything she didn't do would find its way back to him. Question was, how long would she be able to stand it?

She could hear a TV going as she walked down the hall. Probably lying there on the couch in his funky undershirt watching some nonsense. Yes, it was coming from their apartment. She was quiet with the keys, careful slipping it into the lock, as if she'd bust in and surprise him.

The couch was empty, a single beer can on the magazines on the coffee table. The TV was coming from Chris's room, his little portable. She set her bag on the hall table and hung her coat in the closet—patiently, as if she wasn't interested whether he was home or not—and noticed his jacket was missing, one hanger bare.

You're so stupid, she thought, mad at herself for assuming he'd be there. She should have seen it. It was just like him.

And just like she'd thought, the sink was piled high with dishes, spaghetti and red sauce stuck between the layers. The tap dripped because he hadn't put it back straight. Well, she'd be damned before she touched one of them. She fixed the tap and headed for Chris's room.

He had the TV on the bed with him, something she'd warned him about. Since the accident, she had a hard time making her discipline stick. Each time she saw him after being away for more than an hour, the undeniable fact of his injuries returned, and she wanted to take him in her arms. She always worried that her boys would not have a fair chance at life, had spent their school years alert to every potential slight, made sure they had a better opportunity than she did growing up: better clothes, better friends, a better home. A better father—she'd always prided herself on that.

Chris was stuck to the TV, his mouth hanging open. Stoned, she thought. Goddamn. She stood in the doorway, waiting for him to notice her.

He still didn't.

"Hi, Moms," she said, mimicking him. "How was work?"

"Not bad," she answered herself, and he turned and gave her a smirk.

"Hey," he said.

"Where's your father?"

"Out walking."

"How 'bout your brother?"

"Sleeping."

"What are *you* doing?"

"Watching TV."

"Not getting high, I trust."

"No," he said, and she could read it in his eyes, even through the Visine. Just like his father. She'd never met a man you couldn't help but tell was lying, yet it seemed it was all they did, every one of them. It was almost funny.

"It's past eleven," she said. "I'm going to bed. I don't want you staying up too late."

"'kay," he said, and he was lost in the TV again.

She peeked in Eugene's room, the light slicing in around her to show him under the covers, his slacks folded over the back of a chair, his shoes grouped at the foot of the bed, pointed toward the door. She resisted going in, turned away slowly, as if still thinking of it.

As she crossed the living room, she reached for the beer can. It was a reflex, and she had to consciously withdraw her hand and leave it there.

Out drinking, doing God knows what to who.

She cut out the light in the living room but left on the one in the kitchen. The rubber bands she added to the baggie in the junk drawer. Crumbs on the table, a smear of sauce. Stove spotty with grease, orange peel in the sink. She felt helpless before the mess, and turned from it, trying to put it out of her mind.

She took her clothes off in the dark and shoved them in the hamper, slipped her robe on, and brushed her teeth. The tub beckoned in the mirror, but she was too tired. She flossed and did her Listerine, spitting then carefully rinsing the blue drops off the sink.

In bed she checked the clock. It wasn't eleven-thirty yet. Her legs were jumpy, her insteps, but she couldn't sleep. She had choir practice tomorrow, that was some comfort. And where would he be then? She knew he waited for her to leave, stole every second for himself. She thought of him at the Liberty (he wasn't really there, she knew that, but she would not picture him with the woman, the way they laughed, the things they did at this time of night) and then of the wreck he'd made of the kitchen.

Like a pigsty, her mother would say. After her father left, she cleaned house to support them, something both Jackie and Daphne had been ashamed of, guarded from their friends like a dirty secret. Her mother was shocked at how nasty white people were, especially in the kitchen. Their stoves were caked with filth, their counters breeding grounds, swabbed with mucked-up dishcloths. Over supper, she described the horrors of her work for the girls, drumming into them the importance of a clean house. How many times had she heard the old saw: We may be poor but at least we're clean. It was a badge of honor, the only one they could afford. How proudly she wore it! She remembered almost vomiting when her mother told her how white people kissed their dogs on the nose. "And it's not like they don't know where that nose has been," her mother said. "There's one place a dog's nose loves to go, and that is *not* somewhere you want to be kissing."

Wasn't it the same with Harold? She knew where he'd been sticking his nose. Now, defenseless, with nothing to distract her, she briefly envisioned it, the raw pornography of what he was doing with this other woman, pictured the two of them, or just Harold bent to her, and she thought she would be sick. He was bringing that home with him, rubbing her face in it, wiping it on these very sheets, infecting everything. She could feel the disease seeping into her skin.

She flung the covers aside and heaved up out of bed. For a moment she stood on the carpet, holding herself, then hurried down the hall to the kitchen.

She crossed the floor to the sink in her bare feet and slapped the tap on. She had to pour the cold water out of the top dishes and set them on the counter to make room to do the pots, the big serving bowl with the worms of spaghetti stuck to the lip. The cuff of her gown got wet and she rolled it up. "You keep your dirt out of my house." She did the bowls, the glasses, and finally the silverware piece by piece, clouds of steam rising around her, until the drainboard was full.

She wiped down the counters with a green pad and then a sponge. She did the table, saving the stove for last, lifting the burners, digging at faint, old stains with a Brillo pad. Always clean from the top down, her mother instructed, and now she looked at the floor, scuffed with a week's worth of dirt.

First she moved the chairs into the hallway, then she swept, discovering a few Cheerios. She squirted the cleaner in snaky waves, dunked the mop in the bucket.

It was almost one when she finished. She had the mad idea of cleaning the fridge, throwing out all the green cheese and watery sour cream, but the shine of the floor and the stove was enough to satisfy her. She stood with her arms folded, surveying her work with a violent pleasure. Her mother would be pleased, she thought. See, she wanted to say, I learned. I did listen.

After a few minutes, she went to the silverware drawer and then turned off the light and lay down on the couch, sweating, her heart thumping from the exertion, a clean boning knife in one hand, waiting for her husband to come home.

EVADING

THE CAPRICE WAS where he'd left it last night, on Wayland, three streets over, behind Sacred Heart, the driver's-side door lock popped. He almost didn't expect it to be there, waiting for him in the rain. He was ready to pass by the empty section of curb, nonchalant, or even a police tow truck lifting the front end, the stubby screwdriver hidden like a knife in his pocket, the see-through plastic grip sweaty in his palm. But here it was, leaves plastered to the hood, the windshield beaded, the radio still in place.

LJ looked back toward the corner, checking the wet, redbrick street and the heavy trees, the porches of the crowded row houses—their barred picture windows all watching him—then cut between the parked cars. Another look the other way and he grabbed the handle and swung himself in, knees bumping the wheel, locking the door behind him, sealing in the quiet. He ducked down, lying half across the new-smelling seat to see what he was doing with the steering column. Rain ticked against the roof. The plastic shell was cracked and jagged, the sky-blue white where it had snapped off. He fit the blade of the screwdriver in the ignition and twisted. It started on the first try.

He'd found the car three days ago over in Homewood, after a party, him and Cardell and some baby Treys they were breaking in. It was just a way home, a way of keeping the night alive until something else came up. He didn't mean to keep it so long. It was stupid, he didn't need it for anything, he wasn't going to sell it, it was just something he'd started doing, driving around the city. It got him away from the neighborhood, away from B-Mo, who he knew was looking for him. It got him away from Nene's things and from his Granmoms and from U, coming over the house at night and talking all kind of God nonsense, like he was trying to save him. Out of respect LJ listened, but he didn't hear him. There was too much going on, too much noise from everyone after what happened, including himself. He'd gotten used to riding around with the radio off, letting the rhythm of traffic sift his thoughts. He knew it couldn't go on forever, that it was dangerous, but every morning he came back to the Caprice, and there it was.

Today he decided to take a different route, across the river and then toward downtown, maybe drive around the North Side a while. It was neutral ground as long as he stayed down by the water. Go too far up into the hilly streets and he'd be in Riverview Crip territory, all projects. Nothing but dead ends and fences, concrete stairs leading nowhere. Didn't want to be caught slipping, not by them.

He wasn't strapping. He wasn't going anywhere he'd need it, and if the cops popped him, it meant time. Without it, the most he'd get was sent to Schuman again. He still had another year as a juvenile.

There was a railyard near the prison. Maybe he'd sit there and watch the trains headed off for Cleveland, Detroit, Chicago, cities he'd dreamed of without ever seeing. No, you couldn't stay in one place that long, people'd get suspicious. It was the one rule of boosting cars: You were only safe as long as you were moving.

He liked it better when it rained. He drove slow, leaving his seatbelt off in case he needed to ditch. The big Caprice rolled through the turns, cruised high and quiet along the tight side streets, eating up the bumps. Blocks of low, brown-brick row houses, telephone wires dipping in threes. The porches with their steel railings slid by like endless boxcars. It was cool for September, the rain steady, and he set the heater to the far side of the red stripe, the fan to the first dot. The radio was basic, no CD or cassette player, and he left it alone. The wipers swept the water off the glass, paused to let more collect, then squeegeed it clean.

For the first few blocks he thought nothing, concentrated on signaling for his turns, an eye out for Five-O. The sidewalks were empty, and he liked that—no one trying to make his face. Once he swung it around Penn Circle and past Sears and down Negley Run, he'd be onto the long stretch of Washington Boulevard beside the old driver's-test place, and free of the neighborhood. He could be from Blawnox or Penn Hills for all people knew. He could be going home to a big house in Shaler where his mother would be vacuuming the living room, his father at work downtown in the PPG Tower, his office with a view of Station Square where the fake riverboats docked. Nene would be at Penn State — or no, working downtown in another building, maybe Gateway Center.

What would he do there? Something with money, a desk with a computer and neat stacks of paper, contracts from other businesses.

But Nene wasn't good with money, he was always getting behind with B-Mo, asking him for another week, doing all his product then begging B-Mo to front him some.

He couldn't picture it, Nene in some fine suit like the prom or the awards dinner he missed. This was always the hard part, finding him a job. Cleaning him up was easy; he remembered in eighth grade girls phoning him every night, so many their Granmoms said he couldn't take calls after nine o'clock. She locked him in his room after she caught him getting into it on the back porch with Danita Coleman — the same Danita Coleman who turned into a straight head-hunter later, skanky raspberry who'd do anything to get her mouth around that glass dick one more time. What was the difference between her and Nene?

She was alive, tricking downtown. Nene was over in Homewood Cemetery, under the mud. That was the difference.

At Highland LJ had to wait for a bus, and he turned down the heater before pulling across the oncoming lane. The streetlights were still on, even though it wasn't that dark. He was out of the side streets now, no longer protected, part of the overall flow of the city yet hidden, safe behind the thin windshield. He sat up straighter in the seat, as he imagined race-car drivers did, checking his mirrors without turning his head, keeping the needle at the precise speed, following the car in front of him at a reasonable distance. He took pride in facing the danger quietly, of being the only one aware of it, separate from the other drivers, and at the same time felt part of a larger body, the Caprice one cell in the blood of traffic pumping through the country, every street and road and interstate open to him, a possibility, as if he could leave. It was an illusion. He was nearly invisible, yet a second could change that, drag him out onto the wet pavement facedown, police's knee in his back, a gun to his ear. No other feeling seemed so true to him, and it filled him like a drug, gave him strength.

Around Penn Circle now, staying in one lane past the basketball courts by the cop station, the cruisers lined up outside, parked on the sidewalk. They had Caprices too, it was like a joke to him; maybe that was why he couldn't get rid of the car. He flicked his eyes at the rearview mirror; none of them had moved.

He caught the light at Baum Boulevard and headed up past the Chevy dealer where U worked. He glanced over at the rows of used cars, the rain dotted on their fresh wax jobs, and wondered if U would have to do them again. O.G. Trey cleaning up after white folks, all because of Jesus.

"'s fucked up," LJ said.

He stayed sharp across Penn and around the other side of the circle, over the muddy busway and past the old-folks high-rise. The lights were on in the laundromat, some mothers filling the machines. There wasn't much traffic, just enough to keep him busy, making sure he knew where everyone was behind him. He turned the heat off and got in the right lane to go straight on Collins, but the light was changing and he had to brake and then stop.

Beside him, a raggedy station wagon pulled up, a jitney, an older woman in back with her groceries, the driver waving his hand and laughing, telling tales. With the rain it was tough to see, but for an instant LJ thought the woman was his Granmoms, and a rush of panic shocked him, then evaporated, leaving him weak. The light dropped to green and he let the jitney beat him down the straightaway to Negley Run where it made the light and was gone.

She was keeping Nene's clothes for him. She didn't have to say it. They were almost the same size. He used to borrow Nene's Raptors jersey, but now it didn't seem right. He'd open the closet and under the sweet cedar and harsh mothballs he could smell him. And forget about shoes.

The hard part was over. Negley Run was a bypass cut out of the hillside; it connected East Liberty to Washington Boulevard so people could book out of there faster. No sidewalks, no shops, no stoplights, just grass and trees on both sides of the slope, and LJ laid back against the headrest and let the weight of the Caprice take it downhill through the long, easy curves.

At the bottom it T-boned Washington by the fire school, an empty brick building they pretended to burn down each week. He was going left, toward the river. If he went right, he'd end up in Homewood, and now he wished he did have a gun to settle his beef with B-Mo, bust some caps in his dumb, ugly ass. It didn't matter that Fats had his soldiers smoke those two punks. Everyone in his set was waiting for LJ to take care of his business.

He could see it. He'd spent the last week thinking of it—here, at home, just hanging on the corner. It's what everyone was thinking, but it was up to him to put it together, to put the shit into effect.

He couldn't do it alone. He'd have to get someone to drive—Cardell, cause he was always talking garbage. Nighttime, a Friday while it was still warm enough to party outside. A dark car, four-door. He'd be in the backseat with the window open, Tek Nine ready in his lap, extra clip between his knees.

"Pull up," he'd say. "Pull up here."

There'd be people hanging out on someone's porch, smoking on the steps, lounging on someone's brokedown couch, passing a 40 of Private Stock and clowning on his brother, how they wasted the cluckhead motherfucker. "Sliced and diced," they'd be saying, Master P booming out the windows.

"Ha! Chipped and chopped that trick-ass bitch."

"For real."

He'd roll down on them, serve them straight off the top.

"Show 'em what you got," Cardell would shout, and the shit would be on.

He'd see B-Mo sitting there with that fat, ugly grill of his, skeezer hanging off his arm, trying to figure out who was sweating his clique.

It wouldn't be a secret; LJ would turn on the light inside so they'd know. "What's up, punk?" he'd say. "My name is L-to-the-motherfucking-J," and they'd see him and know what was up and try to bounce, but he'd have that Tek spraying, holding it with both hands, ripping that shit up, saying, "What's my name?"

"Yeah," he said, taking the left. "That's right."

There was another version where he walked B-Mo down Moreland to the spot Nene had fallen, holding a chrome magnum under his chin. People came out of their houses to watch. No one tried to stop him; they knew it was justice, point-blank.

They got to the spot and LJ moved the muzzle to B-Mo's forehead, pressed it in so it left an O. He had him up against the fence, and people were crowding around.

"You got any last words?"

"I—"

"Shut the fuck up," he said, and blew his whole head open. Then they tie-wrapped him to the fence and let the birds pick at his brains, let the little wannabes cut him for fun.

While he was driving around, these dreams of his soothed him, as if they'd already come true. He could pretend he'd already avenged his brother, that he'd earned back the respect they'd taken from him. He could drive like this all day, he knew, but eventually he would have to turn around and go home, and Cardell would be there, asking him what he was going to do, how soon.

U knew that. Everyone knew that, but U was the one asking him not to do it. U was asking him to forgive B-Mo's people.

"Fuck that shit," LJ told him. They were in his living room, and he was trying to be polite.

"You can't keep living like this," U said, like that was some kind of answer.

Now he was gliding past the old state police barracks on one side, the road up to Schuman on the other. He'd been in there once, GTA, possession and evading. It was basically the same thing he was doing now, except that time he was dumb enough to have some bud on him, so he had to do drug school too, read these stupid pamphlets the social worker gave him and take tests. He had to pass or do the course over, so he read the stuff. Wasn't anything he didn't already know.

Down alongside the driver's-test place, deserted now, a sign on the chained gate saying they moved. Spray kicked up from the car in front of him, misting the windshield, and with a touch the wipers slapped it away. A flat, dirty patch on the road was a squirrel. He got in the right lane so he'd be in position to get on the bridge, made the light and jogged the car into the chute for the on-ramp, the traffic in front of him bunching up for the turn even though they had their own lane. He braked, swearing at them, but once he was on the bridge itself and the view opened up, he forgot everything.

It was like flying. A hundred feet below, the Allegheny ran high and wide and gray as mushroom soup, poured frothing over the low dam. On the far shore a fleet of derelict barges bobbed, one half sunk in the mud. Upriver stood a black railroad bridge he'd only seen a train on once, and beyond it on the near shore, topping the wooded cliff like a ship, the VA Med Center. Now he wished he could slow down to absorb everything, to appreciate the way it filled

his mind so he didn't have to think of anything. He knew if
he stopped the car in the middle and got out and stood at
the rail that the view would lose its power and he'd turn in
on himself again, think of Nene. He had to keep moving,
that was the one rule; why did he keep forgetting it?

Toward downtown there was an island with nothing
on it, just a rusty dredge that had been there since he was a
kid. He used to want him and Nene to build a cabin there
and swim all the time and make rafts and fish for their dinner. When he told their Granmoms, she laughed out loud.
"I don't think you want to eat anything that comes out of
that river," she said, and he was hurt, his plans demolished.
He'd never been there, and the island still held some mystery for him. He would never get there, he thought. It wasn't
right. The thing was so close.

At the end of the bridge, the ramp for downtown curled
around a box factory, a lit billboard above it advertising
frozen food that used their product. The car in front of him
went right, peeled off toward Fox Chapel—where he would
be stopped, searched, the cop kicking his ankles apart, a
gloved hand on his neck—and LJ stayed left, gunned the
Caprice up onto Route 28, headed downtown, flying along
beneath sheer cliffs covered with lovers' graffiti, the rock
dark in the rain. On the other side the shiny streets of
Sharpsburg passed below, the houses just roofs, antennas,
chimneys smoking as if it was winter. Pigeons sat on a tar-
nished cross atop a church's greening dome. By the river, a
scrap-yard magnet rocked its load toward a waiting gondola
car, silently dropping rusty beams like straight pins. He
could see across to Highland Park, the houses crowding the

hills of Morningside. A mile beyond that lay his neighborhood, where Cardell would already be on the corner, slinging rock, his beeper set on vibrate.

He wanted to tell U he knew he couldn't go on living
this way. He wasn't stupid. But what was he supposed
to do?

"Turn yourself around," U said, "or someone or some-
thing is going to do it for you, believe that."

He believed it. All he had to do was think of Nene.

"That right there should be enough," U said. He shook
his hand before leaving, thanked his Granmoms, all official.
He was putting together a group down at the church, he told
her. He'd be real happy if Leonard—if LJ—might give it
a try.

"Tell me what time," she said, "and he'll be there."

The first meeting was tonight. He hadn't decided what
he was going to tell her, what kind of lie. Why bother? U
would come by after, so she'd know he didn't go.

He thought of driving out to the airport and watching
the planes take off, an endless line of them, all going somewhere he'd never been. No, you had to pay for parking, and
there were cops everywhere.

Past Etna and down toward Millvale, where the road
changed and the lights started again. On his right, between
peeling billboards, a few houses were pushed up against the
hillside, set on top of buckled retaining walls. In one yard,
a chained dog stood on top of its house, barking at the traffic. Farther on, an old white lady with a black scarf over her
hair sat in a bus shelter, waiting with her purse, and he
thought of his Granmoms at the library, pushing the cart

along, helping shelve the books. She was the only reason he stayed.

He could admit it here, alone in the Caprice. He didn't have anyone else.

Nene used to tell him stories about their mother, how beautiful she was, how she loved to hold LJ when she was eating. Their Granmoms would tell her to leave him in his crib when she came to the table, but she'd just cut everything with the side of her fork and sit there rocking him. Nene always thought she loved LJ better, but it was just because he was the new baby.

"Jealous?" Nene'd say. "Why I wanna be jealous of you? Stringy, big-head motherfucker. Look like a Tootsie pop and shit." Then they'd slap fight. LJ could never beat him, with those long arms. "Stick and move," Nene'd say, making him flinch.

He'd show LJ pictures of her, taking down their Granmoms' albums and sitting on the couch.

"Hold up," LJ would say, needing to look at every page a little longer, to hear the story of where and when just one more time. So he'd know. Now his Granmoms had Chris's drawing of Nene framed and hanging over the fireplace, like it was something from the past. It was — but not that far past, he wanted to say. It was like the drawing was the same as the photo albums, like Nene was gone like their mother, and that wasn't true. He could still feel Nene leaving him.

He'd drifted close to the white line, and he straightened his nose out. He was almost across from downtown now; he could see the skyscrapers, the top of the Gulf Building flashing blue to let him know it was raining. The Heinz plant came up on his left in a wall of steam, the tilted bottle on top spilling neon lines of ketchup above a clock. He checked his gas—a little less than half. Even self-serves were too risky. When he ran out, he'd have to ditch it. Another day, maybe two if he didn't go too far.

The road dropped down to the level of the neighborhood streets, the North Side pawn shops and sports bars around the stadium. Bail bonds, checks cashed. Painted on the sides of old brick buildings, faded signs advertised stores that had closed before he was born. The road gained another lane, then two. He could see the white concrete tire of Three Rivers ahead, the desolate parking fields under the curved ramps of the Fort Duquesne Bridge. The Pirates were out of town, so it was possible the Steelers were there, practicing for Sunday's game in the rain. He and Nene had gone once, with the church. Their Granmoms gave them five dollars each to get whatever they wanted. The lines at the concession stand were endless, the steps of the upper deck dizzyingly steep. He remembered dropping his hot dog when they finally got back to their seats, and wanting to pick it up, but Nene stepped on it on purpose, squishing it, then ripped his own in half and gave him the bigger piece. And still he cried, thinking he'd been mean.

That was the Nene he'd remember, not the one who sold his Gameboy on the corner and then twenty minutes later came back looking for the games. Not the one who smashed in the back door after their Granmoms changed the locks on him. Not the one stressing his friends for a dollar on the way to school, his lips silver from huffing aluminum paint. Not the one peeing on parked cars like some old drunk. Not the one under the sheet on the sidewalk, the can of ice tea he'd been drinking lying in a chalk box next to him.

Driving, he remembered not just good things or bad things, but everything. That was why he did it, he figured. Sometimes he even pretended Nene was with him, riding shotgun, talking shit about the places they'd been. They'd lived their entire lives in the city, and every street had some of them in it. He was coming up on the high fences and concertina wire of Western Pen. "Remember when we went to visit U that time and they wouldn't let us in?" LJ would say, and Nene would help him tell the whole story. "'member the time Granmoms ran over Cardell's bike?" and they'd laugh and laugh.

The Caprice was quiet, the Ohio flowing muddy beside him, downtown filling the rearview mirror. He turned on the heater again and blinked, the air drying his eyes. Ohio River Boulevard ran out past Western Pen and along the railroad tracks. He crossed into Bellevue and then Avalon, quiet towns, the supermarket lots full of Jeep Wagoneers and Ford Explorers, not a face like his anywhere. LJ had never been this far, but there was nothing new or interesting here, only a barge pushing upriver. Somehow he'd gone too far and lost Nene, lost the feeling he needed. For the first time, it wasn't working.

At Neville Island he crossed the Ohio and came back, driving by the chemical plants pumping out clouds, the waste-treatment facility, a graveyard in the middle of nowhere. He took West Carson Street back in, crossing the Fort Pitt Bridge for the postcard view of downtown, then swung onto the Parkway East, the Mon on his right, all bridges and old steel mills. The hill of the South Side looked gray in the rain, cheap company houses crammed onto steep streets, clouds right down on top of them. He had nothing to be back for, yet he was heading straight home, the needle on 65. Most days it worked, driving around. What was different today—the rain?

It always rained in Pittsburgh.

In his disappointment, he couldn't think of any one place to lay the blame. He was tired of thinking, maybe that was it. He needed to find another way to take his mind off Nene.

And he'd thought this one would last him, that was the sad part. It was the one place he felt safe.

There was nothing he could have done, that was clear. He'd been watching TV at Cardell's when it happened. He'd even heard the shots and then the car taking off, or he thought he did afterward. It was *Comic View*, and they were laughing at something dumb. He didn't know until twenty minutes later when Mrs. Brown came in holding a hand over the phone and told him it was his Granmoms. He took it into the hall so he could hear. At first he couldn't understand what she was saying, and then it all fit together like a puzzle. He ran out of the house, leaving his Seahawks jacket; the next day Cardell brought it over, saying he was sorry.

Everyone was sorry.

The Oakland exit came up fast, and he slowed for the ramp and merged onto Forbes. Traffic was bumper to bumper between the lights, trucks double-parked and unloading on both sides. The sidewalks were busy here, even in the rain—students from Pitt, street people hustling change outside the Giant Eagle. There was a cop car there, facing the street, and he kept his eyes straight ahead.

He was through the first light when the siren came up behind him. He squashed the urge to look back. He was boxed in, there was nowhere to go. The sound was louder, and a streak of red light bounced off the storefronts. He would not fight them. He would not say a word, just sit in the caged backseat like a killer, the handcuffs biting his wrists.

Was that what he wanted—to use that as an excuse?

He knew he should have killed B-Mo the same night, or died trying, should have brought an army of Treys down on his shit, all of Spofford mobbing through Brushton.

The siren gave way to a blast of noise like a horn, and the van beside him pulled over to make way.

It was an ambulance, probably for one of the hospitals up on Fifth. He angled the Caprice beside the van to let it through, then spun the wheel and gunned into the open space.

At Craig he cut over to Centre, sliding by a whole row of churches and expensive funeral homes. He'd cried at Nene's service. He didn't expect to, and then when he was helping their Granmoms up to see him, his whole body turned to rubber and he couldn't breathe. Nene had a new suit on, and someone had done his hair. The shotgun had left holes in his face but they'd covered them with makeup, and he looked like the Nene he wanted to remember, not the Nene who ripped him off, the Nene who shorted him a quarter ounce, the Nene who dared him to try and get back what was his.

"Fucking step up or step off, bitch," Nene said in front of his friends, and LJ backed down. "Yeah, I thought so."

"Fuck you," LJ said, walking away, and Nene got him in a headlock so his Pirates hat fell in the mud.

"Don't you *ever* mess with me."

Cardell just stood there, waiting for him to let go.

"Don't know why I fuck with your punk ass." Nene threw him to the ground and walked off, not bothering to do his pimp strut. Because it wasn't a joke. Cardell picked up the hat and gave it to LJ. There was mud on the gold button, and rubbing it off just rubbed it in.

"I'ma *kill* that motherfucker," LJ said, and Cardell didn't say anything. Because he knew he wouldn't do shit.

He was almost home now, driving past Shadyside Hospital and then the projects, Centre empty, beer bottles caught in the storm grates. Ahead, the light went red for no reason; the intersection was deserted, not a car in sight. Babyland had closed a few years ago but no one had rented it; the sign was faded, the name spelled out in children's blocks. The bar next to it was open, the metal door scarred, half kicked in. He sighed and waited for the light, careful now that he was so close.

Did he really think he could get away from it? He could drive all night, all the way across the country, nonstop, and Nene would be sitting right beside him. Always would. The best he could hope for was talking with him once in a while, remembering when he was still his brother.

The circle, then Highland and into the side streets. Stop signs, no cops. Long puddles in the alleys. The windows of Sacred Heart glowed yellow. He signaled and turned down

Wayland. His parking spot was there; everyone was at work. It took him two tries to get it right, riding up on the curb. He looked around before pulling out the screwdriver, carefully replaced the cracked shell over the hole.

The one door he left unlocked. He crossed in front of the hood, a drop falling on his cheek, making him blink. As he walked away he looked back at the Caprice like he owned it, like someone might steal it, like this was the last time, and he thought maybe now he really was finished with it. Like U said, he had to stop. He had to change. It made sense.

The wind kicked up, and a loud shower fell from the trees. LJ shoved his hands in his pockets and ducked his face against the rain, headed home, knowing he'd be back tomorrow.

CRY ME A RIVER

HE CALLED ANDRE from somewhere over South Dakota, fuzzy, saying he'd be in around midnight and there was champagne in the liquor cabinet.

"Don't put it in the freezer," Michel said, as if they'd never done this before.

He wanted to say no, he needed his sleep, but the machine was across the room.

"And if you could, on your way over pick up some milk for breakfast. I'm sure mine's cottage cheese by now."

"I'm not staying for breakfast," Andre said into the article he was reading.

"See you soon," Michel said, and the line cut off. The machine clicked and rewound until the green light flickered.

Andre slowly got up and walked over in his slippers, the *Advocate* hanging open in one hand. He stood there with his finger on the button, frozen, as if trying to decide.

He'd told Harold he wasn't seeing Michel anymore. It wasn't a lie; he was off in the Pacific, pulling three full months of Bangkok, Hong Kong and Tokyo. The flights were long, and the time difference was tough to get used to, so they kept the crews together, then gave them two weeks off to decompress. When they were living together, Michel always came home exhausted, happy to see him, even when they were having a bad time. For a night, a day, a week, everything was forgiven, but then a backhanded remark, a chipped dish, an overdue bill, and they fought like dogs, each of them lunging for the other's weakness, digging their teeth in. Andre wanted to say he'd finally left, sick of his constant criticism, but Michel never gave him the choice, shouting and pitching his things down the stairs in the middle of the night in just his underwear, like some overdone Tennessee Williams thing.

It had been nearly a year now, and they'd made up, seen each other around. Twice, late spring nights in Shadyside, Andre had ended up in his bed—not drunk, just sweetly buzzed on Campari—and things had been good. Michel knew how to love him, where and how much and when to be still. It seemed to both of them a mistake that they'd broken up. How did it happen, they asked; we're so good together. Then Michel had to do his Pacific route. He promised to call, though Andre said he'd rather have a letter. Of course he hadn't heard from him until now, when he wanted Andre.

Like takeout, he thought. It's late and he's hungry and there's nothing open, just me.

He did miss him, he couldn't deny it. Harold asked about him all the time, suspicious. Have you talked to him lately? Gotten any interesting mail? It was so typical, that hypocritical straight-guy possessiveness; secretly for a while Andre kind of liked it, but finally it wasn't romantic, just another hassle.

Michel called Harold Mrs. Jones, after the Billy Paul song. He'd sing it every time he mentioned him — "We got a thinnnnnnnng goin o-on." As usual, he thought Andre was being foolish, leading with his heart. "Or maybe it isn't your heart?" he insinuated, and Andre told him to fuck off.

"Married men." Michel shook his head. "My little homewrecker." It was a joke to him, and Andre laughed, but deep down he accused himself, and had all along. He could see how futile it was from the outset, how damaging. He promised he'd never ask Harold to leave his family, but from time to time, alone in his apartment, he thought it was only fair: He wanted the man he loved to be by his side. It couldn't help but slip out, and then it became this big thing that ruined their few hours together. After a while, all they did was fight. Even their lovemaking was part of a larger argument, a test of their true feelings. And though they proved again and again that they fit perfectly (despite the age difference and Harold's chronic worrying about his body), this knowledge only bred resentment. The whole thing was pointless. Finally they decided to just stop seeing each other.

It had been a week now of sitting home alone, a week of opening novels and ending up watching TV. He was used to killing time, waiting for Harold to break free of his wife, but now there was no possibility of his feet on the stairs, his knock at the door, his arms. So many times this week Andre had caught himself checking the time as if expecting him, then sighing, disgusted with everything, and he felt stupid.

Just as Michel warned, he'd let Harold mean too much to him, and now nothing satisfied him.

He hit the button and the machine whirred, deleting Michel. It was already past ten. He sat down with the *Advocate* and read about Jodie Foster finally coming out (duh!) as if nothing had happened, as if he wasn't thinking of Michel's down comforter, his clean sheets. There was an art to drinking in bed. He imagined the shock of a cold mouthful, the bubbles tickling his skin, and he thought of Harold at home, too timid to give in to love.

When he was finished with the article, he went into the bathroom and turned on the shower. He waited for the steam to pour up and curl in a thin layer beneath the ceiling. He wanted it scalding.

He closed his eyes and let the water pound down over him, trying to pretend this wasn't a mistake. He let his arms go limp, bent his head and stood there until there was nothing but the warm spot on the back of his neck, continually repeating. Did he resent Michel for assuming he'd be waiting for him? He wasn't; he was still waiting for Harold. But wasn't this what he wanted—Michel back and Harold gone? It was probably best for everyone. And the sex was better with Michel, no doubt. Andre was no size queen like some people he knew, but Michel was special, he had the total package—youth, beauty and a long cock with a pretty curve to it. It was what won him in the first place, not so long ago.

He didn't care about the sex.

The thought shocked him so much that it didn't seem true, as if it had come from someone else. There were years when nothing else had mattered, so many wild nights cruising and being cruised, playing the game. He wasn't young like that anymore. He wasn't beautiful like Michel—or only when he was with Harold.

He toweled off and caught himself in the mirror. He hadn't been to the gym in months, and his chest had lost the definition he'd built this spring. No pecs, no sex, Michel always joked, lavishing attention on them. In the mirror, Andre bit a nail and then stopped himself; he'd chewed them down to the nubs, something he hated. Lately it seemed he hated everything—himself, his apartment, this city.

"Stop," he said, because he knew where it all led back to.

He went into the bedroom and got dressed, spending far too long trying to look nonchalant, like he'd just thrown something on. God, he looked awful. He really did need his sleep. He'd been waking up at three and four in the morning and then couldn't get comfortable again. At work he drank coffee all morning so by lunchtime he didn't feel like eating, and then when he got home he had crippling headaches and the damn dog downstairs barked every time he crossed the room.

It was just love, he thought, digging Michel's key out of a tray full of change. He would have to be hard on himself for a while, concentrate on small pleasures the same way he had when he lost Michel.

But he hadn't really lost Michel, he could still have him whenever Michel summoned him. With Harold it was different, all or nothing. He knew it appealed to the romantic in him. His love needed to be abject, devastating, operatic. He was never good at hiding his neediness; he'd cry after

making love with all his heart, clutch at his lover like someone drowning. It always frightened Michel. Maybe he'd
scared Harold off the same way.

He left only the light over the stove on. Miss Payne's
dog yapped at him as he came down the stairs and across
the porch. His Eclipse was untouched beneath the streetlight; the locks clicked when he punched the remote. The
night was chilly and clear, the steering wheel cold even
through his gloves. He purposely hadn't brought a change
of clothes, but now, pulling out, he was unsure. If he stayed
he'd have to wake up early and come back to change.

He shouldn't even be doing this, he thought, already
guilty. He put on Julie London to empty his head. It was a
gift from Michel, a German import, all torch songs.

It's quarter to three, Julie sang, breathy and smoky and
boozy, and Andre sang along, just as crushed. *There's no one
in the place, except you and me.*

It was quicker to go down Spofford, but then he'd
have to drive by Harold's building, and he'd promised himself he wouldn't do that anymore. At the corner he was
tempted to look down the block and see if there were any
lights on on the third floor, but kept his head straight, a
Marine at attention.

Harold would be watching TV, his wife still at work.
Jackie, her name was, and the few times Harold said anything about her, Andre stored the information away, tried,
once Harold had gone back to her, to build a woman from
the pieces. It was like fighting a ghost. None of what Harold
said made sense. She worked nights but was essentially lazy.
She was dirty yet she lectured him about keeping a clean

house. She didn't respect him, she didn't excite him anymore, she was fat and dull and unhappy, and still he chose
her over Andre. Was it just guilt, duty to his sons? The one
was old enough to take care of himself; the other was in a
wheelchair. It was the only reason Andre could see, but he
never brought it up, and Harold never mentioned him.

"Go home to your wife and kids." That's what they said
in the movies, all those showy heroines, the good ones.
Tough, drinking women like Julie London. Cigarette smok-
ers, dames. The weak ones said, "Don't go." They grabbed
at their man's pantlegs as he made for the door, and once
he'd kicked free of them and slammed it, they lay on the
carpet, sobbing in their slips, the unmade bed behind them.
Oh, thought Andre, please don't let me be one of those.

"Honey," he said, "you already are," and turned onto
Penn Circle. Nobody on the sidewalk, just the blank windows of the boarded-up Kroger's. It reminded him of
Bridgeport, the strip leading up to his father's gas station.
The malls had killed the other shops on the block; only the
interstate kept his father in business. At night the street was
desolate, and during a robbery a clerk had been shot. The
security cameras caught the whole thing, but the man had
a mask on and no one was ever arrested. The next week his
father had twenty applications for the job. Pittsburgh was
like that, and there wasn't a day that Andre didn't ask exactly what he thought he was doing here.

He crossed the busway and passed along the bottom
of the park, the hills silhouettes. Back in the overgrown
formal gardens, in the shadows, men knelt on the cold, im-
ported marble and took strangers into their mouths. When

he'd first broken up with Michel he found himself on the stone benches one night, the stars burning down through a trellis of white roses while a Japanese grad student bobbed in his lap. "You make me now?" the boy said, and Andre didn't have the heart to snub him. He'd brought a newspaper to cushion his knees. The boy was so new he actually thanked Andre, shook his hand as if they'd settled a contract, as if they might really see each other again. Oh my brothers, Andre thought, why are we all so lonely?

Now he passed between the two huge churches on Walnut, like medieval gates to Shadyside. Here the sidewalks were deceptively empty. That tall man in the leather jacket walking a beagle wasn't just watering his dog. Neither was the blonde in the next block with the dalmatian. It was what he loved about the neighborhood when he'd lived there—the sudden meeting of eyes as you walked to the bakery for croissants or the hardware for a bracket. Even in winter Shadyside was cruisy, full of students and professional men with the occasional ditzy art-patron widow thrown in for local color. You went out to buy diet soda and ended up in someone's beautiful apartment with a view of the street so the next time you walked by you'd look up at the window and think of yourself looking down, half dressed and satisfied. The only trouble was the money. He would have never exiled himself to East Liberty if Shadyside wasn't so expensive.

And the parking's awful, he thought, searching for a space. *Come on and, cry me a river,* Julie sang in some imaginary nightclub, *cry me a river.* "You tell it," he said, stepping back and letting her do it solo. He had time, so he circled the block, inching along in second, but after trying it twice, he went up to Kentucky and found one easily.

How he knew these streets. Here was where the violinist named Gregory with the handlebar mustache lived—dead now, like so many of his friends. Gregory liked to open his windows and practice; one day while he was playing a Mozart sonata, a neighbor on the other side of Kentucky with a piano suddenly began accompanying him. But that wasn't the end: As in all of Gregory's stories, they wound up in bed. The neighbor was a Russian music student at CMU with gigantic hands. "Well?" Michel asked, because Gregory dropped into a delicious pause. Gregory rolled his eyes like Phyllis Diller. "Let's just say his piano wasn't terribly grand."

And here was Lucien's—dead also, the year before Gregory, with the help of his hospice nurse.

David Holtzman's, positive but still healthy (and having unprotected sex, it was said).

Rick Gary's place, where Michel broke the mixer trying to chop ice for daiquiris. Rick was God knows where, San Francisco or maybe Florida. He always hated how small the scene was in Pittsburgh. "The only new people you meet are students," he'd say, "and I'm sorry, but I am *too* old to get excited about Foucault."

Maybe I should leave, Andre thought. Find some other place, forget all this. Try to live simply, with some dignity.

Like you're doing now, right?

He shook his head to get rid of it. All I want tonight is to be loved. To love someone.

He pictured Harold at home, though he'd never seen the inside of his place. He'd be watching TV, drinking a beer, no glass, his long fingers wrapped around the brown bottle, raising it to his lips. Jackie was at work, the older boy doing something at church, just Harold and the son in the wheelchair sitting there. He tried to imagine what they'd say to each other, what the son would think if he knew his father liked Andre on the bottom, facing him, his ankles over his shoulders; if he knew his father was shy afterward, as if by loving him he'd admitted some terrible secret that Andre had to keep.

He turned into Howe, the street even more densely populated with the dead, the lost worlds of studio apartments and condos, two-room walk-ups and rooftop patios. He'd only lived in this city seven years, yet he contained the history of so many men. A year or so ago he'd lost the will to attend the circuit of parties celebrating the dead, fussy brunches arranged to commemorate friends "the way they'd want to be remembered." It wasn't that he'd lost the ability to feel; he'd just run out of grief. More and more those days he felt he was operating on sheer nerves, every day burning another bundle to get through the bad news. He'd given up on the possibility not just of love but of life. Then Harold came along and everything was new again, fresh.

The blonde with the dalmatian sauntered up the walk, stopping to let the dog sniff a sycamore. The man was Andre's age, but short and somewhat heavy, wearing a pretty cardigan. Marc Antony haircut, fifties hipster goatee. As he came closer, Andre could see he was interested—his eyes searching Andre's for a spark—but instead of the charge that used to thrill him, Andre felt nothing but disgust, and cut him dead, then immediately regretted being cruel. I wish I could help, he should have said, but I have a lot going on. As if that would be any less crushing.

All the man wanted was seven minutes in heaven. Since when did you get so proper?

I may not be proper, he thought, but I'm not common.

He knew it was foolish to argue with himself, to punish himself for the past. His was no more sordid than anyone else's with a healthy libido and a sense of adventure. He didn't understand how time changed that taste for the world into shame, left him hating his own favorite moments, questioning his most intimate judgments. But it did. What he'd thought was daring was stupidity, what was fun seemed sordid, his desires infantile. He wasn't so unsure of himself as to accept it, but often now he found himself yearning for purity. He liked to think celibacy was an option, that he could be that strong, when of course it wasn't true. Look at him now—a phone call and he was on his way.

Michel had stopped the mail, but there were flyers clogging his box, a whole bouquet limp with yesterday's rain. When Andre used to live here there was a garbage can in the vestibule for this kind of shit; it had disappeared, in its place a wrinkled pile of the same flyers. He picked them up, making a face at the fungal smell of wet newsprint. How did people live like this?

Inside, the hallway stank of cooking oil, and the rug was matted, tracked with dirt. He ignored it and headed upstairs, his arms full of garbage.

The first thing he saw in Michel's apartment was the Steuben vase he'd given him on a table in the front hall, holding two dried, dead irises. The lights were on a timer, so the whole apartment was bright. Everything was from the Far East—low and simple, uncluttered. He hadn't thought he missed the tatami mats and the paper screens with their stylized landscapes, the teak table they ate supper from. He had so little in his own place, just secondhand stuff he'd leave when he fled this city. It seemed unfair, as if he'd gotten the raw end of a divorce. He took the flyers into the kitchen and shoved them in the can under the sink, then washed his hands.

The champagne was Moët White Star, good but nothing expensive. He put it in the freezer just to piss Michel off. The fridge was empty—some old juice, a bottle of chili-garlic sauce, a tired head of lettuce—and he remembered the milk. "Damn," he said, then went on cataloguing. There was still time to run out.

Michel's tastes hadn't changed. Here was the Dewar's, the Beefeater, the Absolut—all quality, yet with no intention of impressing anyone. The crystal was Finnish; they'd picked it out together. He chose a tumbler and poured a finger of scotch, turned on the stereo to DUQ for some cool jazz, then went back and cleared out the fridge, put away the clean dishes, all the while sipping.

He threw away the irises and rinsed and dried the vase, set it back on the table in the front hall. The whole place needed to be dusted, so he took the feather wand out of the closet and briskly went over the lampshades and bookshelves, the table in the center of the living room. He'd just started on the mantel above the fireplace when he saw the picture.

It was a shot of Michel and another man on a blinding white beach. It was probably the Caribbean, he thought, because the water was that swimming-pool blue, and the man was darker than Andre, muscle-bound, a red bandanna rolled about his neck like a gaucho. Andre held the picture up so he could look at it more closely, and he realized the silver frame was another present. He'd given it to Michel one Valentine's Day. The picture he'd cut to fit in it was the two of them at Disney World during Gay Week, one of those twenty-dollar black-and-white stills they tempted everyone with after you got off Space Mountain. It was their second time on the ride, and like so many couples that day, they'd timed the final drop so the camera caught them in a deep, soulful kiss. He wondered what Michel had done with it.

It wasn't his business anymore.

Oh, wasn't it?

He drank off the rest of the scotch in one hot swallow and looked at the glass as if it had done something to him, then set the picture facedown on the mantel and went into the kitchen. He put the duster away and stood there, at a loss. It was past eleven. He had to get the milk.

He figured that if he got in his car, he'd probably take off, so he walked down to the convenience mart on Walnut, fending off a parade of eyes. How easy it would be to go with one of them and leave the Moët to explode, or retreat to his apartment and wait for Harold to show up and take him in his arms and make love to him. Or, better, drive right up to Harold's building and ring the bell till he came out, then kiss him hard in front of his wife and children, the whole neighborhood, rightfully claim him for his own.

What would Julie London do?

Oh, no question.

The aisles of the convenience mart were blazing with men, a war zone. They pecked over the neat displays, lingered by the freezer, obvious in their thin T-shirts and ripped gym physiques. Please, Andre thought, I am beyond this. The cashier—strangely, an obese woman in a hideous print muumuu, a poster child for her entire gender—seemed to take forever with his change, and when he was finally out on the dark sidewalk again, he laughed at his panic. Last night he would have given in to one of them simply to rid himself of Harold for a few minutes.

It would have been awful, he thought, and he was glad he hadn't. That was the whole problem—all his solutions were short-term.

And what was this with Michel?

He never said it was a solution.

It could be. Clearly things with Harold weren't going anywhere. That left Michel or someone new, and right now he couldn't deal with someone new.

The man in the picture was just some rough island traffic, a cabana boy, high-priced sport for the tourists, nothing more. He and Michel would have a laugh over him.

Ahead, he saw the blonde still walking his dalmatian, looking forlorn. Oh God, shoot me if I get like that, he thought.

Was he any less desperate, running errands for his ex just for some Moët and a welcome-home fuck?

It was this city, he thought. It had run out of fun. He had to get out of here, go to Savannah and do the party circuit, maybe take a sublet in Charleston, New Orleans.

The blonde saw him and turned around, yanking the dalmatian away from someone's steps. Christ, Andre thought, now I've hurt his feelings. Sometimes he actually wished he could pass for straight. For seventeen years he had, more or less, but lately he seemed to have lost the knack of playing the Menacing Young Black Man. Living in Shadyside did that to you.

He walked past Gregory's and Lucien's and David Holtzman's and Rick Gary's old place, past Brendan the bouncer at the Raspberry Rhino's (yes, dead) and Alan who used to play tennis with them before he got beat up rollerblading in the park and moved to St. Paul. It had taken years, but it seemed to Andre that he'd woken up one day and everyone had left, the town emptied out. No wonder he was mooning over a married man; all the real catches were gone.

A spot had opened up in front of their building, and he was tempted to move his car, but immediately a van noticed it and signaled. He ducked inside before the driver could get out and proposition him, then on the stairs laughed at his paranoia. Below, the outside door squeaked closed. He told himself he wouldn't wait for it to click shut, but when it didn't, he stopped and cocked his head toward the lack of noise.

"Help me," someone said matter-of-factly. "Goddammit," the voice said with effort, "don't just walk away," and he realized it was Michel.

He was struggling with his luggage, propping the door open with it. He still had his uniform on, the jacket with the gold stripes on the cuffs that made him look like a pilot. He'd gotten some color, his hair longer, tinted auburn at the ends, and Andre didn't know which annoyed him more, the fact that he'd been lying around on some beach in Thailand or just how very beautiful he was.

"You're early," Andre said.

"Don't act so happy to see me."

"Sorry."

"Don't apologize," Michel scolded, "just help me."

Andre put the milk down and grabbed a rollaway suitcase. There were only three, but they each weighed a ton, and Michel was tired.

"Didn't you see me?" he asked when Andre brought the last one up.

"I'm sorry."

"Stop saying that."

"I must have been spacing out. It's been a long day."

"Don't I get a kiss?"

He was standing by the mantel, and as they kissed, Andre noticed he'd replaced the picture. Turned the music off too. Michel surprised him with his tongue. Andre tried to respond honestly, then closed his eyes and thought of Harold, how over the months even his noxious cigars became endearing, a part of him.

"How about some bubbly?" Michel asked. "And I'd kill for a shower."

"Go ahead, I'll bring you a glass. I just took one."

"Don't you want to join me?"

"I'll be waiting for you in bed."

"Playing hard to get, I see."

"Never failed me yet," Andre said.

He waited till Michel had the water on before taking the champagne out of the freezer. It was perfectly chilled, crisp. It gave him a deep satisfaction that Michel would never know. How petty he could be, like a child. He found the copper bucket under the sink and filled it with ice, plucked two fluted glasses off the shelf and carried everything into the bedroom. He poured a glass and took it in to Michel, the water drilling the stall. His tan was all over, no lines, and Andre wondered if there'd been any little Thai cabana boys. Michel liked to say they were pretty even if they didn't have anything in their pants.

"Thank you," Michel said, taking the glass by the stem, utterly grateful, apologetic. He was always snippy after a long flight, and it was wrong to hold it against him. Andre thought it was his own fault; he was so wound up over Harold. It would be best to simply admit it, leave, tell Michel he'd be back when he knew what he was doing.

And when would that be?

The water cut off, and Andre retreated to the bedroom. The comforter on the futon was thrown back, the white sheets inviting. Michel would want the lights on, would think something was wrong if he turned them off. Andre didn't want him to see how he'd let himself go, so he pulled off his top and stepped out of his jeans and slid between the chilly covers. He poured himself a glass and tossed it back, poured himself another and left it untouched on the low night table, as if it were his first.

He could leave now, grab his keys and run for the Eclipse.

Michel came out in a mask, a red dragon with flames licking its face. He had on a black kimono, undone so Andre could appreciate him. He stalked over to the bed, hunched like a sumo wrestler, his package dangling. If only he could keep the mask on, Andre thought, not talk.

Michel took off the mask. "I got one for you too. Green dragon." He turned and threw the kimono on a chair, and Andre could see the hardness of his long limbs, his sharply defined back tapering to his waist. Harold was no comparison, thick around the hips, and Andre thought it was unfair. Harold always called him beautiful, as if that was what he loved, not Andre himself, just his skin, the muscles underneath. He was equally guilty of lust, even now, when he thought he was immune to it. Wanted to be.

Michel lifted the covers and lay down beside him, his skin warm from the shower. His hair was still damp. He threw a leg over Andre, his thigh rolling his cock on his stomach, bowing it. Michel rose up, took a sip and kissed him, his hands roaming his chest, and Andre reached around to touch his strong back, pulling Michel against him, their tongues sliding together, wet. His scent was familiar, and Andre's body responded, filled with years of memory.

It was wrong, he thought. He could see himself from the outside, as if he were hovering in one corner of the room, not really there at all. He would not stay the night. He would save something of himself for Harold, keep some part of their lovemaking sacred.

Michel stopped to find a condom, tore the foil with his teeth, applied a dab of Astroglide. At least he was that considerate. He dug a hand beneath Andre and lifted his leg.

Not this, he thought, but his other leg obeyed Michel's touch, rose into the air until his heels were on Michel's shoulders, his knees nearly touching his own. He was hard against the hair of Michel's belly, and he could feel Michel prodding him. There was still time to stop, he thought. All he had to do was say something, ask about the picture on the mantel.

But there was not time, because now Michel had found him, was heavy inside him, rocking, plunging, and involuntarily Andre opened to him. He closed his eyes and pictured Harold above him, Harold sliding into him, his kind face shining with sweat, his kisses afterward, their shared secret an extra tenderness between them. He would be at home, watching TV, thinking Andre was in his apartment. What if he called? He could see Harold listening to the phone ring, standing on the sidewalk under his window, knocking on his door.

The frame of the futon creaked and shuddered, knocked against the wall, banishing Harold.

It's all right, Andre promised him calmly, it doesn't mean anything. Nothing at all, just sex. Yes, he really was being honest, or so he'd thought, because soon, with the two of them slapping together, his eyes tight shut, Andre realized he was actually talking to himself, and even he knew it was much worse than that.

ARE YOU MY MOTHER?

THERE WAS NOTHING wrong with Miss Fisk except she was getting old. Every day Vanessa told herself this, as if she hadn't heard Miss Fisk call her by her mother's name, hadn't seen the milk in the cupboard, the dish detergent in the frigerator.

She was still good with Rashaan. Vanessa checked to make sure he'd eaten, and he had—there was a smear of bananas on his collar, a bowl in the sink with Yogi Bear smiling up beneath a brown crust of something. And every day he was fresh, smelling of powder, his diaper light. Most days Miss Fisk was fine, dropping his big keys and soft blocks in the plastic laundry basket in the corner, going on about how they had a nice stroll over to the park and what they read together and how Rashaan didn't want to go down for his nap, but some days she said things that made Vanessa hesitate to bring him by the next morning, made her start giving him his pills at home.

"I remember when your daddy first came north," Miss Fisk said, beaming, showing her stained lower teeth. "This was right after the war, because *his* daddy worked for the war department down to Virginia—he was a dentist—and the work was over, at least for our people. Even then everyone knew he was something special."

Vanessa didn't correct her, say she was thinking of someone else—her mother's father, possibly (though he was from Texas and worked first in a sawmill and then a meat-packing plant, according to her mother, stunning dried-up Holsteins with a pneumatic bolt gun, coming home smelling of blood, his fingers shaking). Maybe she thought Vanessa was someone else altogether. Vanessa nodded as if she knew this history, as if they were just going over it again together, remembering for the sheer pleasure of it.

It wasn't that Vanessa wasn't interested. Even though their oral history was done (she'd gotten an A), she still came over to listen to Miss Fisk, lingered on the couch, sipping bitter lemonade. It seemed she held the entire history of East Liberty inside her, from the Great Migration all the way up to the present. She took Vanessa back to a time when men were natty dressers, church was the high time of the week, and white landlords hadn't bought up all their property for a song. She looked to the ceiling as if an angel were hovering above them, and Vanessa could see she was picturing the streets filled with fat Cadillacs, the sidewalks lined with businesses long gone bankrupt.

"And on the corner of Highland," she would say, squinting as if to see it better, "there was a shoe shop, a cobbler. Little Jewish fella, name of . . . Goldblum? Goldberg?"

Sometimes she said things even she knew were wrong. She'd wave a hand in front of her face as if erasing them, sending away the messenger that served her memory.

"Some days are better than others," she admitted.

"You tell me if he gets too much for you now," Vanessa said.

"Never. Not my good boy." Miss Fisk stroked Rashaan's smooth head.

Vanessa said she had to get home and start supper so she could study, which wasn't a complete lie. Her mother was making her famous haddock tonight, but she did have reading to do, and a quiz tomorrow on it.

"We'll see you two tomorrow then," Miss Fisk said, and let her go.

Walking across the front lawn and around the porch to the side door of their building, Vanessa wondered what Miss Fisk would do for the rest of the day. The thought of her alone in that big house worried her. Vanessa didn't like the quiet. Even in their apartment, she was afraid of break-ins, burglars holding a sharpened screwdriver to her throat. Miss Fisk didn't have any family around here, no pets, not even cable TV. How did she spend the hours until bedtime? She'd stopped getting the *Post-Gazette* because her eyes were only good enough for large print. Maybe she talked on the phone, wrote letters someone in another state would try to decipher. Bean's mother was her daughter. Vanessa couldn't imagine what they'd say to each other. She had a hard enough time talking with Chris.

They were supposed to be together again, a couple, just because they'd gone to the park twice. He called almost every night, and patiently she told him about her day and then Rashaan's, her work waiting for her on the kitchen table. She wasn't being mean, she really did want to talk to him, but the timing wasn't right. They needed to be together for more than a week before they really started talking. And so every night they went on about nothing in particular, and when it was time to hang up, he said he loved her, just like in high school.

"I love you," he said, and she resented being put on the defensive, having to come back with something. It wasn't a lie to say she loved him, because she did care for him, she'd known him since they were kids, he was important to her, the father of her baby.

"Let's wait a little while on that," she'd say, "okay?"

Or "I know."

Or "You don't quit, I'll tell you that."

Or just "Good night, Chris."

He needed her. Not me, she thought, just someone.

Maybe he'd let it slide and not call tonight. It was a wish, and immediately she took it back. Sometimes she really feared she was heartless, that she didn't like people in general, even herself. Sometimes she thought she was crazy. She knew it wasn't true, it was just her life being so out of control.

Upstairs, she locked the door behind her. The apartment was quiet and gray with the lights off. Her mother was supposed to be home.

She'd left a message on the machine. "Sorry, baby. We've got someone coming in on the Lifeflight so I'm going to have to stay late. Save the fish for tomorrow, okay?"

"Right," Vanessa said, then stood there looking at the cupboard, thinking there was never anything good to eat. Nothing in the fridge either. Soup, there was always soup. She hated cooking for herself. She imagined Miss Fisk eating silently in her tidy kitchen, reusing her teabag from lunch, washing and drying the dishes as soon as she finished. Then what?

She nuked Rashaan's turkey and vegetables, opened a new jar of the plums he loved. She'd make something for herself later. Or not. All of a sudden she wasn't hungry.

She brought her books in and buckled Rashaan into his high chair, stirred the turkey and tested it with her pinkie. Rashaan rubbed his bib over his face. When he wouldn't quit she had to hold it down to feed him, and still it was a mess. "So much for studying," she said.

Outside, the sun was going down, and she heard the chimes of Tony's truck, the programmed, mechanical music drifting up from the street. It seemed too cold, the season over, but Tony liked to surprise them; once he even came the day of the Super Bowl, wearing a Steeler jersey and handing out free Clark bars. She'd been hearing his bells her entire life. "Candyman!" they used to shout, and run for their mothers, begging change. Now she didn't even go to the window, just listened to him cruise down the block, the rubber-coated spoon poised for Rashaan to open his lips.

Cleaning up, she wondered why she was so tired today. It was Miss Fisk mentioning her father again, that was all. Everything else had gone well. Work was work. Rashaan had been good. The haddock she didn't really care about;

her mother always had to work late. It was an emergency room, there were going to be emergencies.

When Miss Fisk said he'd come from Virginia, that his father was a dentist, Vanessa almost wanted to believe it. She was ready to hear anything, everything about him. She knew so little that every scrap was precious. She stitched the smallest offhand remarks of her mother's into a man, and still he was nothing like the Marine smiling down from the picture, young and handsome, almost dead already. Every time Miss Fisk said "your father," Vanessa's heart jumped as if she might hear a deep secret. Miss Fisk could have told her anything—that he drank, that he danced beautifully, that he carried her on his shoulders to church—and Vanessa would have no way of checking it, would have to add it to her stash of clues on faith, at her own risk.

Why didn't her mother want to talk about him? Would she be like this with Chris when Rashaan needed to know everything?

No. She hoped not. She didn't blame her mother for her father not being there, at least she didn't think so. She'd always felt it was someone's fault, and whose could it be— the government's? His own? Her mother had nothing to do with it. You couldn't stop a man from doing something stupid, Chris had taught her that much.

Suddenly she was afraid that this was exactly what her mother worried about, and that she had *let* her worry about it, let it hurt her all these years. She had to tell her mother she understood, maybe then it would be easier to talk about him.

She opened her notebook and wrote the date, cracked and flattened the beat-up paperback she was reading against the table. Professor Shelby was taking them way back, back to Africa and tribal life and the Door of No Return, making them remember the complex and delicate cultures American slavery told them to forget. It wasn't all gone, he lectured them; it was too strong to rub out. Every generation had its griots, every set of young people dug deeper, exposed the hidden connections between African messenger dances and slave chants bearing coded news, the long line of signing and signifying running down through Jack Johnson and Louis Armstrong and Cab Calloway and Langston Hughes and Zora Neale Hurston, into Satchel Paige and John Lee Hooker and Chester Himes and Leroi Jones and James Brown, into Charles Mingus and Muhammed Ali and Bob Marley and Nikki Giovanni and Gil Scott-Heron and Ishmael Reed, into George Clinton and Lucille Clifton and Grandmaster Flash and Public Enemy and Shaquille O'Neal, and all the way up to the present. "Turn on your radio," he said, "and you will hear the voices of Africa."

The quiz tomorrow was on that legacy and the ways people kept it alive, from the Middle Passage on. Professor Shelby would give them five names from their reading and they would have to say how the five fit into the tradition. Vanessa had gotten a sixty on her first quiz, so she needed a hundred, and as she read down the page, she stopped each time a new name appeared and added it to the long column in her notebook, glancing into the living room to make sure Rashaan was okay.

She'd only finished three pages when the phone rang. Chris, she thought, and cursed herself for not leaving the machine on. She let it ring four times before picking up.

"We're done here," her mother said. "I should be home in ten minutes. Did you get something?"

"Just for Rashaan," she admitted.

"I'll pick something up, how would that be?"

"Fine."

"Is everything all right?"

"I'm just tired," she lied, and then when she'd hung up, she really was exhausted. In the other room, Rashaan was slapping the glass of the TV set, and she went in and held him on the couch until she felt better.

Did she really want Chris to call? No, she didn't think so. It was everything—work and school and Miss Fisk. Her father. The usual stuff.

She had reading to do, and she got up and brought the book back to the couch, then sat there with Rashaan on her lap and skimmed the pages. Countee Cullen, Jayne Cortez, Haki Madhubuti. There was only so much she could remember, so she retrieved her notebook from the table and started marking down names.

Her mother brought home Arby's, a Beef 'n' Cheddar and a Big Beef. She gave Vanessa her choice.

"I don't care."

"Just choose one," her mother said, impatient with her. "It's not a big deal." She sighed as if apologizing. "I got those spicy fries you like."

"Thanks." Vanessa took the Big Beef and unwrapped

it at the table, squeezed on some Horsey Sauce. Her mother
sat down and ate beside her, quiet.

"Work that bad?"

Her mother just nodded, chewing. She put her sandwich down and rubbed her forehead with her fingertips, her
eyes closed. "The Lifeflight was this little girl, couldn't have
been older than Rashaan."

"She all right?"

"She'll live. There were six people in the van, and she
was the only one. The rest of them . . ." She shook her head.
"I don't know. It's been a bad week. I keep thinking it's
going to get better."

"I know," Vanessa said.

"How about you, are you all right?"

"I'm just worried about Miss Fisk." She told her about
the detergent in the fridge and what she'd said about her
father.

"I don't know who she's thinking of," her mother said.
Vanessa waited for her to go on, but she took a bite of fries
and wiped her fingers with a paper napkin and looked off
across the living room.

"Where was Daddy's father from?"

"Youngstown, you know that. Otherwise she's fine
though? She understands what you're saying to her?"

"She seems to. It's only when she starts telling stories."

"She's old," her mother said, and shrugged, as if that
explained it, and again Vanessa felt the conversation stray-
ing, sensed her mother's reluctance like an invisible fence,
an unspoken disagreement between them.

"What was Mr. Fisk like?"

"Oh God." Her mother laughed and had to cover her mouth with a hand. "Short! He was shorter than she is now and he always wore a blue suit, didn't matter what time of year it was. They had a Lincoln the exact same color, he ordered it special. You'd see him riding her around Sunday, both of them dressed to meet Jesus." She shook her head. "Must be twenty years now."

The number stopped her, faded away to nothing between them. Longer than your father. Neither of them had to say it.

"Do you still miss Daddy?" Vanessa asked.

Her mother looked up from her sandwich and fixed her grimly, as if giving Vanessa a chance to take it back.

"You've been thinking about him. I thought you've been quiet lately. That's usually what it is."

"Not usually," Vanessa said. "Just lately. I don't know why."

"I know why. It's Chris."

"Not all of it. I was thinking earlier I wanted to tell you I don't blame you. For him not being around."

"That's generous of you," her mother joked.

"You know what I mean."

"I do, and thank you. That's not what all this is about, is it?"

"Yes," Vanessa said, unsure now.

"Nessie." She looked at her flatly, that worn-out, sick-of-working-double-shifts look full of her mother's truth. "I wish he were around too, but you know what? After twenty years, I'm not holding my breath. It's me and you and

Shaanie, and I think we're doing pretty well for ourselves."
She put down her Arby's like it disgusted her. "I'm sorry,
but I can't work any harder than I already am."

"I know," Vanessa said, "I didn't mean that," but it was
too late to apologize. Her mother was up, shoving her
crumpled foil in the garbage.

"Yes, I miss him. Of course I miss him." She stopped,
her head turned to one side, hands out in front of her as if
to calm someone else down. She came over and stood behind Vanessa, her strong fingers squeezing her shoulders,
and kissed the top of her head. "I'm glad you miss him too.
I don't mean to get upset. Let me go take a shower and relax
for a minute, then I'll watch Rashaan so you can do your
homework."

Vanessa wanted to say she didn't have to, but she knew
not to argue at this point, to just let her go. In a minute the
water came on, the door of the shower rolled shut with a
thump. Rashaan gnawed on his fries. She picked at her sandwich, then threw it away too (the Horsey Sauce was too
strong, oddly metallic). She stood at the sink looking at the
tap, and a strange urge took her—to turn it on so her
mother's water would be freezing. Not just once, but jam-
ming the gearshift of the tap back and forth so the pipes
shook with each blast, her mother blinded by her shampoo,
swearing and shouting for her to stop, banging the walls of
the stall.

She didn't, but the idea was there, and it worried her.
Why was she so angry? It was like Rashaan and his tantrums,
blown over in a minute, but when he was swinging his little
fists at her, his hate was pure and she was someone alien.

She wasn't the one being childish, she thought. All she'd done was ask a question.

Her mother was extra nice the rest of the night, getting Rashaan into his jammies and reading him his story. Vanessa could hear her from the living room. "Are *you* my mother?" It was a favorite of Rashaan's, a lost baby bird going to all the other animals of the barnyard—the goose, the horse, the pig. "No, *I* am not your mother," her mother said, doing the cow in a goofy cartoon voice, and Vanessa thought that, yes, that refusal to answer was her mother exactly. Why had she thought she would change?

It was too late to make up tonight, and they stayed out of each other's way. Vanessa didn't get to bed till eleven, the page crowded with names. In the morning, her mother made eggs—a peace offering—and waited while she dropped Rashaan off with Miss Fisk to give her a ride to work.

"How's she doing today?"

"Seems all right," Vanessa said.

"Sometimes they get tired toward the end of the day. Just like us."

Like last night, Vanessa wanted to shift the topic back to her father, but rode along, nodding, watching the park go by, the sunken busway sliding alongside them like an empty river, its concrete walls dark with yesterday's rain. She knew her mother thought she was thinking of Chris, that every time they crossed the busway, every time she even took a bus she pictured him and Bean that night. How could she tell her she didn't? Yes, it came to her sometimes—rain and the barrels with their orange flashers set up to make lanes on the busway, the two of them with their backpacks full of spraycans, laughing, the red-faced paramedic cutting Chris's Steeler jacket off with special scissors — but she could get rid of it, sometimes by just shaking her head or thinking of a song.

Was that how it was with her father? She wondered when she could ask again. Not for a while.

"I'll be home the regular time tonight," her mother promised, letting her off. It was another gift, and Vanessa didn't question it, just thanked her for the ride and went in to face the breakfast rush.

Work didn't let her remember anything, though she fought to keep the names straight in her head. Haki Madubaruti. No, that wasn't it. There were too many poets. She wished she'd made a crib sheet she could check between orders, a notecard to stick in her pocket, cup in her palm like the prices when she first started. As she hustled for a missing ketchup, a handful of jam packets, a large milk, another knife, all the reading she'd done vanished, evaporated like water flicked on a hot grill, and by the time she peeled her uniform off and hauled her jeans on, she couldn't remember why she was taking the class in the first place.

The funny thing was, Chris would know all this stuff. He wouldn't even have to study, you could just ask him and he'd know. Bean too. They were always quizzing each other, singing half a lyric and waiting for the other one to jump in. They knew the groups, the gossip, when the new record was coming out — all before *The Source*. She was terrible at remembering names, especially if she'd heard them only once. She wasn't made for college, she thought, but she knew that was an excuse. She *wanted* to learn, she just wasn't very good at it.

She found her bench in the sun beneath the Cathedral of Learning and went over her notes one last time before class, crossing off the people she knew. Almost half. She had a feeling Haki Madhubuti would be on the quiz, just from his name. The rest she went over slowly, looking them up in the book when she didn't know what they'd done. Curt Flood was a baseball player who stood up for his rights. Coleman Young was the first mayor of a major U.S. city. When her watch said it was time, she wasn't done with the list.

She took the elevator up with a bunch of classmates.

"Benjamin O. Davis," one girl said.

"First general in the regular army," another said. "Gwendolyn Brooks."

"Please," the first said, and everyone laughed except Vanessa. She felt dizzy, as if she'd forgotten to eat. Getting off, her legs didn't move right; she had to consciously think about how she was supposed to walk, and she was relieved to get to her chair. She took out the list but it was useless now, her thoughts zipping all over the place like flies, never settling. She folded it away, giving in to fate. School was always like that, the weeklong dread of the test and then finding out she'd had good reason to worry. There were no sudden miracles or surprising scores. Chris could wait till the night before to crack the books and then ace something, but not her. She knew she wasn't stupid, but she'd never be a student either. She'd never get the degree her mother wanted—that *she* wanted now.

Professor Shelby came in wearing his ridiculous green suit and tie and handed out the quizzes without a word, solemn as an undertaker. He circled around the desk to the board and wrote 10 MIN., then sat down and unpacked his briefcase.

The guy in front of Vanessa handed the quizzes back, still damp and inky-smelling from the mimeograph, the words purple like in grade school. The five people were:

> Angela Davis
> Benjamin O. Davis
> Benjamin Hooks
> bell hooks
> Derrick Bell

She knew the first three, partly because of the girl in the elevator, and also because Benjamin O. Davis was on a stamp. Angela Davis was a Panther. Benjamin Hooks was the head of the NAACP. The other two she had no idea. Another sixty, she thought. Another D.

bell hooks was an important poet, she wrote, *whose poems are about the true inner feelings of African American women.*

Derrick Bell was a famous baseball player who spoke up for his rights.

She knew how stupid these would look to Professor Shelby, and she thought of giving up, just erasing them, admitting she was too dumb for his class, but by now she felt beaten and didn't care.

Around her the others were still scribbling like they were writing essays. There were five minutes left, during

which she made plans to tell her mother she was withdraw-
ing from the class and that she would never be anything.
She thought of her father, how he never had a chance to be
where she was right now, and she honestly wished she could
trade places with him, the same way she wished she could
trade places with Chris.

"Time," Professor Shelby said, and with a rustle everyone passed the quizzes up to the front.

In class she barely listened. John Brown, Jim Crow.
On the bus home she found out she was almost right about
bell hooks. So what? A seventy, with partial credit. She
should have known it and she didn't.

Miss Fisk met her at the door, Rashaan in her arms.
He dove for her shoulder, hung around her neck, and she
smelled how fresh his skin was, how sweet, even after a long
day. He clawed at her earrings, so she swung him around.

"He was very good," Miss Fisk said proudly, as if he
deserved something.

"Good," Vanessa said. She just wanted to go, to close the
door to the apartment and sit down, think of nothing at all.

"He does remind me of your daddy, those big cheeks."
She made lobster claws of her hands, and Rashaan covered
his face and giggled, peeked out between his fingers. "Maybe
he'll be famous too."

She had that crazy, old-lady gleam in her eye, smiling
so the gap in her stained lowers showed her tongue, and
Vanessa thought she wouldn't even ask.

"I've gotta go," she said, thinking it was enough of a
hint, and started for the edge of the porch. Miss Fisk followed, making faces at him, waving baby good-byes.

"Big famous politician just like your grandaddy."

Vanessa stopped on the stairs in midstep. "Like *my* father?"

"Nothing wrong with it," Miss Fisk said. "Long as he remembers who voted for him. Your daddy tends to forget some of the time. Not to pick nits. Can't be easy, everyone wanting you to vote for their bill."

It dawned on Vanessa that Miss Fisk was talking about Martin Robinson, that somehow she'd gotten the two of them mixed up. It was a relief to finally solve the mystery.

"Don't get me wrong," Miss Fisk was saying, "I'll vote for him when I'm in the cemetery, I will, but sometimes I don't understand what his thinking is."

"Thank you for watching him," Vanessa said, patting Rashaan, trying not to be too rude.

"Oh, you're welcome." She waved again, Martin Robinson completely forgotten. Just old, that was all. Vanessa couldn't imagine trying to find day care, paying for it.

Her mother was late again—another car wreck. It was the time of year, between the rain and the leaves and dusk coming earlier. The haddock would have to keep one more day. Vanessa had already started some soup, buttered bread to make grilled cheese. She told her mother about Miss Fisk, laughing and cutting thick, crumbly slices of sharp cheddar. "Can you imagine," she said, "Martin Robinson?"

Behind her, her mother didn't laugh, said absolutely nothing. Vanessa had thought it would cheer her up the same way.

"I mean," Vanessa said, bearing down on the knife, "I'm sure she's okay, but—it's so bizarre, Martin Robinson! Where'd she come up with that?"

I don't know, her mother was supposed to say, and roll her eyes at poor Miss Fisk, or scold her for making fun of someone doing her a favor. But when Vanessa glanced back at her, her mother was just looking at her, tired, stricken, her lips set, as if Vanessa were torturing her, and she wanted to apologize for bringing the whole thing up again.

"I know where," her mother said softly, then left it, a flat admission.

Vanessa stood there with the knife, thinking it must be a joke, that she'd misunderstood what her mother said. Her mother watched her like a guard, waiting for an answer.

Vanessa didn't have one.

Her mother bowed her head, looking straight down into the table, unable to face her. Then she said, "Baby," seriously, and blindly held up one hand, as if reaching out to her—or, Vanessa thought, trying to protect herself. Vanessa set the knife down on the counter gently, like a sleepwalker, like a robot. "Baby," her mother said, "baby, come here," and, turning to her, Vanessa realized there were some even harder things she would have to learn.

(ANDYMAN

TONY KNEW WHO the boy was. He knew everyone; it wasn't bragging, just good business. You knew your customers, your customers knew you. Was there some other way?

So he knew the boy, if he didn't know where he lived. He'd seen him on Moreland and sometimes on Spofford, shooting the bull with his friends, playing ball against the steps while the children rode their bikes up and down the sidewalk. But still a boy. Another year maybe, he would be a man, but not yet. He wasn't a bad boy, not always. Milk Duds were his favorite, the ones in back, door four, first box on the left, frozen so you could suck on them a long time.

The police weren't interested in that. They wanted a name, an address.

Ten years ago Tony knew his name, but that was ten years ago. Now he knew him to see him on the street, to remember what he liked.

The police thought it might be a kind of gang initiation, proof that the boy was worthy. They had pictures, books and books of pictures. They had him sit at someone's messy desk and look through the books. They left him there flipping the tall plastic pages and went out to see if anyone had found the truck yet.

The pictures were just their heads—which made it harder, Tony thought. They were all angry they'd been caught, or sad; you could hear them thinking, see their plans in their eyes. He remembered the boy's hands better, long thin hands, and his coat—Seattle Seahawks, two-toned, the poncho kind with the pocket in front. Tony had just gotten out and was coming around to see what people wanted when the truck rocked, dipped like someone had jumped on the bumper. He thought it was just the children climbing on the running boards like they did, touching the door that looked like the gate of a picket fence to see if it was really wood. Then the engine started up, a jet of hot exhaust flapped the cuffs of his pants, and he ran for the door. The truck swerved away from the curb; he had to dive or it would have run into him. All he saw was the boy hunched over the wheel, his thin hands, the blue-and-green sleeve of his jacket with the team logo. "Milk Duds. The frozen ones." He remembered counting change into his small palm, and then he was on the ground, rolling. He could see the dark curb under the cars, feel the stony cold of the street. People were running over to help him up, brushing the grit from his back. A block away, the bells played.

"My truck," he said.

"You need to sit down," his Vanessa said, and helped him to some steps. The children stood back, holding their jump ropes, suddenly afraid of him.

"I'm all right." He waved and tried to smile for them. "Ah, but your poor candy, someone kidnapped it."

No one laughed at the joke. The children stared, little Nekysha pointing and covering her mouth.

"You're bleeding," Vanessa said. "Let's get you inside."

Renée had been predicting something like this for years, but with him pistol-whipped, a bullet in his lung, or dead, Renée a middle-aged orphan. Finally her worst fears had come true, all her caution justified. They even had his keys. He'd called her first thing, at work, from Vanessa's kitchen. He got the hotel operator. Renée had just moved to the William Penn from the Hilton, and the switchboard didn't know her yet.

"She's in group sales if that's any help," he said.

"Please hold while I connect you."

"Thank you," he said, and he must have surprised her, because she said, "You're welcome," like a question, startled, like it was a strange thing to say.

When he told Renée, she didn't interrupt, just said, "Mm-hm, mm-hm." He could see her nodding, biting her lip, angry that she'd been right. You don't belong there, she argued—fifteen years she'd been telling him. Now she was quiet.

"Are you all right?" she said.

"I'm fine. But the Little Horse." It was their name for the truck; Renée used to call it that when she was just a girl.

"The police'll find it. It's not like you can hide something like that."

The fact hadn't occurred to him, and he thanked God he had a smart daughter.

"She says they'll find it," he told Vanessa.

It was probably just some stupid prank, she agreed. She cleaned the gash on his forehead with a washcloth, squeezed on some cream and stuck two butterfly strips across it.

"Thank you," he'd said, and she said she was glad he wasn't hurt worse—another Renée.

Now, turning the heavy page of faces, Tony thought she must have known the boy's name, that everyone on Spofford knew exactly who he was. They'd kept quiet, protected him the same way no one in Little Italy squealed. But would they take care of punishing him? Would there be a Manfredi or a Ciresi who weighed the boy's fate, whose captains would visit the family and ask the boy to come with them? And what would it be—a knuckle, the pinkie bent back till it cracked? Tony wanted a say in it, to tell them not to be too hard on the boy. But a little something, he deserved that at least. A scare, for a warning.

The policeman returned with a can of soda. "Nothin'. Any luck here?"

Tony started to tell him how it was hard with just the faces, but the policeman wasn't listening.

"Anyway, we'll probably find it come daylight. I'm sure he's not out riding around. You're welcome to keep looking though."

"No," Tony said. "I should get home."

The policeman arranged for another policeman to drive him. Tony had never been in a police car before, and the computer surprised him, the screen and keyboard sticking out from where the radio should have been. The policeman had a St. Christopher medal hanging from the mirror, and Tony remembered his own in the exact same place in the truck. It had been Rita's great-grandfather's; he'd given it to her when she left Trieste, to watch over her during the long voyage. It was shiny from being rubbed. This was the first time it hadn't worked. When the policeman asked Tony about personal belongings, he'd shaken his head and said, "My truck is my business."

And if they didn't find it?

He didn't know. He was tired. He couldn't think when he needed to eat.

Renée was waiting for him, thanking the policeman over and over. She took Tony in her arms, then examined the cut, fingering the butterflies until he winced.

"Not so bad," she said, but he could tell she was saying it for him. The apartment smelled of sautéed garlic. She'd made a Bolognese especially for him and tried to be quiet while they ate. He could see it was hard for her.

"I'm okay," he said.

"Did he hit you?"

"No."

"Did he *say* anything?"

"He jumped in the truck and drove away, that was it. I saw him maybe three seconds."

"And nobody knows him?"

"That's what they say."

"How long have you been doing business, and this is how they repay you?"

He thought of trying to explain the way of neighborhoods to her, but she knew. She would say East Liberty was different, and then they'd get into an argument he did not want to have tonight.

"My friend Vanessa took care of me. Everyone was very nice."

"But they won't say who it was."

He shrugged. "Some punk, probably not from around there."

"I'm sure," she said, and got up to clear their plates. He thanked her for supper and she said he was welcome.

"Don't kid yourself," she said. "They take care of their own."

"Like us."

"Don't go making excuses on their account. They stole your truck."

"One person stole my truck."

"The rest of them are protecting him—it's the same thing."

She left him there while she fixed dessert, lemon sherbet with biscotti, his favorite.

"At least you're all right," she said.

She didn't have to say it could have been worse, that it could have been the police who called her. The cut stung, and for the first time he understood that her worry wasn't imaginary. The truck really was gone.

He went to bed at the regular time, Renée looking in on him, asking one final time if he was all right. In the yellow light from the hall, she looked for a minute like Rita, those big eyes, that nub of a chin, and he thought of her St. Christopher swinging from the mirror, the Little Horse somewhere out there in the dark instead of their locked garage.

"I'm okay," he said, and waved her away, like she was being too much of a mother. The hall light went off.

He'd bought the truck used in the mid-sixties from his cousin Nunzio, who'd painted it red, white and blue and swapped the doors for the gates. Even then it was an antique, a refugee—like him—from the thirties. The dashboard was varnished cherry, the headlights mounted like eyes on the fenders. The first thing he did was rechrome the grille and the bumpers and all the freezer latches so they shone on bright days. In the morning he'd go out in the driveway with his creams and soft cloths and rub it lovingly—like a horse, Rita said, like a pet. The Little Horse, Renée christened it. He'd repainted it three times since then, and lately he'd had problems finding leaded gas, but the engine was still strong, the frame straight and unrusted. Whenever Renée talked about him quitting, he just shrugged it off. "When the Horse goes, I go," he'd say, not really meaning it. Now he wondered if it was a prediction. His mother claimed their branch of the family had The Sight.

The police would find it, Renée said so herself.

He thought of the boy and what he would do with the truck. Nothing. Brag to his friends. He couldn't sell it.

The pointlessness of it hurt him. It would have been easier to understand if the boy had robbed him, torn his change apron from him, the pockets bulging with silver, or if he'd pushed him to the ground, shouting something, jabbing his finger at him like a knife. Yet even as he pictured it differently, the same facts came back to him, erasing all possibilities. The truck pulled away, swerved to miss the parked car, and he dove so it didn't hit him. He had not fought, had not been beaten. He had lost his truck, and in his mind there was no doubt that it was his fault.

Maybe Renée had The Sight, because the next morning after she left for work the police called and said they'd found it, not far from where it had been taken. It was in the impound yard in Brushton, they'd had to tow it over there. "There's been some damage," the man said.

"A lot?" Tony asked.

"You're insured?"

"Yes."

"Then you should have no problem."

"Can I come down and take a look at it?"

"It's not a safe neighborhood," the man warned him. "It might be better if you let your garage take care of it."

"I know the area," Tony said.

Reluctantly, the man gave him the address. "We can have one of our people accompany you."

"That's all right," Tony said. He thanked him and hung up and went to the desk in the front hall to look for his policy.

He called Renée and told her he was going over to see it.

"Do you want me to come with you?" she asked.

He said no, mostly to protect her. As a girl, she'd loved the truck like the pony she dreamed of. Weekends, she helped him, ringing the bells from the passenger seat, making change. Every year until she was in middle school, she'd bring him in to talk to her class. It wasn't until she was in college that she started asking things like "Doesn't it get boring? Don't you ever want to do something more, something different?"

"No," he'd say, knowing exactly what she meant—that she was ashamed of him for not being rich and important like her friends' fathers. She still loved him, that didn't change, but he could feel her disappointment, and for a while it had become his own. His cousin Nunzio was his wholesaler; Tony drove a delivery truck for him in the winter. He could easily get a position with him, sit at a desk all day in a shirt and tie down in the Strip, buying and selling truckloads of nuts and jelly beans on the phone. It was not what he wanted, but without Rita around to help him make decisions it seemed almost reasonable, and he would have asked except that fall Nunzio had just divorced his wife—Rita's cousin Terry—and it would not have been proper to do any new business with him. After college, the subject never came up. Renée was in New York, using her degree, trying to be a dancer. He sent her a check every month, and once in a while she mailed him clippings from shows he'd never heard of, her name highlighted far down at the bottom. Then the clippings stopped and she moved to San Francisco. Then one day she was waiting in the vestibule for him, her bags at her feet, a complicated knee brace on one leg like a football player. "I'm back," she said. A week later she got a job at the Oakland Howard Johnson's, in reservations. That was almost ten years ago. He didn't have to ask her if her job was boring, if she didn't ever want to do something more. Maybe now she understood, he thought, but they no longer talked about it. They got up, they went to work, they came home.

All this flew through his head as he gathered his policy and his keys and his jacket. It was raining out, gray. The

cut stung. If the truck wasn't bad, maybe they could have it
ready for tomorrow. Or would it be like her knee, ruined,
never the same again?

He took the good car, the Lincoln. The Big Baby,
Renée called it, because he hardly drove it. It was plush,
quiet inside, only the wipers shuttling back and forth. He
didn't know the street the yard was on, but he had an idea,
he had a map.

The neighborhood was no worse than East Liberty, he
thought, though the road the map finally put him on was.
The row houses on one side stood abandoned, their doors
and windows holes, tar-paper fake brick falling off in
squares. On the other side, there were bars on the doors and
windows, an old three-toned Toyota with fancy chrome
wheels the only sign of life. The houses gave way to an abandoned plant of some kind, the parking lot weedy, then an
auto-body shop with a high fence topped with razor wire,
and then, at the dead end, the impound yard with its fence
sandbagged around the bottom so no one could dig under
it. There was a concrete-block garage surrounded by cars
and auto parts. A sign on the locked gate said to honk for
service. He looked in the rearview mirror before he did.

He was about to honk again when a black man in a
zipped-up jumpsuit came out of the garage and waved without actually looking at him. He was short and squat and it
took him a while to cross the yard, wiping his hands with a
rag, stepping around puddles. His glasses were large and
made him look owlish, wide-eyed. He unlocked the gate with
a key chained to his waist, then slid it aside so Tony could

drive through. He locked the gate behind him, wary, eyeing the street as if preparing for an attack.

Tony got out of the car. The man just stared, waited
for him to say something, blinking.

"My truck's here somewhere. An ice-cream truck?"

The man laughed—just a snort, like he'd said something ridiculous. "You're the guy, huh? They said you'd be
coming down." He waved for him to follow and stuck the
rag in his back pocket.

They walked around the rear of the garage, past a
doorless Cadillac full of batteries, a rack of hoods stacked
like books, a doghouse with a rusted chain. The puddles
were rainbowed with oil.

As they cleared the corner, the man stopped and
pointed. "That the one?"

Tony came abreast of him and saw the truck—his
truck, he thought, yes, because it took him a minute to recognize it. The headlights, the entire front fenders were completely missing, just the tires and red wheels sticking out.
They'd spraypainted the hood and the sides: *SRT* in red fluorescent, over and over. He walked toward it, stunned, oblivi-
ous of the puddles, his hands out in front of him as if trying
to heal it from a distance.

The grille was gone, and the doors made to look like
gates. He opened the hood and saw they'd taken the plugs,
the distributor—everything but the battery itself, still tied
down, the screws stripped silver. The seats were slashed,
the stuffing wet, and they'd gone to the trouble to smash the
gauges, every last one, the cherry dash splintered and

gouged around them. He looked up to the rearview mirror but it was gone.

"Bastards," he said.

The man nodded, goggle-eyed. "They did a job on her."

The freezer was littered with broken glass, a few malt liquor bottles. They'd tried to set a fire. All of his boxes were gone. *SRT*, it said across the Fudgesicle decals.

"Left the wheels," the man noted. "You're lucky it's so old. None of this stuff fits anything."

Tony didn't ask him about the keys, figuring he'd laugh at him again. He'd brought an extra set, and started to climb up on the wet seat; the man stopped him and pulled out his rag and brushed away the blue cubes of glass.

"Thank you," Tony said, and the man nodded.

He turned the key but nothing happened, not even the starter kicking in. He didn't expect anything. He sat there feeling the wet seat beneath him, wondering how much it would cost to fix everything. He'd have it done at Sal's, right there in Bloomfield. Nunzio would loan him the money.

At his age, it didn't make sense. Absently, he tried the toggles for the lights, the hazards and turn signals, none of them working until he switched on the bells and the music came chiming out of the speakers hidden in the canopy. The man bopped his head to the tune and smirked, as if it figured, the one thing.

Tony shut it off and climbed down. "You have a phone I can use?"

"Inside," the man said, and led him past the Caddy again.

"Fucking niggers," Sal said over the phone.

Tony glanced at the man at the other desk as if he could hear. "How long you think it'll take?"

"Depends on parts, you know with that thing. Could be months."

Spring, Tony thought. It wasn't that far off. "Okay," he said. "If you could send someone over."

Leaving, he thanked the man again and shook his hand. The man unlocked the gate, let him back the Baby out, then rolled it closed again. Driving away, Tony wished he'd gotten his name.

At home, he called the police about the St. Christopher and the rearview mirror. He wanted to know where they'd found the truck. Maybe they were around there somewhere.

"I don't think you want to go there alone, Mr. Giuliano," a different policeman said.

"I know the neighborhood, Officer."

"That may be so, but —"

"It's not a bad neighborhood."

"I'm just suggesting it might be better if we send someone with you."

They made him wait half an hour, and then the man they sent couldn't find the street. He couldn't find it because it no longer existed. It was behind the Nabisco factory, back by the railroad tracks, cut off from its other half by the new busway, a wasteland. The officer walked him into a vacant lot crowded with naked weed trees and speckled with trash — pink egg cartons, rusty tar buckets, the white chunks of a Styrofoam cooler, the ribs and skin of an umbrella. Plastic bags flew from a fence edging the busway. The officer motioned toward the corner where a set of bedsprings leaned on a tipped-over stove, and they made their way for it, tiptoeing around bald tires and swaths of sodden carpet.

"Right around here," the officer said, and scanned the ground.

There was too much junk to see anything. Doughnut boxes, the head of a broken broom, puffy triangles of diapers, desk drawers, bike tires, a crooked barbecue cart. He saw one of his boxes among the flood of junk—the anonymous brown cardboard soft and dark now, *CHERRY* stenciled on the side.

They searched for twenty minutes in the rain but found nothing else.

"I'm sorry, sir," the officer said, and Tony said it was all right. On the way home, they talked about the truck. The officer seemed genuinely sympathetic. He said the graffiti meant Spofford Rolling Treys, a local street gang.

So they had known all along, he thought. They knew who it was and they'd said nothing, watched him get knocked down, his truck taken away.

When he got home he called Sal to see if he'd done an estimate yet.

"What, are you kiddin' me? I got no idea what these parts are gonna cost, how'm I supposed to do an estimate?"

"Good," Tony said. "Don't do anything. I don't want it fixed."

"So what do you want me to do?"

"You can have it."

"Tony, no disrespect, but I can't use it."

"Sal, listen. What do you usually do with something like this?"

They went back and forth on who would pay to have it taken away. Finally Sal said he wouldn't charge him for the towing, seeing he was a good customer.

While he was on the phone, Tony had been pacing. Now when he got off, he had to sit down. That was it, he thought. He'd retire, spend his mornings at the St. Clair, read the paper over a cup of coffee, play the numbers every day like those old bums, smoking their stogies by the bowling alley. Outside, the rain came down, beading the telephone wires. The apartment was dark, and he imagined this was what the rest of his life would be like—Renée coming home tired from work and having to cook him dinner. All because of the boy.

How many times did he have to replay it in his mind? The truck dipped, and he still didn't suspect anything. Then the exhaust hot on his shin, his surprise that the tire was moving—the emergency brake, he'd thought, the children, one of them could be crushed—and he turned and ran. The memory had become a dream, the one scene repeated in the slow motion of a nightmare. He would run and run yet never reach the door, he'd only see the boy, his long fingers on the wheel, the Seahawk's fierce beak, and then he was falling, waking up.

He was thinking of Miami, of himself in a bathrobe on the beach, when the phone rang. It was the police. They'd picked up a suspect, if he could come down and identify him.

"Of course," Tony said, like he'd thought hard about it.

He tried not to drive too fast, and then it took him forever to find a parking spot outside the precinct house. The sergeant at the desk pointed him through the doors with his pen, and there was the officer who'd helped him look for Rita's St. Christopher. He had a clipboard and talked while they walked down the hall.

"We got an anonymous call that this juvenile might be involved," he said, and Tony thought it had to be his Vanessa. She'd saved him twice now, he'd tell Renée.

The officer led him into a dark room with a single window, a heavy green shade pulled down in front of it. "We need to know if this is him, so you need to be positive. If it's not him, you need to tell us that."

He pulled the shade up, and there in the window sat the boy in jeans and a Steeler jacket, the same kind. Where did he get all these jackets from? He was in a hallway by a candy machine, watching people walk past, and Tony thought he didn't look anything like the men in the pictures. There were no plans in his face, just a scowl, half pouting, like a child. When the hall was empty, his face changed, and he looked around, worried, and stubbed his nose with the heel of his hand, sniffed in with his shoulders as if he had a cold. Tony thought of his frozen Milk Duds, his hand out for the change.

"Is that the one?" the officer asked.

"What's going to happen to him?"

"So that is him."

"Yes."

"Seeing as he's a juvenile, he'll probably be sent to a juvenile detention center, depending on his record."

"Not jail."

"Not the jail we think of as jail."

"I don't want him to go to jail."

"That depends on the judge, but I'd say that's rare in this type of case."

He had to sign a form on the clipboard, and then he was free to go, suddenly outside and in the Big Baby, shaking from the swiftness, the finality of the whole thing. He wondered what they were doing to the boy, if they would take his clothes away and put him in a cell, call his mother. He resented the boy even more for forcing him to do this. He didn't want to, even after seeing the truck. He had no choice.

Back home, he thought it wasn't right that he should feel bad after what had happened. He wondered if Vanessa or whoever it was that called felt the same way. Probably not.

No, probably, because they knew his people.

He called Sal and asked him if he'd done anything with the truck.

"You just told me not to."

"Hold on to it, all right?"

"Make up your mind."

"A day or two," Tony said. "I'm in no condition to make a decision here."

He told Renée everything over dinner, and found himself downplaying how bad the truck was. She asked how much it would cost, and he said Sal couldn't give him a number.

"I knew they'd find it," she said.

"And someone did turn him in. You know that wouldn't happen around here."

She pointed her fork at him, chewing. "Around here no one would steal it."

"Someone called, that's all I'm saying."

"Why do I think you'll listen to me? Because maybe I'm your daughter?"

"I listen to you all the time—what do you think, I don't?"

"Ahh," she said, and dismissed him with a wave of her hand. "You'd be back there tomorrow if it was running."

It was true, he thought, if the weather was good enough. Why did it surprise him that his daughter knew her father? At one time she hadn't. That was past.

The next day it was brilliant. All afternoon the temperature climbed, the sun cutting in the windows, angling down the hall so it lit a strip of his dresser. The butterflies came off, leaving a gray patch of adhesive he scrubbed with rubbing alcohol; already the cut was healing. He pulled on his work clothes—the white pants and the shirt with his name sewn in red over the heart, the white gloves—and made sure he had enough change for the apron. He took the Big Baby, a cooler in the trunk, filling it with popsicles at the Giant Eagle.

He turned down Spofford and saw the children chasing each other along the sidewalk, jumping double-dutch, a group of mothers and older girls sitting on the steps in the sun, enjoying the last of Indian summer. He slowed and put his captain's hat on, rolled his window down and stopped in front of them. He wished he had his bells, but his horn made them turn around. They gave him this look like *Who are you?* No one moved until he got out of the car to open the trunk. Then they recognized him.

The mothers stood up, digging in their pockets like always. The children quit their games, dropped their balls and jump ropes and came running, laughing and jostling and calling his name. "Candyman!" they shouted, "Candyman!"

"Yes, children," Tony said, as they flocked around him. "Yes. The Candyman is here."

THE PAYBACK

EVERY TUESDAY AND Thursday after work he went with Chris in the city van, bumping his chair down the front stairs of their building while Chris lay back like an astronaut, staring up at the sky. It was not his choice; Eugene had gotten a job out at the airport, Jackie was back on first shift. Five days a week, until dinner, it was just Chris and him.

Besides this trip, Chris only left the house with Vanessa, Saturdays, their walk in the park. The city had finally started work on the lift, the workers mysteriously appearing one morning, then gone the next. Harold thought Chris had gained weight, his head resting on an extra lip of chin, but didn't mention it to Jackie. At rehab he was learning how to do for himself, cooking on a special stove he could reach, doing laundry in an ingenious pair of machines, but at home Jackie didn't let him near the dirty clothes, left him lunches already plastic-wrapped for the microwave. Harold was just as guilty, popping up from the couch during commercials to see if Chris wanted anything.

He didn't. He stayed in his room, working on his mural. He'd taped together pages from his big sketchpad and tacked them across the back wall at chest level so he could lie on his bed and pencil in figures. There were famous people and people like Bean. "And right there," he'd say, "I'm going to put in Benjamin Davis."

"Who?" Harold would say, and Chris would show him a picture from one of the books Vanessa brought over. The face on the wall looked exactly the same, but of the thirty people so far, Harold only recognized Bean, Minister Farrakhan with his big-ass glasses, and Curtis Martin, number 28 of the Patriots, who grew up here. He thought of his own father, how disappointed he'd be that Harold had wasted his education. He had no excuses, only a few useless tales of Vietnam—and actually they were from Thailand, from the airbase where as a mechanic he assisted the plane captain of an A-6, bucking rivets and drizzling stripped fasteners with Loctite so they didn't pop during bombing runs. He'd had a shot at college when he came back, VA benefits, but it seemed childish after Thailand, so he got a job, married, raised his children. It was a full life, despite what his father or Dre might say. There was still some honor in it that might be salvaged, if he could just keep his eye on what was important.

That was his hope now, especially on Tuesdays and Thursdays, and today, sitting in the van with Chris, he suddenly felt calm, at peace, as if the war inside him between Dre and Jackie had been decided (not by him, he couldn't say that, but by events) and he'd been given a fresh start. He honestly felt, for an instant as they turned off Penn

Circle, that the life he needed to live was the one he desired, that he would grow into it like a beautiful suit. Beside him, Chris sat hunched over a book in his chair, old photographs of jazz greats, some of them from Pittsburgh, like Roy Eldridge there.

Harold pointed at Little Jazz. "Your grandfather used to go see him at the old Hurricane Lounge. He'd come through four, five times a year when his mother was still alive."

"You ever hear him?"

"Few times. Man could blow fire."

Chris seemed happy at the fact, impressed, and as he turned the pages, tipped the book toward Harold to ask if he'd seen Erroll Garner, Stanley Turrentine, Ahmad Jamal. He nodded, told stories, though mostly they were second-hand. His father had heard them, an aficionado, his 78s clean as dishes. He'd hole up in his study and crank the Victrola, sit at his desk, smoking and nodding along with solos blown years ago. When he died, his mother drove the collection over to the church rummage sale in the back of the wagon, as if glad for the opportunity to clean out the house. How many thousands of dollars? Harold had been in Thailand, though the distance didn't matter; they'd hardly talked since he quit school to enlist. Despite everything, his father would be pleased that Harold was sharing some of him with his own son, and this seemed further proof of the rightness of his new life.

At the rehab he watched Chris struggle with a device like they used in old grocery stores to reach things on the top shelf. It was about ten feet long and retractable, and had a pistol grip you squeezed. They were doing it in a model kitchen, just one wall; the thing was supposed to save you from having to roll back and forth all the time. As he watched Chris fish for a pepper shaker, his own face wrinkled in concentration, his own fingers clenched an invisible grip, and when the shaker fell and spilled a spray across the stovetop, like Chris, he wanted another chance.

This was what a father was supposed to do, he thought, not the other thing. Was it so hard to remember? And yet at times he wished he was outside, lost in a cigar, night falling behind the streetlights, the steeple of Presby a black knife against the sky.

They couldn't fix Chris; the money wasn't the problem.

Chris gripped the pepper shaker, hit the button so the arm retracted, then slowly, carefully, dropped the entire thing into the boiling pot of noodles.

"Fuck this," he said, and made to spin away, but his therapist shoved the brake on so he froze.

"Try that again," Willa Mae said, tough, as if he'd meant it personally. She was one of those wiry, sexless women Harold had always been afraid of. Dried-up-looking, skin grainy and flaking to ash on her hard forearms. Women like that took a switch to their kids, killed their own chickens. She plucked the shaker from the pot and set another on the counter, this one a little closer, the angle that much easier.

Chris lifted the device like a speargun, touching the button so the slide inched its way over the counter. When he was close, he opened the hinged gripper. Clicked the button once, twice, little baby steps, afraid he'd knock it over. Chris was getting tired; the gripper wavered. Another touch of the button. Harold tilted his chin, giving it some English, and it bracketed the pepper neatly. Chris pulled the trigger.

"Beautiful," Willa Mae said. "Now bring it back and you'll be all done."

Chris didn't acknowledge her, just thumbed the button so the shaker zipped back to him. He swiveled in his chair, facing the stove, and, turning one fist like jerking a kite away from a tree, added a dash of pepper to the water.

"Very good, Chris," she said.

"Nice," Harold added, patting his shoulder, but Chris just handed the device to her.

In the van, Harold said Willa Mae thought he was making real progress.

"Oh yeah," Chris said. "I'm gonna be the next Chef Boyardee."

Back home, Jackie had left a chicken pie in the oven and a note by the phone; she and Eugene were at church, her at choir and Eugene running his new youth group. Harold knew this; it was just her way of saying she was thinking of him, implying she forgave him. Generous of her, and kind to remind him again, as if for one merciful second he might forget. He laid out the plates and the two of them sat at the kitchen table. And this too was right, that he should have to face his failings instead of running away, outside, into the night or someone else's arms. He didn't know what to say to Chris, never had, and now most of the usual subjects seemed cruel—What did you do today? What are you going to do tomorrow?—and so Harold relied on the two things Chris was still interested in.

"Who'd you draw today?" he asked.

"Elijah McCoy." Chris let it sit there, teasing him. He swept his food in, his mouth low to the plate. It was one reason he was getting so big, he ate way too fast.

"Okay," Harold said, "I don't know him."

"He invented the automatic oiler for train engines. People tried to copy his design but theirs always broke, so to make sure they got his, the mechanics would ask for the Real McCoy. That's where that comes from. You learn about him in Black History Month, in school."

"Not when I went to school."

"What did you learn?" Chris asked, and Harold had to think. It was so long ago.

"Not much," he said. He'd wanted to say it like a joke, but it didn't come out that way. "So," he said, "are you and Vanessa doing anything special this weekend?"

"I don't think so."

"She's coming over though."

"We'll probably go to the park."

"Good," Harold said, trying not to be too much of a cheerleader.

"I'm done," Chris said, and set his napkin on the table.

"I'll get your plate."

"That's all right," Chris said, and Harold knew he shouldn't have offered. He ate while Chris maneuvered around the table, the chair whirring, his plate in his lap. "I'm going to go work a little."

"Okay," Harold said. He watched him fit the chair through the door, then turn sideways so he could close it. In a minute his music came on, thumping the walls. Harold

looked at the mound of chicken pie left in front of him. The
Real McCoy, huh? He gently laid down his fork, stood up
and scraped the plate into the garbage. He even did the
dishes slowly, brooding over them though there was no
point. Being here was his choice, Dre always said; now he
believed it, at times even saw it as honorable, yet when
Harold dropped his guard, he pictured the days marching
on like this, his life an endless series of tiny self-denials chip-
ping away at his heart, sadness and rainy days his one comfort. Pitiful. He remembered wrestling with Dre in his sunny
sheets, drinking naked at his table, laughing at Sister Payne's
dog yapping at them. When was the last time he'd been
happy like that?

Life was not about happiness, he thought on the couch.
A man had obligations. A father had responsibilities. He had
the TV on, a bad reflex. He never really watched it, it just
flowed past, eating and tracking time like some loud, expensive clock. Someone passed in the hall, and he looked toward the door, panicked for a second that it would open and
he'd be caught.

But he'd done nothing wrong. It was a habit now, feeling guilty. Even the night he came home late from the Liberty—okay, he'd had way too much, but it wasn't like he
was with anyone except Earl, telling him he needed to close
up, to go home while he could still walk. Even that night he
wasn't completely surprised to find her waiting up for him.
He didn't see her at first, so drunk his eyes only focused on
what was right in front of him (the key, the wandering doorknob and keyhole), but then he heard her long-drawn snoring—like a wet undershirt slowly being torn to shreds—and

found her on the couch. In the deep cup of his lush, sentimental buzz, he thought it was nice of her, waiting up, sweet
like she could be (it had been years, so his own hope now
surprised him, seemed equally sweet), and he sat down beside her, careful not to crush her arm. For some reason she
had a knife in her hand, and he removed it. "Dangerous,"
he said, carrying it to the sink, puzzled but not yet questioning its presence, just accepting it and acting, following logic
as in a dream. He understood only when she woke up and
began hitting him—no, really after that, when he could de-
code what she was screaming at him. Lying motherfucker.
No-good two-timing dog just like her father. Worthless
piece of shit.

   "Wait," he said, "hold up," trying to stop her flashing
arms, but it was dark and a fist caught his nose, crushing it
down, hot, bone and cartilage twisting, a feeling he knew
from so long ago, so far within his body's memory that he
could not stop his own fists from instantly finding its source.
Thank God he'd only hit her in the chest, had caught himself immediately. She cried, wailed like she'd been shot, and
he was saying he was sorry, baby, please baby you know I
didn't mean it, breathless, and then Eugene had him by the
neck, slammed back against the wall as if he'd witnessed
everything.

   "Let me go, son," he said.

   "You come to *me* next time," Eugene said, and pushed
him away.

   Chris's light was on; he was calling, asking what was
happening.

   "Nothing," Eugene said. "Daddy's drunk."

Son of a bitch, if he could have that one night back.

He couldn't. He could never apologize enough for it to anyone, least of all his sons. Every morning when she got dressed after her shower, he saw the bruise he'd left, just above her left breast, just below her shoulder, wide as a pie plate, a bull's-eye still changing colors. His nose was fine, not a thing wrong with it. What would his father have said, him striking a woman. There was no man lower.

What would he say about Dre? At times, months ago, in the haze of love's first dreamy intensity and surrender, he imagined his father might be like himself—that, away from the daily punishment of his mother's high hopes and disappointment in him, he found some comfort in the arms of another. All right, yes, he could admit it: another man. Wasn't his reserve, his fastidiousness and personal privacy, the sign of something? He was certainly not common (for that very reason would be disappointed in him). Now though, he could not see any chain of reasoning that led him to that conclusion, only high spirits and wishful thinking, the hope that his father's life was more than his own, not just a war with his mother he was bound to lose. It wasn't realistic, this hope: He wanted his father to be freer than he was. Now he thought of him closing the door to his study as a way of barricading himself in, and wished he'd been able to help. He imagined some collector still owned the records, picked up cheap at the rummage sale, kept his special treasures cataloged, the sleeves wrapped in plastic, probably never played them.

The TV slogged along, a swamp of commercials. *ER* was on in a few minutes, so he got up and paced around the kitchen like a security guard, making sure everything was neat for her. On the top shelf of the right-hand cabinet his bottle of Johnny Walker waited patiently, strictly forbidden, the pencil line on the side proof of his selflessness. Crumbs huddled under the toaster oven, and he wiped them away with a wet paper towel.

He tucked his shirt in, looking around the living room. The arms of the couch were going shiny, the TV ugly, at least ten years old. Next to the end table the rug was stained where Chris had spilled a glass of grape juice a few years ago, and Harold thought of his mother's formal living room (never used) with its intricate Persian rugs, the almost sterile cleanliness she insisted on. His father's study was a mess, and every spring he had to defend it, his mother standing at the open door in her apron, threatening to take care of it if he didn't. Out back she hung the rugs from the line and gave Harold the wire beater; an hour later, after his arms had turned to clay, she came out and made clouds jump from the Tabriz. Trumpet vines twined around the garage's downspout, flowering in the heat of summer, and his father would take them driving along the river in the Mercury, cool air rushing through the windows, his mother holding her hat on her lap, the ribbon flapping, trying to fly out. What had happened that those people seemed so foreign to him, their existence strange, barely to be believed? Something had slipped, he thought, missed somewhere. There had to be a mistake.

He could not be thinking this when Jackie came home, so he banished it, turned his attention to *ER*, one of the few shows he actually watched with interest. He sat up straight, his posture another sign he wasn't thinking of the other woman, that his confession had washed him clean. She'd been greedy for details (later that same night), and so he'd chosen a woman from work, absolutely imaginary, and when he saw how intently she was listening, he knew Sister Payne hadn't suspected anything. He fabricated their affair, yet in a way he was telling the truth; he never strayed far from what had actually happened between him and Dre. And they had broken it off, they hadn't talked in weeks—the important things were true, or had been then.

ER was just going into its opening credits when they came in, her first, Eugene right behind her like a bodyguard. He sat up straighter, ready for whatever test she had for him.

"How was practice?" he asked.

"Good," she said, handing her overcoat to Eugene, who looked at him with no emotion, like he was waiting for him to make a mistake. "Sister Payne says hello."

"You gave her my best, I hope."

"Of course." Behind him now, she peered into the kitchen. He waited for her to appreciate it—indicated by her silence, the time it took to look over the shining counters. She came back in and leaned a hand on the back of the couch. "I'm tired so I'm going to bed."

ER was back on, and he actually did want to watch it, but he clicked it off. Everything was a measure of his guilt, his willingness to pay, take his punishment. In his heart he knew it was the right thing to do, despite what he sometimes felt. Hadn't his father taught him that?

He went in to say good night to Chris (no dope smell), and motioned for him to put his headphones on. Eugene was in the kitchen, pouring himself some milk.

"'night," Harold said, and Eugene said it back, polite. It was hard being around him now, but as he closed the door of their room Harold wasn't relieved that it was just between him and Jackie, that the rest of the world didn't exist.

"You can stay up," Jackie said from the bathroom.

"That's all right."

"Isn't *ER* on?"

"It's a repeat." Hell, maybe it was; he couldn't tell. Every show they ran around with the crashcarts, someone died, people fell out of love.

She came out in her nightgown, her arms heavy, eyes tired. He went in to brush his teeth, still dressed. It was too bright in the mirror, and he looked old. Yet Dre had called *him*, not the other way around. After the barren weeks, the madness of not seeing him, he could have left any message. His name looked funny in the department secretary's girlish script. Just a box was checked: *Wants you to call.* It was wrong, it was harmful. He had to try three times before he got through, and then, with one word, everything returned and he could breathe, no longer hopeless and alone.

The lights were off when he slid in beside her, the sheets chilly. She seemed to be on his side, her legs rubbery against his butt.

"How was rehab?" she asked when he'd gotten settled.

"It's tough. You know."

"But he's trying hard."

"Yeah," he said, positive, but thought that that might not be enough. Chris knew it too, Willa Mae's toughlove didn't fool him for one minute.

She reached a hand over, and he almost flinched. He was tense whenever she touched him but wasn't allowed to show it, and her fingers on his skin were torture, the scent of her strong and rotten under the covers. She expected him to reach for her, so he did, feeling the slackness, the fat, not Dre's hard body. She was kissing him, and he pushed Dre from his mind, thought of nothing (his father driving, looking in the mirror to see how he was doing in the backseat). Her hands worked him up clumsily; after so many years, he thought, she should know how to touch him. His hands strayed across her back, trying to find neutral ground. How selfish he was, what a terrible man.

Her hand left him and the light clicked on.

"Open your eyes," she said. "Look at me."

She wanted him above her, she said, where she could see him, and Harold could not say no. There was too much at stake—Chris, and Eugene, the life he needed to provide his family. The bruise accused him, livid. He had no defense in its presence, least of all his feelings. She took him into her, pulled his face down to her mouth. "Tell me you love me," she said, and he did, thinking Dre would forgive him. "I don't believe you. Show me." She wanted him to be with her completely, to stop thinking of the other woman, and trying to put some heat in his kisses, to fool his own body (not his heart, no, it knew the truth), he wondered how much of his life he had to sacrifice. All, he thought. She wanted it all.

KiLLiNG ME SOFTLY

HE KNEW WHAT they'd do to him, and how it felt. The boiled food, the cold floors, the stiff jeans and blue uniform shirts starched so hard they scratched the back of your neck open. Fights in the dormitories with hidden pencils, the sharpened butts of toothbrushes, a soap-in-a-sock bolo. Eugene had been in Schuman three times, so he knew what it was like coming back after you thought you were done with it. They all thought you were stupid, a loser. Either that or hard-core, and with one look Eugene could see Little Nene didn't have that. He wasn't straight insane like his brother—he just wasn't thinking at all, Darrin would say.

His Granmoms called Eugene first thing, and he said he'd go down and help out at the scheduling, though he was sure there was nothing he could do. The hearing was immediately, that night. He shaved and put on his good suit, and Smooth came and picked him up in the Regal.

"z'at a Bible?" Smooth asked.

"Yeah."

"What are you gonna do?"

"I don't know," he said. "Represent, I guess."

"You're not gonna preach now."

It was supposed to be a joke, and though both of them laughed, Eugene couldn't explain why he'd brought it along.

Even at the Public Safety Building he wasn't sure what he was doing. He was surprised when the defender pointed to him and the judge asked him to stand up. With her glasses on a chain and her hair pulled back, she reminded him of Mrs. Roby, his old social studies teacher at Reizenstein.

"Mr. Tolbert, what is your role here?"

"I'm here to represent Leonard's family. His grand-mother couldn't be here. His older brother was killed a few weeks ago in a murder."

"Gang-related, is that correct?"

"Yes, ma'am."

"Is there a male guardian in the household?"

"No."

"Are you proposing to assume guardianship?"

"No, ma'am. I run a youth program for teens at risk that Leonard's hoping to enter. I've been in the system myself and I want to help him stay out of it."

"I see," she said, and looked at a piece of paper on her desk as if it said something about him. "Thank you."

He sat down, feeling their conversation wasn't over, that she'd call on him again.

She didn't. She set the date for the hearing and released Little Nene on bond (Smooth helped him with this, the old place by the bus station), and an hour later the three of them were in the Regal, going home.

"Guess they din't have room for you," Smooth joked. In back, Little Nene didn't laugh.

"Ay," Smooth said.

"My name is LJ."

"z'at right?"

"That's right."

"Listen to that shit."

Eugene and Smooth couldn't get used to it, so they didn't call him anything, just laughed at his good luck, warned him there wouldn't be a next time.

"I ain't kidding," Smooth said. "Cause they'll bump you up to that next level, they don't care you're a juvenile. Three strikes and that's it."

"Seriously," Eugene said, "what do you think you're doing? An ice-cream truck."

"*Tony's* truck," Smooth said, shaking his head at the stupidity of it. "And why you have to go and tag it? Damn!"

Eugene looked back at him to show him no one understood what he'd done. It was dark until they went under a streetlight, and then a sliding stripe showed him Little Nene looking out the window, giving him the side of his head.

"You got an answer for that?" Eugene asked.

"I don't know," Little Nene said. He'd been listening, quiet the whole time. "I don't know why I even took it. I was just walking down the street."

"That's how it happens," Smooth said. "You're just walking down the street one second and next thing they're locking the door on your ass. Shit happens to me all the time." He was being harsh partly because he'd been shot at last week in the Regal, a round taking out the back window as he was riding by the park, probably from another car, B-Mo's people. He'd spent Saturday getting it replaced, and didn't mention it again, but on their way to work in the mornings, Eugene noticed he didn't like to sit at the lights on Penn, the line separating Homewood from the white neighborhoods. At work he was fine, but when he let Eugene off, the two of them didn't sit there and talk like they used to.

They didn't tonight either. Smooth pulled up in front of Eugene's building, and he and Little Nene got out. They thanked him for the ride, he waved and he was gone.

"Tomorrow night you're mine," Eugene said, and Little Nene nodded like he'd been caught. "You be there early to set up."

"Okay," he said, shoulders hunched, like Eugene might slap him.

"All right," Eugene said, releasing him.

The boy didn't even say thanks, just walked off, leaving Eugene looking at the way he shoved his hands in his pockets, his Pirates cap tipped to one side, Trey-style. He pimped like a jitterbug, bopping his head (that's right, I'm bad, come on if you got it), ready for anything. It made Eugene chuckle and cover his smile with a hand. Really, the shit was sad, little dude reminded him so much of himself, thinking he could kick the world's ass, that it hadn't played a million of him already. That it was just waiting for him to step up and try that tired shit again.

He'd covered that bet, he thought when he'd gotten inside. Lost it and paid it off. Wasn't much to spare, but here he was, still young, and smarter, stronger — walking, talking proof.

Moms was out shopping, Pops wherever it was he went (it was a woman, on the under, and Eugene thought he should just leave; with his new job he could cover the rent himself). Chris was in his room, working on his mural. Eugene was hoping the group could get funding and put it up along the busway, get the state to buy the supplies; it seemed he had all these ideas now, just no way of getting them done.

They said hey, and Eugene went into his room, set his Bible on the dresser. In the mirror he caught a glimpse of himself in the suit, and he could see how he might look impressive to the judge. He held the Bible up in front of him like a prize, as if the papers were taking his picture. He looked, maybe for the first time in his life, how he felt he should look. Serious. Capable. He thought of what Smooth said—if he was going to preach. If it would help someone, then yes. He'd thought about it in prison, falling just short of pledging his life to the ministry. Then, he began each day dedicating every breath to Jesus, but now it seemed he hadn't committed himself fully, that out of doubt or selfishness he'd held some small part of his heart back, and it puzzled him.

Run either hot or cold, he recalled, for if you are lukewarm I will spit you out of my mouth.

He closed the door, made sure it was locked and got down on his knees in his suit, bent over nearly double, the Bible squeezed in both fists, his forehead resting on its pebbled jacket.

The week before he was arrested, he'd killed a man. A boy really, no older than Little Nene. They were just riding around, Fats and them, when they decided to cruise Westinghouse Park over in Homewood. It was a dare, just stupid stuff. They'd been smoking and goofing on some car sounds and they were amped. Smooth had this little .22 pistol, and all night U was waving it around for a joke, little peashooter thing, saying they were going to take out those dudes from Larimer with it, they were so weak. "Now we up, see?" he was saying. "SRT up. They straight simps. They simpin'."

"Truth, dog!"

"This is your Minister of Information speaking," Fats said.

It was no one's idea, or all of theirs, or maybe the car was drawn to the park the way rain ends up in the river. The courts were still busy even though most of the lights were broken; the players' shadows reached through the fence, flew in transition, then bunched under the boards. Fats eased the car along, the windows humming down with the touch of a button, and the person Eugene had been leveled the little pistol at a crowd in one corner bent over a flame. He steadied his wrist on the door, waited until they cleared the whalelike shadow of a parked Continental, then let loose.

The gun sparked in front of his eyes, blinding him like a flashbulb, throwing a blue halo over everything. It took a second shot into the crowd before they started running (he heard girls screaming, what he thought were return shots), but by then he wasn't looking, just pulling the trigger, emptying the clip at them, laughing, and Fats hit the gas and they were swerving out of there.

The next day it was in the paper. A sixteen-year-old named Dawayne Perry. Eugene didn't even read the article, just looked at the picture, flipped to the box scores to see if the Pirates won. Freak shot, it must have been (he would read in the prison library that it hit him in the eye, drove straight into his brain). It was the boy's fault for being there; he knew the risk like everyone else. Casualty of war. But months later, in group, when Darrin asked them to remember the time they were most ashamed of themselves, the one thing they'd done that couldn't be forgiven, that night returned to him and he had no way to shrug it off. He went back to his cell with the boy's face in his mind, the smiling school picture they'd used to make him look even younger, more innocent. The case was never solved, nothing linked to him, yet nightly Eugene tried himself for the murder of Dawayne Perry, found himself guilty, and, kneeling on the cold stone floor of his cell, a cheap, donated Bible in his hands, pleaded for mercy before the only court he trusted to deliver justice.

Now he opened his eyes, lifted his head and stood, not at all absolved—if anything, more deeply beholden. He set the Bible on his dresser again and carefully hung up the suit. He cut the lights and lay in bed, wondering if he saw Little Nene as payment for Dawayne. It wasn't that simple. He still had to pay for himself, and that would take his entire life. Longer, he thought.

The phone rang in the living room. Chris couldn't get it, so he got up and wrapped a towel around himself, unlocked the door.

Chris hadn't moved at all, still working on his mural, as if it couldn't be for him.

It was Nene's Granmoms, thanking him for getting Leonard out of jail. She was crying like it was a miracle.

"He still has a hearing next week," Eugene reminded her. "Did you read his papers?"

"He's home," she said. "That's all that matters. Now that you're helping him, I know he'll be all right. He'll listen to you."

In bed again, he thought she really meant something different—that Little Nene didn't listen to *her.* Eugene was flattered she had confidence in him, but wasn't so sure. Drifting, he imagined what it would take to save the boy. He could see the two of them at some banquet, having come through it, receiving an award. Contributing, like Darrin said, giving back. They smiled for the flash like father and son, like brothers. But exactly how they'd gotten there was a mystery, and in the morning he woke up with the feeling that he hadn't thought hard enough, had come up with no real answers, only dreams, and that nothing was settled.

At work he had time to think. When he wasn't crawling in the dirty bellies of planes or chucking luggage onto a conveyor belt, he sat on a baggage tractor in his headphones and fluorescent vest and plastic knee pads, his gloves in his lap, skimming a discarded newspaper and sipping his coffee, trying to come up with what to say. He remembered Darrin in group. The group did all the talking, Darrin just stepped in when they needed to be set straight. Potential, Darrin always talked about. Using your natural intelligence. What else? Every meeting it seemed he said something for Eugene to think on, something he'd take back to his cell and turn over like a puzzle. Simple things like: What do you want? How are you going to achieve that goal? What are you going to do if that doesn't succeed?

A flight was coming in, and he folded the paper away and tugged his gloves on, picked up the orange-tipped batons and walked out to guide it in. On the ground were stenciled markings for the different planes—737, DC-9, A300. He liked the job, except for the wind and the noise and the blue uniform that looked like a janitor's. The rain was a bitch, but otherwise Smooth was right, it was easy money. You could earn free tickets by working overtime, and every day he pictured himself inside one of these planes, in the cushioned hum, going somewhere like Atlanta or D.C., a Chocolate City with strong churches, a history of struggle and belief that would rub off on him, keep him strong. He'd never been anywhere except Indiana, visiting their grandmother, and she'd been gone almost ten years. Since then he'd been stuck in Pittsburgh, and now it seemed he'd been trapped in the city as much as in that misguided life he was living. Leaving might lift that past off him, give him the perspective he needed, like Malcolm jetting to Mecca. But to go, he'd have to ask his parole officer, and he didn't see that happening. Patience, Darrin said. Things don't change in a day. Now, waving the plane in, he saw the pasty faces of the passengers and envied them. Their leisure and freedom, how they took it for granted while he had to fight for the littlest thing. They looked down at him, unseeing. He shoved the sticks in his back pocket, chocked the front wheels and got busy, trying to put that spite out of his mind.

At lunch in the cafeteria, he could have anything he wanted as long as he paid for it. The first week he'd been astonished by the prices, but now he found the walk along the steaming chafing dishes secretly funny, so close to how it was inside, except he was out now. Sitting down to his soup and sandwich, he was truly grateful, and again, in that moment of saying grace, he felt saved.

Already chomping on his burger, Smooth stared at him like he was out of his mind. "Can I ax you something?"

"Huh?"

"You for real with that shit?"

"Why," Eugene said, "'m I making you nervous?"

"Naw," Smooth said. "I got you. Just ig me, a'ight."

"Since when you know me *not* to be real?"

"Never."

"Well there you go."

"It's just strange," Smooth said. "It's just different, you know?"

"It's different," Eugene agreed. "But it's all right."

Later, dropping him off, Smooth called after him, "Keep it real, man," and from habit Eugene stretched his arm out, palm down, and shot him with the gun of his thumb and finger. He saw what he'd done, and wondered how long he'd been doing it. Like Darrin said, you had to be conscious all the time, you couldn't let yourself fall into those old traps.

He kept that advice in mind when Pops helped him with the dinner dishes, washing while Eugene dried. Since it happened, the two of them hadn't talked about it, probably never would. Nothing would change, except this, and that wouldn't last long. Again, he thought he should have the words to break through, make a difference. Wasn't that what a preacher did? Pops had a scratch above one eye. He seemed older to Eugene since he'd been out, his face thinner. Before he could look at him, Pops looked away. The dishes clunked underwater.

"How you doin'?" Eugene asked.

"I'm all right," he said wearily, relieved, as if he'd been waiting on something worse.

"You know the two of you have got to work something out."

"I know."

It didn't go beyond that. It didn't have to. They were busy with their hands, and then they were done, each of them wiping down the counter on their side of the sink.

By the time he got off the church van in his suit, he'd convinced himself the same straight-up approach would work with Little Nene. He'd just lay out the facts, put down the Bible and testify from his life. The key was exactly what he'd told the judge. He'd been in the system, he'd made the mistakes and paid the price. Maybe if Little Nene would listen he wouldn't have to.

In the basement Sunday school room he set up the metal chairs in a circle. First twelve, then eight, then he compromised at ten. He wasn't sure how many would come. He'd stapled flyers to bulletin boards and telly poles all across East Liberty, and Reverend Skinner had announced it before the sermon, so ten was a guess. He had enough Lemon Blend for twenty, and brownies from the women's auxiliary, a two-liter bottle of pop he'd bought himself, a bowl of ice from the kitchen. He arranged the stacks of cups and the napkins on the table, then poured himself a glass of Diet Pepsi. Upstairs, the choir softly rumbled, clapping and stamping their feet.

He drank the pop down to the ice, from time to time checking his watch. It was still five minutes before the time, so he set the glass down and went upstairs to see if people were wandering the halls, having trouble finding the room. The only person he came across was Reverend Skinner in his office, who used the opportunity to give Eugene the book on grant proposals he'd been recommending. Eugene had told him about Chris's mural, and Reverend Skinner thought he ought to try Martin Robinson's office.

"Make sure you run it by me before it goes out," he said, and Eugene promised he would.

Outside, the parking lot was lit a sickly orange, shadows hunched between the cars. The four corners by the stoplight were empty, and he wondered if Little Nene had slipped in while he was with Reverend Skinner. He waited another minute, watching a cop car cruise through, a big Caprice slow as a shark, then went downstairs.

No one had come. The chairs sat there, the overhead light reflected in the punch bowl full of Lemon Blend. It seemed a waste, and he had a glass, dipping the scratched plastic ladle in. So sweet it hurt his teeth, turned them gritty. He felt stupid in his suit, surrounded by the second grade's cut-outs of Noah's Ark, the crayon drawings of Harriet Tubman. The ice had melted so there was no way of saving it, and he dumped the bowl in the teacher's sink, poured the Lemon Blend over it.

Nene's Granmoms thought Leonard was at the meeting with him. She sounded shocked that he wasn't, but only

for a minute. Then she was all promises, telling him she'd
be on him when he came in. When was the next meeting,
because she would see to it that he was there if she had to
drag him there herself.

"It's Thursday," Eugene said. "And don't tell him, but
I am personally going to come over there and escort him if
that's all right."

"Bless you," she said, but after he'd hung up he found
he was angry with her, though he knew it was impossible
to stop the little hustler. It was his own history; why did he
think he could change it?

Because he had. You're living proof, Darrin said, all
of you. Use that.

Where would he start? Boosting cigarettes from the
Giant Eagle. Hanging on the corner with his partners, selling some bud. None of it seemed that scandalous, and then
he was strapping every day, moving TVs, riding down on
Dawayne Perry that night. It was too easy to blame it on
the rock. It wasn't like Nene. It wasn't the Treys either. He
couldn't say for sure exactly what happened.

"How'd it go?" Moms asked him in the van, and he
told her.

"It may take a little while," she said, and patted his knee.
Riding beside her, he thought she must know so much about
patience that her advice had to be right.

Wednesday it rained and they wore their yellow slick-
ers at work, the hoods useless. The planes dripped, the
jetways, and even drawing the rubber curtains of the carts
didn't stop the bags from getting wet. They were cold coming out of the planes, and Eugene's fingers hurt like frost-

bite. He squeezed into the glassed-in cab of the tractor, staring out at the brown lakes of the runways while Smooth wondered aloud about the Pirates' slim playoff chances. The season was ending, and Eugene had missed it; he wanted to take Chris to a game like old times. It had been at least ten years, since they were kids.

The stink of burnt diesel drifted up from the pedals, warming his shins. He would tell Little Nene he couldn't remember when he stopped caring about anything. It snuck up on you and then you were in the middle of it, you weren't sure how, but that's what happened, and it could last a long time, your entire life if you were unlucky.

"Think he'll show tomorrow?" Smooth asked as he dropped him off.

"I'm not going to wait and find out."

"I hear you."

When he got out, Eugene gave him an old-school power salute that Smooth laughed at.

"Power to the people, baby."

Again, Pops helped with the dinner dishes, quiet for a while, then asking Eugene how he was doing. Moms made a Mrs. Smith's pie, and the three of them ate it watching TV, unable to tear Chris away from his mural. Eugene told them about the grant book Reverend Skinner lent him, and they agreed that it would be good for Chris. They didn't have to say they were worried, that the only time he left his room was when Vanessa came over. Eugene watched them watching Damon Wayans, laughing on the same couch they'd fought on, and wanted to understand. The pie was better than frozen pie should be. He thought he should start on the book and left them there, closing his door so he could concentrate.

The key to writing winning grant proposals is the dynamic presentation of ideas in a clear and concise manner. If applicable, charts and graphs are preferable to lengthy paragraphs of explanation. He yawned above the page, felt his jaws pop. Rain tapped at the window. He'd been going to bed earlier and earlier since he got the job, and his sleep was deeper, dreamless. He'd lay down and the next thing he knew the alarm was going off in his ear, as if it had only been minutes, his back knotted, and then he needed coffee, sat dazed in the Regal with a tall cup between his legs while Smooth motored along the Parkway, picking sleep from his eyes.

He closed the book and got ready for bed, made sure he had a clean uniform for tomorrow. He would come home and put his suit on, go straight over to Moreland. He'd have Little Nene, even if no one else came. He knew exactly what to tell him now.

In the morning it was still raining, the trucks on the Parkway blinding them with spray, making Smooth turn the wipers up to high. They didn't bother to talk, just rode with the heat on defrost. At work there was nothing to do. The east coast was socked in, JFK and Logan closed; everyone missed their connections. They tended the few puddle jumpers that came in from Dubois and Ligonier, the bags barely filling their cart.

At break Eugene stayed in the dry cab while Smooth put his hood up and went off to buy them coffees. He'd brought Reverend Skinner's book with him, but it just made him tired. *Establishing nonprofit status is imperative for maximum tax exemp-*

tion. He took off his cap and hung it on the gearshift, rubbed his hands over his hair and watched the drops make their way down the pane. The rain was harder now, bouncing white off the tarmac; nothing was coming in today, and he wished the tractor had a real heater. Maybe he'd catch up on his sleep.

Smooth came back early from break, running and ducking the drops. Eugene thought he'd take a long one, warm in the bacon-and-egg smell of the cafeteria, but here he was, hood flapping, sprinting like B-Mo's crew was after his ass. Eugene laughed in the cab, and when Smooth got to the door he held it closed for a joke.

"Cut the shit," Smooth yelled through the glass, banging it with a fist, and Eugene let him in.

"Fuck you playing around for?" Smooth said, all serious. He shoved the paper at him, flattened it with a slap. "I was trying to show you something if you'd listen." He jabbed at it with a finger.

EAST END MAN DEAD IN POLICE CHASE, the headline said.

"Musta happened last night," Smooth said, but Eugene wasn't listening, was falling through the article, caught on the name—*Leonard Jenkins, 16, of East Liberty.*

His face burned, the skin of his cheeks and his forehead. It had to be a mistake, a misprint, and he backtracked and then read on, dizzy with the impossibility of it. He was seeing him tonight. His Granmoms would have called. Vehicle reported stolen, a brief exchange of gunfire. This was exactly the kind of shit he was going to tell him about.

He stopped and started to read it again from the beginning, as if beneath a more intense concentration the words might change or mean something different. Early morning, the North Side. But there was no reason for him to be there, Eugene thought.

where the suspect then crashed at high speed into a utility pole.

"'s fucked up," Smooth said, as if there was nothing anyone could do.

It was true. It was not his fault, Eugene knew, but still, somehow he had lost him—had failed to save Little Nene as Darrin had saved him. He'd barely even tried, and now everything he had to say to him seemed fake and useless, an empty lesson.

Police say the deceased had various misdemeanor charges pending in juvenile court.

The story refused to change.

He still didn't fully believe it.

He folded the paper and laid it on the dash, unable to fit his thoughts together, to see anything but Little Nene jumping from the cracked, steaming car, running. He didn't picture an exchange of gunfire, just the police drawing down on him, the boy falling. For a car—but it was not about a car, it was about him: Little Nene or Eugene, or Nene, Dawayne Perry. It was about all of them, and the knowledge made Eugene get up and push past Smooth and out the door into the rain.

"U man," Smooth called, but he was gone, splashing across the concrete for the terminal, then inside, out of the rain, in the scarred corridor that led to the big belts. The light was dim in here, and his footsteps echoed dully, like the inner ring of a basketball. He walked the length of it, swinging his arms, wanting to punch something, or someone, holding and letting go his breath until he realized he

was making a wet, seething noise in his throat. He had nowhere to go, and he turned and walked back to the end just
as fast, turned again, slower, the feeling leaving him, seeping like adrenalin from his muscles.

"Motherfucker," he said, but quiet so it didn't echo. He
was suddenly tired. The walls were black with skid marks.
It was too late to do anything, and he walked back outside
into the rain, stopping to feel it against his skin, looking up
at the low clouds as if they held some answer. Nothing but
gray, the drops falling white and cold.

He got back in the cab, and Smooth scooted over.

"You all right?"

"Yeah," Eugene said, because it was easier. Smooth
knew what he meant.

The day moved too slow. He needed something to do,
but the coast stayed closed, only Chicago feeding them con-
nectors, a few commuters from Erie. After lunch he spent
most of his time reconstructing what happened from the
paper, each time believing it more, and by the time Smooth
dropped him off, it seemed to have happened weeks ago, like
Nene. He didn't wave to Smooth, just said, "Tomorrow,"
and closed the door.

Chris was in his room.

"You hear?" Eugene said.

He hadn't, so he told him.

"Man," Chris said, "I don't know. It's gettin' insane out
there."

Eugene was disappointed in him; he'd wanted him to
be shocked. But what did Eugene expect after what had
happened? For Chris this was normal.

He'd find a place on the wall for him, he said. He pointed with his pencil. He'd move Fred Hampton over so he could be right by Nene.

"I'm sorry," Pops said at dinner.

"It just shows how much we need your group," Moms said, then went on about poor Alberta Jenkins. Eugene thought he'd have to visit with her, sit in that beautiful living room with Chris's picture of Nene and eat cheese and crackers, chips and dip. She would thank him, make him feel comfortable, would somehow know what to say, and then he'd leave her, the door of the house would close and she would be alone. No more "Where you goin'? When you gone be back?" He would visit her again, and maybe once more after that, but finally he would stop going. He'd walk by the house wondering if she was home and wouldn't know, wouldn't bother to knock.

After dinner, Moms put on her makeup and came out to see if he was ready. He was wearing his hearing suit, still crisp from the hanger, in need of a dry clean. In the van, neither of them said a word, the streets rolling by glazed with rain.

The doors of the church were open. He went downstairs and turned on the lights. From the walls, Harriet Tubman looked back at him, the scar on her forehead a dent under her bandanna. He poured the Lemon Blend and laid out the cookies on a plate, made two stacks of cups and a fan of napkins. Upstairs, the choir rocked, praising God. He set the chairs in a circle, then sat down himself and waited to see if anyone would show up.

FAVORITE SON

WAS HE SO OLD?

Yes, seventy-three. Each time he came back there was less he remembered, and he missed the Pittsburgh he'd known as a child. Genteel. Professional. A world of topcoats and long brunches at the Crawford Grill, black Packard sedans and day lilies in crystal vases. Was it possible his father's house was still gone, hadn't miraculously grown back in his absence, the ivy green on its mock-Gothic arches, the leaded windows of his mother's sewing room open on the garden? As the limousine slid by Spofford in a drizzle, Martin Robinson was tempted to peer up the street, but didn't, knowing he'd find only the soulless faces of brick apartment buildings instead of his cloistered boyhood.

"The community center's tricky," Sylvia was saying, going over her clipboard. "Their funding's been cut, so no promises."

"Discretionary money?"

"Nothing. Then at one you have the new state senator."

"Combes," he guessed.

"Goines. Friend, definitely. You met her last year at the library anniversary."

He remembered nothing of it, another in the chain of sectioned days—interviews and photo shoots, speeches faxed to him in the car, doctored in the front row while the locals spoke, then delivered with lofty, heartfelt conviction, his trademark oratory. His father had schooled him in Cicero and Frederick Douglass, brought him into the study to critique his performance, leaning back in his calfskin swivel chair, long dentist's hands folded over his chest. "Deeper here," he'd coach. "Okay, now slowly," and Martin tried to do it right, ride the waves of self-righteous fervor, skim across the calms of intricate reasoning. The worst was when his father laughed and told him to start over—no instructions, just his hands flapping up like gulls, scattering his words. But he learned.

"Two-thirty: pictures at Nabisco; three-thirty: downtown to petition city council."

"Petition," he asked.

"The Jenkins case."

"God, yes." Excessive use of force. How many of these had he presented? His first had earned him the seat back in the sixties, though no one had been convicted. Few had been through the years, but there were some, little victories that kept the papers—if not the cops—at least partly honest. The Jenkins boy was someone's son. Heartache, etc., a gross disregard for human life.

The limo turned onto Highland, its tinted windows drawing stares, splashed down the long straightaway past the half-demolished Sears with its blue panels of sheet metal bent like playing cards. An ugly landmark, it had been bought up by Home Depot, who brought in Korean contractors from upstate New York to fulfill the city minority hiring quota. The unions and usual local groups bonded together in protest (strange—and strained—bedfellows), and the city asked Martin's office to help with the talks. In the end he'd brokered a deal neither side liked, five jobs short of the number prescribed by law. Twenty years ago he would have gotten the five plus heavy concessions, maybe cut a sideways deal with the unions finally making it possible for people from the community to get bonded for construction work, but everyone knew he'd taken a hit on the busway he'd never recover from. The city bringing him back for the dedication was repayment for years of being a pain in the ass, a way of reminding him how far he'd fallen. No one forgot in politics, just as no one forgave him. Thirty-six years. Sylvia was the one he felt sorry for, only in her mid-forties, though she insisted she'd be fine.

"What's the community center again?"

"Day care and after-school programs for single working mothers. Your bill."

"And funding's done when—fiscal ninety-nine?"

"First of the year."

He would still officially be in office then, for three more weeks. He thought of Armstrong's transition team moving new furniture into the cleaned-out suite, the troughs left in the rug from the cherry file cabinets, Sylvia's desk, and he could feel the hotel danish from this morning knifing upward, its jagged tip lodged just under his heart. Thirty-six years of public service. And it was his own fault, that was the sad thing. Stepped on his own dick, that was the phrase they used on the hill. He imagined it felt about the same, but with the crucial difference that at some point you stepped back off it. He patted his jacket for his roll of Tums, but it was gone.

Magically Sylvia offered him one from her bag. The orange-flavored, his favorite. She thumbed one out for herself, a habit she'd taken up recently and for which he felt responsible.

"Do we get lunch?" he asked.

"At the center. Sudanese cuisine by the sixth-graders."

"Peanut-squash soup again."

"I brought the Maalox." She flashed him just the top of the bottle—the mint.

"What would I do without you?" he said, with too much truth in it, but she just shrugged it off. It was one reason he loved her: She refused to be sentimental. He could keep her on as his personal assistant, they both knew, but it would be a different life (as if this was exciting). And Muriel didn't want anyone around. He was unsure if retirement held anything for him other than boredom and then, mercifully, death. The idea of writing his memoirs offended him as it would his father, a man with no patience for vanity. He supposed he would be in the same demand as now, the congressman emeritus, the gray eminence, but without the funding or the clout the position seemed untenable, pathetic, like Hall of Fame ballplayers buttoning up their uniforms to run around potbellied and wheezing on old-timers day. Muriel expected them to travel—Europe, Africa, the Far East. Ten

years ago she'd left the rubber-chicken circuit unceremoni-
ously, simply refusing to attend another fund-raiser. The
society pages made a fuss for one season, speculated about
her health, and then she was free, at home with her roses
and her bridge club (bid whist, really), visiting Terrence and
the girls without him, becoming, unopposed, the true rep-
resentative of the family. When, he wondered, had he begun
to envy her?

Ahead, a single photographer lurked outside the community center, a low bunkerlike cube of raw concrete the
rain turned the color of a shopping bag, and with a shame
not quite equal to an earlier pride Martin read his own name
engraved above the front doors. The driver rolled up slowly,
giving the photographer time to plant himself in an oppor-
tune spot, setting his bag down on the wet sidewalk between
his feet as if someone might steal it. Martin prepared to smile
heartily, tonguing his upper bridge in place. He imagined
the captions that would run under this shot for the next few
months. ROBINSON SAVES FACE, QUITS.

"Are you quitting?" his father would say when he went
silent in the face of his criticism, when the boy he'd been
looked at his shoes, at the tendrils and leaves curling repeat-
edly in the pastoral world of the rug. "Or do you have something else? If you have something else, then I would be very
interested to hear it."

By then he would be seeing the room through a wavy
curtain of tears, some falling on the carpet like raindrops,
darkening the suede uppers of his shoes in spots. "No sir. I
have more."

"All right, let's hear it then."

And this time he would get it right, or more of it, so they would be forced to go through the same routine again — five, ten times, his father pretending to be reasonable, even patient with him — to the end of Demosthenes' defense of Athenian freedom, Roosevelt's New Deal speech.

He had nothing more now. His own feasibility study of the busway had given the city the means of shoving it up his ass. That they'd doctored their own environmental impact studies of the other two (white, middle-class) sites was a moot point. He should have buried his or simply aborted it. How it got out he wasn't sure, and that only hurt worse. Like Sylvia said, it's one thing to be ignorant, another to be dumb. The pundits implied he was senile, though they were careful not to use the word.

He tongued his bridge again and checked his pocket for today's remarks — brief, and actually written by him (though, of course, for another occasion; it was an all-purpose piece, plug-and-chug).

"The name of the director," Sylvia tested.

"Mrs. Lane."

"Belva Amos. Ms. Mrs. Lane's with the city now."

"Like everyone else," he said.

When he stepped out into the wind, he smiled and gave a little wave past the photographer. There was no crowd there to greet him, but he knew from experience that he would look better in the paper, more authoritative, the center of attention. Sylvia had turned it into a joke: the invisible majority. Lately they were all he had left.

Inside, Belva Amos was waiting with the children, all of them swaddled in Kente cloth. A boy and girl had been deputized to wrap him in it as well, as if he were royalty. He smiled as the photographer lined up another shot, shook Ms. Amos's hand with a solid but not steely grip (flash, *poof*), and followed her into the gym for the dance program, Sylvia by his side.

A good crowd had turned out, the bleachers filled with young mothers dandling babies on their laps, a few older folks still wearing their jackets despite the heat. A percussion ensemble warmed up at half-court, the children in their Kente outfits finding their assigned spots on the floor. Beneath the sharp smell of sweat and floor polish, he could make out a touch of cardamon from the hall, a bite of curry powder, and the danish leaned on his heart like an iceberg.

Sylvia saw him wince and gave him a concerned look, and now it was his turn to shrug her off. The Tums would kick in, give it a minute.

The drums thunked and flammed, and the children went into their dance, flinging their arms above their heads like pitchers, doing energetic kung fu kicks. He was sweating up by his hairline, and above his lip.

"This is an ancient harvest dance called Capeoira-Angola," Ms. Amos confided, and he nodded. He recalled seeing a dance of the same name during a trip to Zaire years ago, but it didn't resemble this. The children seemed to be enjoying themselves though, and the crowd was bouncing along, mothers clapping their babies' hands together. It had taken him so long to enjoy moments like these, always worrying about what needed to be done back at the office, that now they struck him with an odd melancholy, as if he'd wasted the richest part of his life. He was too serious, too caught up in his job. It was an accusation Elise, his first wife, had leveled at him and that he, at the time, accepted with pride. When she left him, he delighted in proving her wrong by becoming addicted to Percocet and gin and making a fool of himself with any pretty woman within his vision, not a small number.

Watching the dancers whirl, he thought of detox, the generosity of his constituency, the twin miracles of Muriel and Sylvia. Another chance. He would always be saved by a woman, something his mother had never done for him, though he could see her love of quiet in himself, her wish for a sane and elegant world in which to live her days. But overwhelmingly he was his father's son. That turned out to be the answer to so many questions, like today's. Why was he here? Why did he insist on completing his term? What did he think he could accomplish? Everything went back to those afternoons in his father's study, the lesson being not simply diction but never quitting, never giving up, no matter what the cost. He'd learned well.

The drums stopped, and almost simultaneously the dancers. Applause, whistling. He stood, and so everyone else around him did too. The photographer decided it wasn't a shot, went back to dig in his bag for another lens.

Next was lunch, his words of encouragement ("You know they're screwing me. Good luck getting any funding from that bastard Armstrong!"), then a tour of the classrooms, and finally a chance to talk with some of the children. Congressman Robinson's schedule was tight, Sylvia reminded Ms. Amos, so they all hustled out into the hall and headed for the cafeteria, into the heavy scent of boiled squash and cardamon, the crowd bunching up behind them.

The tables they sat at were designed for schoolchildren, and he hunched over his soup. It was thick and hot, not as spicy as the real thing, but still the first bite landed in his stomach like a shot of scotch. He looked to Sylvia, who knew.

"It's very good," he said earnestly, taking another spoonful to prove it, following it with water. It was filling at least, and after half a bowl he could plead that he was stuffed. Lots of stops, had to travel light.

He was looking over his remarks—an actor's trick, rereading them constantly so the words were closer to you, more concrete, less likely to confuse you with their meaning—when a woman materialized behind him. She was younger than Sylvia, pretty but with a hardness about her mouth. A cold wave and lipstick. Beside her stood a young mother in braids, obviously her daughter, hefting a baby in a blue jacket.

"Hello," he said, searching for Sylvia, who had just as suddenly vanished.

The woman snaked out her hand for him to take. "I don't know if you remember me. My name is Ruth Owens."

He waited, leery of answering.

"We dated a little, way back in the eighties."

A bad time, he wanted to say. "That *is* way back."

"This is my daughter, Vanessa, and her son, Rashaan."

"Hello."

"I know this is going to sound crazy," she said, her daughter swaying beside her with the child, "but," and though this had never happened to him or anyone he'd ever known, he knew exactly what Ruth Owens was going to say. He was beginning to remember, in the same way his father's house came back to him, the face she wore beneath this one, her muscular back, the scent of her breasts. It had not been a bad time but a strange one, full of places he'd never be again, nights that ended well into morning, cabbies paid with hundred-dollar bills, the change too complicated, stuffed uncounted into his pockets. One day he woke up in his closet, a dozen suits pulled over him like a quilt.

"I was wondering," she said, "if maybe we could speak privately."

"Not today," he said, checking on Ms. Belva Amos, still spooning her soup.

"I wrote down my number. I figured you're in town until Sunday. We would really appreciate it if you could call."

"Thank you." He slipped it in his jacket. *We.*

"I'm sorry," she said. "I didn't think I'd ever do this."

Sylvia was coming back, apparently from the ladies' room, because she had her bag. Ruth Owens stood above him, waiting for an answer. The daughter looked at him with contempt, gave him the side of her face as if disinterested. The boy played with her braids.

"We'll talk," he said.

Sylvia took her seat and immediately sensed trouble from them. "Can I help you with something?" she asked. "I'm the congressman's press secretary."

"No thank you," Ruth Owens said, and led her daughter away, only the little boy looking back over her shoulder.

"Who was that crew?" Sylvia asked.

"An old friend of Elise," he said—sufficient cover because the subject was off-limits, as if it had happened to someone else, a respected, dead friend.

Throughout dessert, a yam tart bursting with brown sugar, he contemplated what it would mean if she really was his daughter, what it would mean to Muriel and their plans. Up at the lectern, it was impossible not to pick them out of the crowd—her, really. Pretty, and strong, capable of shutting him out. He tested her face, her head, for any resemblance, but found none. Not that he would call Ruth Owens a liar. At that time of his life he was capable of anything. Not murder perhaps, but certainly the worst, most reckless negligence. This would be it.

He could not remember her name, and, prematurely, it shamed him. He could not recall a specific night with her mother, a room with a bed, music with supper, how they'd met; there was just the memory of her face beneath his, her skin smooth under his fingers. Ruth, a name he liked. She had been beautiful, he knew; you could still see it. *Too late, too late*—wasn't that how the poem went?

The applause for him was polite, though no one stood. He was hot in his suit, a result of the lights, but also the surprise. Ms. Amos came on and thanked everyone for coming, and when they made their tour of the rooms, he strained to find the three faces, for the boy would be in a sense his grandson. *Would* be his grandson. They were gone, and not waiting for him outside by the limo. It was still spitting; the photographer had disappeared at some point, flown off to a more important story. He waved anyway, smiled for Ms. Amos and the children.

Inside, as he sat with his belt cutting into his stomach, the danish seemed to have moved behind his heart, squeezing it forward against his ribs. The soup bubbled underneath it like a sea of lava, and he clutched his gut.

"Want the Maalox?" Sylvia asked, already pulling it out.

He twisted the cap, loosening a few threads of white crust, then tipped the mouth to his. Going down, it coated his organs like spilled paint, made the clog that much more solid. They were headed west on Highland, back toward the Sears.

"What's next?" he said apologetically. Forgetful. Maybe the pundits were right.

"Goines."

"Ah, my friend." It was hard to breathe, and he touched a button but the window refused to budge. He tried another, and a fleck of rain caught him on the cheek, the swish of the tires loud now. He thought he might vomit.

"Martin," Sylvia said, "are you okay?"

He felt her hand on his arm and leaned toward the cool air, the bones in his shoulder burning. For a moment he couldn't see, nothing but an electric checkerboard glowing like a test pattern, a flashbulb's dazzle. A spike of lightning shot up one biceps and landed in his chest, spread like fire. And then, like fog lifting, it stopped, dissipated like rain, his skin chilly. Sylvia still had his arm.

"I'm all right," Martin said. "Just a little heartburn."

"Where's the nearest hospital?" Sylvia asked the intercom, and the driver told her. "Take us there."

"I'm fine now."

"You lost consciousness, Martin."

There was no use arguing with her when she was right. He leaned back in the seat. He felt like jelly, spineless (hadn't Armstrong called him that after the busway debacle?). They were going by Spofford, speeding, but even at fifty he could see there was nothing left, that the only place he could retreat to was his memory. The front hall with its marble-topped table, his father's natty houndstooth hat doubled in the mirror. His father, his mother—everything he loved was gone. Now East Liberty.

He was tired and closed his eyes. The danish stayed there, butted up against his heart, throbbing like a rotten tooth. It would not be such a bad thing to die here, where he'd come from.

But he couldn't die now, he thought; he was a father, he had responsibilities, a new grandson to take care of. Violet, the girl's name was. Ruth Owens. He needed to call her, the number was in his pocket.

He tried to say this out loud, reaching for it, and Sylvia stared at him in terror.

The pressure knotted around his heart and twisted again, making him take a deep breath.

"Martin," Sylvia called, far away. And then it was like his memories of the nights he'd forgotten, when he'd become a man even he despised, let alone the ghost of his father. It could have been Ruth Owens, it could have been anyone. Midnight, and someone trying to break through the numb

armor of his drunkenness, the Percocet sealing him in like
ice. Like now, he could sense her hands on him but he
couldn't feel anything. And both times—this was a new
admission, after all his talk of selflessness, his indefensible
principles—he really didn't care if he did die. The job was
all he was, like the speeches that appeased his father.

The fist clenching his heart eased, and he could see
again. Sylvia's face was inches from his, her fingers in his
mouth, then gone, nothing but the ceiling. Somehow he was
lying across the seat, trees flying in the windows, telephone
lines. He was someone's father, someone he didn't know,
someone he'd never shown love.

"Help me," he said.

O HAPPY DAY

THEY WOULD HAVE understood if she didn't want to sing at the thing. Friday night Jackie could feel the other sopranos timidly seeking her out when they practiced their three numbers, listening to see if she'd learned her parts. She'd have to be an idiot not to after so long.

No, she didn't mean this; she wasn't angry with them, only their well-meaning pity. They were her friends.

They'd practiced every night this week, and tomorrow they were doing a full dress rehearsal at the dedication site. Some of them seemed surprised she was still with them, every practice expected her to be missing, as if her presence at the ceremony would be an affront, bad manners after what had happened there.

Most of those who wondered about her were younger, girls just beginning their families. Women closer to her age understood: Tragedies would come and go, only faith stayed the same. This was the one time each week she could call her own, the time she felt closest to her true self. It was a

time for forgetting the rest of the world, even and especially
her worst troubles. Sunday wasn't quite like this — only the
altar and the nave lit, the rest of the church dark, pews running back into blackness, saints looking down like stony
ghosts from their niches, and when Sister Turner had them
stop in midnote, their voices echoed, caught in the vaulted
dark. There was peace in singing, in being alone in God's
house, and she needed it now.

And strength, Lord. Tomorrow she would be seeing the
spot for the first time, and she knew these same people
would be watching her, checking for the littlest sign of grief,
waiting for her to give way. She'd glimpsed the bridge in
passing, riding in the van, or from the bus on her way to
work, but she hadn't walked down the freshly lined exit
ramp and stood there looking up, imagining that night — the
rain and then the flashing lights of the ambulance. She knew
that Eugene had, and understood just as keenly that Harold
didn't dare. In that, at least, they were the same. Parents.
Helpless. Tomorrow she would be there without him, in her
robe, as if on a lone pilgrimage.

She was. She knew she couldn't run from it forever,
pretend it didn't affect her every hour. Like Harold stray-
ing, it needed to be faced before she could gather her courage and go on. She needed to know the worst before she
could overcome it. And she would. Hadn't she gotten used
to cleaning Chris, dressing him, lifting him into his chair?

No, not honestly. She liked to think she had, but like
Harold she was afraid of his skin, his dead legs. She wondered what was secretly going on inside of him, how it was
possible that only half of him was alive. Once, propping him

on the bucket-shaped stool in the shower, she'd barked his shin against the edge of the door; he didn't flinch, and then the blood welled up and overflowed, ran in a line down his calf. The water was already on, and he concentrated on the spray, eyes closed, holding a towel across his lap out of modesty. When they were done, the cut was just a lip of skin, bloodless, a nick on a piece of furniture.

But she was used to draining his bag, if not how the catheter needed to be greased to fit up into him. She was accustomed to toweling him down after his shower, the backs of his knees growing dimpled with fat. She found Cheez-It boxes tucked under his bed, orange crumbs in his sheets. He didn't laugh at the TV the way he used to, just stayed in his room all day, drawing on the walls, reading books Vanessa brought from the library. What frightened her was how fast he'd turned into this different person, as if her Chris was gone, her Smiley buried inside him like the memory of his legs.

Singing, she wondered if the others were right, if she should even be here. Lately her worries followed her everywhere, and rather than being a sanctuary, practice was just another reminder of how everything had gone wrong. She was fine as long as she was singing, but when she had to wait for Sister Turner to straighten out the tenors (like now), her mind wandered and found nothing but troubles.

Harold had to come back to her, that's what it came down to. She could see her turning into her mother—bitter, despising her mindless work, going through the days without hope.

And there was no one to talk to since Marita's little dog died. Wednesday Jackie had processed the check herself, read it like a telegram bearing bad news. Nine hundred dollars to bury him. Jackie had gone over that night, but her lights were out and it was late. She hadn't seen her since then, and when she didn't show up at practice, Jackie thought she understood that too. She'd been so tempted to give up, to hide herself away from everything (again, her mother in their falling-down house, screaming at the Meals on Wheels lady, calling Daphne three times a day). It was not possible, she'd found. Her heart kept pumping. The world did not stop.

The three songs they were going to sing were "I've Got to Praise Him," "He Is My Rock," and "O Happy Day." The first two were staples; the last they were learning new for the ceremony. It didn't seem fitting, with Martin Robinson in the hospital, but they'd been practicing for weeks, and it was too late to change. Reverend Skinner said it was even more important they show their support for him now; the *Courier* expected a big turnout, all four TV stations.

"Sopranos," Sister Turner called from the piano, "it's 'When Je-suh-hus waa-haashed,' not 'waa-haa-haashed my si-ins away,' all right? Two syllables, not three. And give 'washed' a little hesitation just a scoosh behind the beat and really make it swing. Get up there and stay up there. Better than the record, all right? All right, one two three four."

Sister Turner knocked out a few bars of intro and they all joined in. "O happy day. O happy day." Jackie had always liked the song, fell into the groove of it with the rest of the row, clapping, moving foot to foot. "When Je-suh-hus waa-haashed, O when he waa-haashed, when Je-suh-hus waa-haa-haashed—"

Sister Turner banged the keyboard, breaking them up, drowning them out. She jumped up from behind the piano. "So-*pran*-os!" she scolded. "What did I say? How many syllables?"

No one dared answer her.

"Two, I said. Two, not three. It's two all the way through." She stalked back behind the piano. "Let's see if you remember it this time. One two three four."

They did until the second chorus, when someone— Mildred Tolliver or Vivian Broadus, to Jackie's ear— stretched it to three again. Eventually they got it, swinging it high and hard, but still Sister Turner kept them after dismissing everyone else.

"Sopranos," she lectured them after a long pause, "are supposed to be our strong suit, if you follow me. Tenors come and go, and altos. None of you are new. I know it's a new piece, but it's not a hard piece. You've been hearing this song thirty years, some of you. I do *not* want to go out there tomorrow and hear what I heard tonight. I don't think that would be respectful to Martin Robinson or to the rest of us. All right, tomorrow at ten. We'll meet here and walk over, and I want all of you sharp. How many syllables?"

This time they all answered.

Eugene was waiting for her in the front hall, in his suit. It was shiny around the shoulders and elbows; she'd been meaning to take it in to the cleaners. He'd been talking with Reverend Skinner about getting some city money for Chris's

mural now that Martin Robinson was ill. No one was showing up for his meetings, and she knew it hurt him. She recognized his desire for a saving faith — his need — as her own.
How she wanted to tell him: For every hope in this world
there was an even greater disappointment waiting (oh,
wasn't that her mother's voice she heard?). But he was an
adult, he had to know that by now, had come to grips with
it the same way she had. She was pleased he had something
solid to build his new life on, not like Chris, who seemed to
be betting everything on Vanessa. Harold she could see was
lost all this time. In the end it came down to faith.

"He says they only take applications once a year," Eugene said on the van. "The deadline's the end of January."

"That's not far," she said, because, really, it wasn't. Still,
he seemed downcast, as if he'd hoped to start tomorrow. He
worried about Chris as much as she did, and she put her
arm over his shoulder. "Be patient. You'll get it done."

"I know but . . ."

"Everything takes time."

They were coming up to the busway. It was like a moat
circling East Liberty; at some point you had to cross it. The
bridge had a chain-link fence on both sides, the top curled
over the sidewalk so you couldn't throw things. It had been
a bridge like this one, she supposed, the boys using the fence
for a handhold, the toes of their sneakers slipping on the wet
metal. What did they think they were doing?

"You want me to come with you tomorrow?" Eugene
asked.

"That's all right."

"You sure?"

"Yes," she said, then wished he would ask her again.

When they got home, Harold wasn't there. She tried not to be surprised, but her first thought was that he'd left for good, skipped like her father. How long, she thought, did she have to live her mother's life?

Chris said he'd gone out a little while ago, during *Millennium*. She figured the time, imagined what two people could do in twenty minutes. Anything, everything.

"Remember," Chris said, "I need my shower early tomorrow."

"I haven't forgotten," she said, and went into the kitchen. He wanted to be clean for Vanessa, and Jackie worried that he'd be hurt if she decided to leave him again. Because she might, a good-looking girl like that. A nice girl too. Chris couldn't ask her to stay, he had to know that.

He did. Of course he did.

She ran a glass of tap water and was standing at the sink drinking it when Harold came in, jiggling the key. Eugene stepped out of his room in his shirtsleeves like there might be trouble. Harold had a gallon of milk and a box of doughnuts.

"For tomorrow," he said. "I know everyone's getting up early."

He seemed so pleased with himself she couldn't tell if it was a lie. He could walk to the 7-Eleven in five minutes, leaving him ten, maybe fifteen to meet someone. If they had a car, then a full twenty minutes in a parking lot somewhere. She'd grown so tired of checking up on him that it was easier to believe he was lying about everything. It was *his* job to prove his innocence, not the other way around.

"Good night," Eugene said, and closed his door.

"Good night," Harold said to the door, and she could see the two of them would be like this for a while. She wanted to tell Eugene that his father had not hurt her—or that him hitting her was nothing compared to how she felt. She had honestly wanted to kill him that night; now she wondered if she'd been insane. He wasn't worth it. But wasn't he everything, wasn't her entire life with him? If only she could care nothing for him, the way he felt about her. It was unfair. That's what hurt the worst: that he'd tricked her into loving him, and now he'd disappeared. Twenty-five years, and every one a lie.

She looked in on Chris again. He was in bed, saving his strength for tomorrow's walk in the park. She was tempted to sit down beside him, tell him not to get his hopes up so he wouldn't be crushed, but how could she truthfully do that when Harold was waiting for her?

She wanted to be wrong—she was not her mother.

"Sweet dreams," she said, and he said it back, a reflex. What did he dream of—running, driving a car? She cut the lights in the living room, then the kitchen.

"You all done in here?" she called, and Harold said yes.

He was already brushing his teeth, wearing the bathrobe she'd given him for Christmas. They were shy around each other now, their bodies no longer common property. It might have been exciting if she didn't know the reason why.

Stop, she thought.

"You just decided to go out and get some doughnuts," she asked despite herself.

"We needed milk anyway."

It might have been a real answer. He might have actually done it out of boredom, just to get out of the house, away from all the reminders of his life with her. Every time she imagined his girlfriend, she saw an airy apartment with hardwood floors and slanting light, jazz seeping from the stereo. No children, no bills. They made love all day in clean sheets, ate gourmet food she fixed for him buck naked. Now here he was in the bathrobe she'd gotten on sale then hidden in the closet for six months, the bow gathering dust. And *she* wanted romance?

While he covered himself with a lover's sense of privacy, she kept to herself out of shame. He didn't want to see her body, its sags and pouches, its heaviness. She only shed her robe as she slipped between the cold sheets, and then she didn't search for his warmth, thinking instead of the doughnuts, why he didn't get them earlier. Just once she wanted to come home and find him right where he said he'd be.

Cattin', her mother called it. "Man starts cattin' around, you got to lock your door on him." That simple. But her father was long gone by then; she was locking the door on nothing. Wind.

She thought of Marita, how she needed to talk to her, and then of her little dog. She'd have to go see her. They could lean on each other.

"Hey," Harold said softly in the dark, "you going to be all right tomorrow?"

"I'll be fine," she said. Like you care.

His hand crept across her stomach, and she rolled away. He let it rest on her ribs, stilled. "I'd like to come with you." But the way he said it wasn't convincing. It tempted her to make him go, rub his face in it.

"I'll be fine," she said. "You go ahead and do whatever it is you do."

He sighed and withdrew his hand, and then she wished he hadn't. It only verified her worst fears—that he hated her even more now, that she was pushing him away. Didn't he understand she couldn't help herself, that she had to keep at least some of her pride? She'd let him lie to her for so long, even as she felt him moving away from her, escaping the gravity of their marriage, flying off to someone else. She'd lied to herself, pretending at first that it wasn't actually happening and then that he would see things clearly and come back to her. Now *she* could see clearly that he had no reason to return to her, that his life would be so much easier without her, and by this kind of logic discovered why he'd strayed in the first place.

Not that it was her fault, no, it was all his, but she could see his side of things, selfish as it was. Heartless. Sometimes at night she wanted to punch him in his sleep, stop his snoring by splitting his lip. Because that was how it felt, being blindsided and knocked out of your life, and not for anything you'd done. She had to be satisfied with a few elbows, an occasional knee as they rolled over, with pushing his hand away as it reached for her, and still she was just punishing herself.

"Why do you give up so easily?" she asked now, and his hand reached for her again, on cue. She shoved it away. "No," she scolded, sad. "I shouldn't have to tell you."

"I'm trying."

"You shouldn't *have* to try." She wanted him to come to her desperately, like a lover, everything new between them. Why was she surprised when that didn't happen?

She needed to be won again, but he didn't seem to know this. And even if he did, would he feel the need to? Could he?

"I love you," he said seriously, as if she could believe it.

"You're not *in* love with me," she said, emphasizing the difference, though he continually refused to acknowledge it. Did it seem simple only to her?

They did not talk beyond this, just turned the same circles they had for weeks now, knowing they'd be tired tomorrow morning, that it was pointless. Strangely, she felt most intimate with him then, in their shared failure, their admission of how important it was to find an answer to her problem. Because that was how it felt now, as if it were her fault for not letting him back in. That he was probably still seeing the bitch—that her paranoia could not be verified one way or the other—was conveniently ignored, forced into its own separate court in which he pleaded innocence while she threatened him, stormed, cried.

They slept then, or lay awake, waiting for the release of sleep. The anger she'd felt all day dissolved into emptiness. Surely Daphne's marriage had these loveless minutes. Everyone's did. The hardest part now was looking back at those old beaus like Alvin Reese and Gregory Mattison and realizing they were phantoms. Harold was the one love of her life and she had lost him, he had betrayed her—it didn't matter; whichever way you looked at it, she was alone now and would be for the rest of her life, unless—and this was ridiculous—she could win *him* back somehow. She felt powerless. Everything seemed to be in the past, nothing up ahead but days and nights she would have to fight her way through. For what, more of this?

There was tomorrow, seeing where Chris had fallen. What else was she looking forward to?

In her dreams she was running through an abandoned building, a school or an old factory, racing up the stairs and then down again, pursued by a mob she could only hear, and then she was in a car in Los Angeles (how she knew the city she couldn't say, maybe from TV), riding along with the windows open, the summer air pouring over her skin, parked cars glinting, the scent of taco stands, then something about Harold's fingers, the palms of his hands turned up to reveal his lifeline. In the morning, she thought she could almost make sense of it—something to do with her worries—but after her first cup of coffee she couldn't bring back the connection.

Did it matter? It wasn't something hidden that was troubling her.

Chris's chair didn't fit through the bathroom door. She had to wedge the shower stool in the corner of the stall and then, with Chris's help, deadlift him across the few feet of floor and prop him on it—really a job for Harold. His ankles were tangled, and she had to bend down and reposition them, feeling the watery heaviness under the skin, as if they were filled with blood. He wanted a towel to cover himself, and she gave him one. She ran the water onto her hand, shielding him until it was just right—like making a baby bottle, she thought. He grabbed the soap and started with his chest, giving her a look that said she could leave. It went faster if she did it, but he didn't like her touching his skin, stiffened when she reached behind him. She drew the curtain.

"Let me know when you're ready for me," she said.

It didn't take long. There was only so much he could do.

The steam rose up around them. She soaped the washcloth, keeping it between her hand and his skin. They'd installed a handheld showerhead with some of the insurance money, and she went over him with it (she could not stop the thought) as if watering a plant. She had not gotten used to the scars or to the wasted thighs, each week narrower, the knees seeming to bulge out further. He was heavy in the chest now, and his gut was round, his belly button a tunnel. Even his face was slowly becoming someone else's; only his hands were the same, stained with Magic Marker, fingers slashed with ink. He turned away as she did his bottom; she rinsed him with the showerhead, then clicked it off, as if her efficiency had saved him some humiliation.

But it did not stop there. She had to haul on his underwear and then his jeans, the legs baggy and then so tight at the waist they no longer buttoned. She tugged on his socks, fitted his feet into his sneakers and double-knotted them like a toddler's. He could barely manage his shirt, and even that she had to pull down in the back, tuck into his jeans. There were no thank-yous, no bitter jokes as there had been at the beginning, just an abiding silence between them.

Vanessa was right on time, with Rashaan in her arms. Except for a brief greeting at the door, Jackie stayed out of their way. Chris asked after Martin Robinson, who was in

Western Penn where her mother worked. Vanessa shrugged, uninterested. Nothing new, she guessed.

Jackie tried to read the way she approached Chris, alert for the smallest hint of pity, watching where she let her hands land and then rest. She gauged Chris's stiffness, listened for any tremor in what Vanessa said, any false giddiness, knowing Chris was in no mood. She compared the girl's composure to her own. Was it selfish, thinking she was better with him, or just jealousy?

Chris held Rashaan on his lap, doing a Daffy Duck voice, trying to smile for him, but as soon as he looked up at Vanessa, his face snapped back to serious, as if it were an effort.

"Ready to jet?" he asked, and she was. They never stayed long. The city had finally installed the lift they promised, so he didn't need Eugene's help with the stairs. He could go out every day if he wanted, but he never did, just Saturdays when she came over. Jackie knew not to walk them out, waited for the hum of the elevator, the clash as it rolled open its doors.

What did he feel, she wondered. What did he miss? Sometimes, walking across a room, she paid attention to her movements, how easily they came to her. Harold said some of the people in Chris's therapy were learning to walk again. How did anyone learn in the first place?

A doughnut and then it was her turn to get ready. She zipped her robe into a hanging bag, made sure she had some honey-lemon cough drops in her purse. Harold and Eugene both asked if she wanted them to go with her, but she held fast. One thing all this trouble had done was make her stronger. If she had to rely on herself, she could. Wouldn't her mother be proud?

She stopped by Marita's place first. There was no mail in the mailbox, no *Courier* slipped inside the storm door. She rang the bell five times, then stood on the porch, listening for her. Nine hundred dollars, she thought. She must have really loved that dog. Maybe she'd paid in advance and the burial was today. She hoped so. All the other explanations Jackie could come up with were too depressing.

The van was full of altos. They went quiet when she got on, and she took a seat in back by a window so she wouldn't feel stared at. It was cloudy out, and Penn Circle was empty. They were finally tearing down the Sears. Crossing the busway, she looked down and caught a glimpse of the road, workers grooming the dirt on both sides, then pulled back as if she might fall.

No one was looking at her. She was ready to freeze the first person that did, but everyone was talking and drinking coffee, bumping along. So that was how it was going to be. People were such cowards.

She thought of Harold, how he couldn't say it to her face. When she demanded to know her name, she could see he was lying. Did he really think that would satisfy her?

Nothing would. Not for a long time.

The truth.

They changed in the basement, zipping each other up, going over the hard parts. Jackie stuck with the sopranos, pretending like the rest of them that this was just another

practice, as if it were possible not to think of Chris. This
wasn't betraying him; this was something she needed to do.
Sister Turner had just had her hair done, shiny waves caught
in midbreak rising above a skirt of bangs. She had new
glasses too, clear frames with a red tint, the lenses square
as TVs. "Give me tenors," she said, and had them line up
before sending them off. "Baritones, you're next."

They marched to the site like troops, drivers honking
at them, children waving. She watched the altos ahead of
her, their feet hidden beneath their robes as if they were
gliding. She was walking without even thinking of it, lifting one foot, putting the other down, over and over, the
muscles working automatically, triggered by a signal, a
chemical. She thought she should be grateful for it, stop
taking it for granted like the rest of them, but it only made
her angry, as if she'd been cheated.

The closer they got to the site, the more she realized
she'd been mistaken. People were looking back, stealing
glances at her. It reminded her of going to school when the
other children found out her mother cleaned houses —
whispers, fingers pointing from the swing set. But she'd
had Daphne then, and that had not been her fault.

Did they really think this was?

Some of them did, she was sure. A mother, she would
always be judged by her sons.

Ahead, the tenors were turning down the exit ramp,
the baritones right behind. They seemed to be hurrying, and
when she slowed down, someone stepped on her heel. She
stumbled, then rescued herself, an arm flailing out for bal-

ance. The shock brought a sudden heat to her face. She would give them nothing, she thought, become that child again, pinched and closed over, hard as an Indiana winter.

The road was wider than she expected. They walked down the middle of the ramp, a white line peeking out from under their robes. Below, men in blue Penndot jumpsuits were spraypainting the dirt green, the silver cans on their backs making them look like deep-sea divers, spacemen. From here, the bridge didn't seem so high, and Jackie thought it couldn't be the one. Eugene had said there was graffiti, but she didn't see any.

She looked up as the flock of them crossed the busway, shielding her eyes from the light. The workers had stopped to watch. Nothing, just a bridge, a curved chain-link fence. What did she expect?

A makeshift stage stood against the far wall, a maroon curtain behind two rows of folding chairs, a dais with a microphone. Their risers circled the back, and Sister Turner herded them on by tiers—first the tall tenors, then the baritones, the altos, and finally the sopranos up front. Jackie was turned away from the bridge, facing a long swath of green dirt. The road was so new it shone white.

Sister Turner fitted her music stand together and spread out her papers. Jackie waited, trying to ignore the eyes sneaking a peek at her. She could feel the bridge lurking behind her, fought the temptation to turn her shoulder and glance back at it, Lot's wife. She wished Marita were here, just to have someone to talk to. She thought she was doing okay so far. She looked around at the raw concrete walls, the absolutely flat mud strewn with hay, interrupted by the cages of sewer drains. Was that it? Was that all she had to contend with?

She'd imagined what happened that night over and over—Benny's hand slipping, Chris reaching for him—but always she saw it in the dark, in the rain, the streetlights and the blackness beneath them dramatic. Not this barrenness. If she didn't know it had happened here, she never would have guessed. This didn't seem frightening, and yet she knew that this was the right bridge, that it did happen here. Chris on the wet road, his legs motionless, the paramedics rolling the stretcher. The very blandness of the busway disguised the truth, like Harold watching TV or bringing home a box of doughnuts. That was how the world worked. How could she explain it to Chris? Things seemed normal and then the masks came off, the trapdoors gave way, and you were falling. Your life could be swept up in invisible currents. Yet, even hidden, the truth still announced itself. You avoided it at your own risk. Her mother would understand.

It seemed so clear here:

Harold didn't love her. Chris would never walk again. Vanessa would leave him eventually.

Good, she thought. It was better to know these things. Was it really?

"All right," Sister Turner said, raising her hands. "'O Happy Day.' Sopranos only. One two three four."

Yes. The time for lying was over. No more of this go-along-to-get-along mess.

She turned her head and there was the bridge, solid as fact. It did seem special now, different, though she couldn't pick out anything specific. It held her eyes longer than she wanted, refused to let go, as if it might change, become something else, divulge another, deeper secret she needed.

The others were clapping, stomping their feet so the risers shook.

They could look all they wanted, she thought.

Their voices lifted, rich and filled with praise, making the bridge seem small and far away. She looked back, and there was Sister Turner stabbing a finger at her. Yes, her. She wanted to hear her, to see if she'd learned the hard part. She was testing everyone, digging for the weak spot like any good director. She raised her palm for more volume, cocked a hand to her ear, her face a question. The others were waiting, staying in rhythm, but softer, giving Jackie room, almost like a soloist.

What choice did she have?

She gathered her breath and sang.

GIANT STEPS

THEY CAN'T RIDE in the van with him, so Crest is alone again, Han Solo going into the deep freeze. Not alone alone, that would be too easy, they got him in with the old biddies, it's getting so he knows them — Miss Phillips locked in beside him, munching her gums like she's chewing a plug of Skoal, Mrs. Morris right up next to her, wheel to wheel, listening to her books on tape, the player making a munchkin voice in her earphones, Mrs. Mackey smiling away up front, pleased to see him. Crest sits his mirrors on the bridge of his nose and chills, arms folded, doing a Huey Newton. Smells like a drugstore exploded, every cleaner under the sink mixed together and then cat pee on top of that, a million dead anchovies left for a month in the sun. He's the only man (and half of one at that, he thinks), the only one not going back to the nursing home when this is over.

"Good morning, Chris," Mrs. Mackey says.

"Hey," he says, not too cool; he knows they don't go for that. He had a grandmother once, hasn't forgotten how she'd just glance at that willow switch and your calves would sting for a week. Could hit me all she wants now, he thinks.

Damn lift is still going down, Mr. Washington with his thumb on the button. He wears gloves to move their chairs, then takes them off when he drives, like he might catch something. Almost as old as the biddies, goofy white sideburns like he's fighting the Civil War, looking like Ossie Davis in *Do the Right Thing*, Da Mayor and shit. Drives slow as a mo too, makes Crest want to jump up front and commandeer the motherfucker, *Speed III*, baby.

Outside, they're looking through the door at him, Vanessa and Rashaan, Pops and U, waiting till he's all in. Go 'head, he wants to tell them, but they wait by the steps in their church clothes like it's his funeral, V silked to the bone in that black suit, looking like home cooking, hair done up in braids, little man stylin in his bow tie. They wait till Mr. Washington slips the pin in to secure the lift and thumps the double doors shut. Vanessa waves Rashaan's arm, and Crest waves back.

"That your little boy?" Mrs. Mackey asks. "He's a peanut."

"Precious," Miss Phillips says, "little, chile," smacking her wet lips between words, weighing and tasting each one before letting them go like they might be her last. They just might. Her hands shake when she picks them up from the armrests, wiggle like Ali's. He was going to put The Champ up, but now, with Martin Robinson dead, he's rethinking everything.

Vanessa told him this morning before church, quiet, like it was a secret and not the headline in today's *Post-Gazette.* She wanted him to be more upset, like he was the real Martin or something. He thought she was taking it too hard but didn't argue. Her mother had been on shift when it happened. They're all coming in her car, not that there's going to be parking. It's turned into a big thing, the dedication, a tribute to Martin Robinson.

That's what he wants the piece to be now, a tribute to those already gone, to the people that brought them here across the years, the ones that need to be remembered. He's had to rethink the whole scheme of the piece, move around names and faces, even leave spots blank for the time being. No Louis Farrakhan or Kordell Stewart, no Spike Lee and Michael Jordan. Let someone else remember them. He wants people who gave up something for the people. Everyone's going to be dead, like on the Vietnam Wall.

But The Champ, he thinks, The Champ took us a long way.

He'll go soon though. Have to leave room, put him up right by Nene whose Ali used to break everyone up. Dancing all stupid, whistling jabs, doing the rope-a-dope. *I'm sweet! I'm pretty! I'm a ba-a-a-d man!*

Put Bean off the other side of him, then someone big in the middle. Not Martin, not Malcolm. Martin Robinson? He'll have to read up on him, get Vanessa to help.

Things have been better between them lately, even though nothing's changed with him. Times he wants to say don't if it's just to cheer him up. But she's changed too, gone smart on him, talking all this college nonsense. U God-struck, Pops dressing up for church first time since Crest was a little kid—'s like everyone around him's on the pipe or something, Invasion of the Body Snatchers and shit.

Mr. Washington guns the van, leaving the key turned so the starter screeches, and everyone steps back. How he got the job Crest will never know. S'pose no one else wanted to drive the old biddies around.

"Hold on, ladies," Mr. Washington says, and now U and Pops wave too. Crest doesn't bother waving back. It's stupid, they're going to see him in ten minutes.

Off down Spofford, out from under the trees so the sun cuts in the window and hits his face. The brake's on, and his chair's clipped in; if they hit a telly pole and catch on fire they'll all be meat. Watching too much TV, he thinks, just like Moms says. Taking too many meds. It's not even fun anymore, that stand-still feeling the pills give him, like time is stuck right on him, locked on to that minute, and he can ride it, hold that note, keep that sweet feeling before it turns into shit again and someone has to remind him to empty his bag, change his bed for him, take him to the park like a dog. It's gone sour on him now so when that sweetness hits it's like it's already over, like he can see past it.

It's like his dreams, he thinks. He can walk, run, fuck. Not like he's the Six Million Dollar Man, but it's all right. Last night he was chasing flies through rooms, smashing them with superhuman accuracy. Waking up, he thought: Naw, not this shit again.

Think The Champ thinks that? Mrs. Mackey? He looks at Miss Phillips, her head bent over like a dead flower, and he doesn't know.

Left onto Taine past the Liberty Grill, brown and green beer bottles on the barred windowsills, a sagging plastic banner advertising ladies' night. He tries to picture his ladies in the Liberty, oiled up, wheeling around the pool table, packing the booths. Can't see himself in there either; he'd never get up the one step. Have to do his drinking in the park at a picnic table, nursing a 40 in a sack like Nene, like U before he cleaned up. His bag would be full before he even got a buzz on, nasty, all foaming and shit, no, he ain't going out like that.

It's bright outside, kind of day for a playoff game if the Pirates didn't get eliminated last week, cheap motherfuckers. (Roberto Clemente, definitely; Jackie Robinson he's not sure.) The Charlie Brown Halloween special's been on TNT twice so far, but it's still warm in the sun, the trees keeping their leaves. They all fall at once, he knows from raking Miss Fisk's yard, Bean and him getting paid ten dollars, going to the movies Saturday afternoon. Remembers seeing *Jurassic Park*, the two of them hiding behind the seats in front of them, watching Samuel L. Jackson with one eye, figuring he'd be killed, only brother in the picture. The whole Bellmawr booed too, knew it was a ripoff. Shit, you see *Juice*? Samuel L. Jackson is *bad*, I don't care, no old dinosaur gonna take him out.

Crest slips the temptation to think of Bean the same way, gives him a little juke, slick little stutter-step, and he's behind him and gone down the sideline. Only takes one step—like Wile E. Coyote going over the cliff and knowing it. Bean man, can you get to that step?

Now when I step up in the place, ay yo, I step correct. Woo-hah, woo-hah! I got you all in check.

Sometimes at night—okay, in the day too, you want to know the truth—Crest tries to move his toes. Stops what he's doing and concentrates on the big one on his right foot, thinks he remembers how to send a message to it. Move, you fucking piece of shit. The doctors have got to be wrong sometimes (like with his dick). He watches his clean Filas sitting on the footrests or his bare feet lying in the sheets, ashy ankles. The muscles in his head flex he's thinking so hard, he can feel them bunch up at his temples. Come on now, just a wiggle, it's not like he wants to pick up a sock with his toes. But he's got nothing, lets his breath out like he's exercising, the same noise he makes at therapy when old Willie Mays is working him hard. He can make his own lunch now if Moms didn't leave him one every day. He can find a job in computers. He can do anything.

This kind of shit isn't getting him anywhere, mize well be dreaming about some dumb flies, so he watches East Liberty roll by slow outside, Mr. Washington coasting light to light on Highland, past the black iron fence of the seminary with the spikes on top to keep people out. Remembers the time Bean and him—

But everything's a Bean story, if you let it. Like the two of them are everywhere here, sometime in their life. Street corner, cemetery, Original Hot Dog Stand. Sometime today, two, three times maybe, Crest knows he's going to see Bean's name and his own up on a wall, the side of a truck, an overpass, a billboard, and he'll remember how it was to run down the train tracks with his pack on, Krylons dinging, climbing the rusty fence behind the tool and die at night, a barb catching the cuff of his jeans, his fingers all cut up the next morning, burning when he soaps them in the shower. Remember how they'd race to see who could tag a new section of fence or fresh-painted wall first, or just a clean bus window, slashing that candy with his purple Mean Streaks. Search and destroy, boy. The feel of shingles slanting under his Filas. The view of Highland Park from the roof of the projects. The way paint sticks to concrete. How pressure-treated lumber sucks. The full bathtub sound of the water tower when you bump against it. The smell that gets you high so the big pieces seem better than they really are at the end. All of it will dump on him like a flood, and he'll just sit there and let it, like watching a rerun. Fuck's the point?

"Look," Mrs. Mackey says.

He's heard they're tearing down Sears, now here it is, a skeleton blocked off from the street by a wall of plywood. No one's touched it, or just a weak blast from EYZ, some punk he doesn't know. Y'ain't fadin nothin over here with that shit. From the jump he's thinking horizontal, killing, what to fill the space with — a worm, a train, a bus — and how to fuck with this trick-ass EYZ, fit them into the mix, make them just a reflection in the eye of a snake, a face in a cage. Damn, it's the right height too, he could do it from the chair, and the waste of it hits him.

"I used to work there," Mrs. Mackey says to everyone — really to Crest, because Miss Phillips is nodding off,

Mrs. Morris deep into her story, the little voice going on like infinity. "In pets."

"I used to go there all the time," Crest says, trying to remember a pet department, a solid wall of fish tanks and guinea pigs. One thing he's learned from riding the van: Old people will make stuff up on you when there's no way to check it. All he remembers is the escalators, the smell of the perfume counter, the stiff Toughskins Moms made him try on.

"Everyone did," Mrs. Mackey says. "I don't know why they have to tear it down."

Because it's old, Crest wants to say. Because no one goes there anymore. Look across the street, all the store-fronts are for lease except the laundromat, and there's no one in there, the doors from the dryers hanging open in a line. Busted windows, signs for old GOING OUT OF BUSINESS SALES, MADAME WALKER'S BEAUTY PRODUCTS. The Kroger's closed up; in summer they use the parking lot for the flea market. Everything's down the mall now.

"I don't know," Crest says.

"Well I think it's a shame," she says, and he agrees, for real. A tight squeeze, but he can see how he'd do the ugly blue tower in between Little Nene and George Jackson. And what about Kroger's? The Original Hot Dog Stand. The Bellmawr, a total crack spot now, smelling of piss and pigeon shit, waiting for some rock star with a torch to burn it down around him. Crest tries to think who's still up, who's dead. Arthur Ashe, Sojourner Truth. U's showed him a picture of the wall where the plaque's supposed to go, but Crest needs to see what kind of room he's got to work with. He's greedy, he wants the Bellmawr now, for Bean.

So this is a scout, basically. It's not the only reason he's going, but it's the one he tells himself. He's seen Moms sing, just saw Vanessa yesterday. He doesn't know Martin Robinson besides his picture in the *Courier*. It's not like he wants to go back and peep the place, lay a bouquet of flowers or anything. He doesn't have to go anywhere to see Bean, he's with him all the time, can't get a second away from him. Won't till he gets him up, nothing superstitious about it either.

Just like the Vietnam Wall, finally give these people their props. Makes sense, since it's a war.

Traffic backs up as they come around the circle. He can see police up ahead at the top of the exit, a big crowd gathered around. Probably frisking people. Smooth got his car shot up yesterday in Garfield; he's fine but that hooptie of his is looking strictly pitiful, mize well stick a target on it. As they nose closer, Crest sees the cops are all brothers and sisters, a smart move after what they did to Little Nene. Johnny Gammage, he's up. They're making folks unzip backpacks and flip open the lids of coolers. It's like a carnival. The WAMO van is handing out balloons, and there's Tony's truck three deep with kids. Mr. Washington tries to slide over to the curb, but people are streaming between the cars, families coming straight from late church, gussied up, bonnets and fedoras like the forties. Dudes macking against the fence, checking out all the sisters. Damn, girl, who fried that hair? There's Cardell fronting hard as always in a pair of mirrors just like his, Fats right beside him, looking like Biggie in his leather jacket and cap.

He'll get Biggie and Tupac together, East meets West.

Marvin Gaye, no doubt about it.

Medgar Evans.

Goddamn, seems all the best ones are dead—cept The Champ. Champ just gonna have to wait.

Mr. Washington grinds the hubcap along the curb like the *Titanic* so everyone stares at the van. Jumps out and comes around. When he opens the door, Al Green is singing and a rush of barbecue smoke just crushes the stink, and breakfast seems like yesterday. One of those Colemans bopping around in a T-shirt that says *Property of Jesus*, a balloon tied to his wrist. Ay, Crest wants to call out, waving an Abe, ay little man, go get me some of that Q. But there's a spread waiting at home, he knows, smothered chicken and macaroni, homemade potato salad, Moms went all out.

Ladies first. Vanessa is waiting there with her mother, and Al Green's singing *Hay-ay-ay-ay-ay-ay-ay, let's stay toge-thuh-uh-huh, lovin you-ou whe-thuh-uh,* and then Mr. Washington fucks it up by getting the lift stuck halfway, and everyone walking by pinning him like he can't see. Fuck you looking at? Like he's Roy Campanella and shit. Is Teddy Pendergrass dead yet? Pops and U each take an arm and muscle the chair down. They leave Mr. Washington still punching the buttons like that'll fix it.

There's the bridge. From this angle he can't see if their piece is still on it. He can remember if he chooses to, it's not like he's forgotten anything.

The ladies all have pushers, but Crest doesn't want one. A Port Authority guy with a walkie-talkie leads them down the exit ramp, saying there's a space up front for them. At

home his chair is fast, knocking into the frigerator before
he can stop it, but now, going downhill, it seems slow. His
face is level with everyone else's stomach, which is okay with
Vanessa, but . . . It's been a while since he's seen this many
white folks in East Liberty. He's afraid of running into
people, clipping their Achilles tendons with his footrests.
"Comin' through," the PAT guy says, and people turn and
look down, surprised, giving him that I'm sorry vibe he
hates.

"Sorry," Crest says, secretly replacing the footrests with
buzz saws like on the Mach 5. Out the fucking way.

And boo-yah, there it is, BEAN in wildstyle on a
Penndot water truck, blowing up like nitro. Shoulda known
he'd represent. Shit is raw. Crest remembers doing the other
side, the two of them walking around it to check each other's
pieces. Beam me up, Bean, it's your world.

But it's not. It's just his now.

Down on the road things clear out a little, and he can
see they've erased their piece, buffed Kenny's weak shit too.
The bridge is clean all the way across, and the walls as far as
he can see. It's his. He wants to pop out of his chair and start
mobbing, burn the motherfucker up, MDP back in effect.
Instead, one front wheel gets hung up on a reflector cemented
into the middle line, and his chair tips, he leans to regain his
balance, and only Vanessa saves him from going over.

"I'm all right," he says, slapping at her hands, but V's
on override, straight ice. Girl got it going on in that suit.
Why's she still with him, just because of Rashaan? She
knows she got his nose open and there's nothing he can do
for her.

They've sprayed the mud with something green, but the smell comes through, reminds him of that night, the road hard on his cheek as he lay there. The police said someone heard him screaming, but he doesn't remember it, only the cold, the sound the rain made on the concrete.

Cardell shows up beside him, leans in to give him a grip—straight, not Trey, cause U's right behind him. "S'up, man."

"You know," Crest says, "just kickin it."

"A'ight," Cardell says, "keep it real," drops a nod to Pops and U and Vanessa before he jets. For some reason it makes Crest feel better; he never thought Cardell was like that, but he is.

Up front, the choir's already onstage. The curtain behind them's nearly the exact size of the piece. He's got it gridded out at home like Michelangelo, broken into squares a yard long. From here it doesn't seem like enough room if he's going to do buildings too. Maybe just Sears and the Bellmawr. Maybe he doesn't need Marvin Gaye.

Fuck yeah he needs Marvin.

John Coltrane.

Miles Davis.

Billy Strayhorn, who grew up right here. Billy Eckstine too, and Romare Bearden. (See, now he's dropping some knowledge on y'all.)

The TV people have run a bundle of cables across the aisle and he needs Pops to wheelie him over it. Keep moving.

James Baldwin, a beautiful dead motherfucker. And Thelonious Monk, another one.

On the way they run into Miss Fisk, all done up with
this shoebox-looking hat with a veil on it. She's wearing
gloves and carrying an old funeral-home fan with JFK and
Martin Luther King on it. Vanessa's mother hugs her, then
wipes at her eyes with a tissue. Vanessa gives her a kiss and
hands her Rashaan. He clings to Miss Fisk, gives her some
sugar too, and they all coo over him, then laugh at their
harmony.

"Chris," she says, taking his hand. Her gloves are soft,
and she squeezes his fingers gently, like they might break.
She holds on to him, doesn't let go. "I haven't seen much of
you."

"I don't think I can get up your steps." But it's too late
to make like he doesn't understand. They both know. Why
can't he just say he's sorry, let it go at that?

"Maybe I could bring Rashaan around during the day,
if you'd like that."

"It's not like I'm going anywhere."

"All right," she says, like it's a deal, and takes her hand
back.

They keep inching toward the front, where the rows
of folding chairs give way to a roped-off swath of green dirt.
The PAT guy nearly has the ladies there. Crest imagines the
piece already done, that it's the reason everyone's here, the
big unveiling. They're going to do it even if they don't get
the money, U says, and Crest thinks that's better anyway.
They'll have to come down here at three in the morning,
undercover, sneak by the abandoned generators and graders and water trucks, work by moonlight. The other way's

fake, just another government okey-doke. They'd want it all don't-worry-be-happy and shit, uplifting, like that bogus grass they got going. Cardell's telling the truth, you got to keep it real, square business.

Gonna need like a hundred cans, all colors, and he can see Fats racking the whole display down at the True Value, old Poindexter boy frozen behind the counter, watching him walk out with it.

PATman comes back to block for them, and they get there. Crest picks a spot and they open the folding chairs around him. Vanessa's right by his side, Rashaan climbing on him, then back to her lap. Her mother's still sniffling and wiping her eyes. Pops and U are sitting on the other side of him, waving to Moms, who Crest finds in the front row of the choir like every Sunday, except Sister Payne isn't right beside her, just an empty space. He waves too, and Moms waves back.

They all talked about it earlier, when Moms was ironing. Sister Payne's dog died and she can't deal, so they invited her for lunch after; they're supposed to cheer her up—if she comes. No one's seen her all week. "Why doesn't she just get another dog?" Pops said, and Moms gave him a look that made him take it back. Crest thought it was good he apologized, that it meant things were better. Now U's the one who's worried about them, keeping his eye on Pops.

"Scuse me," U says, and gets up and walks off.

"Where's he going?" Pops asks no one, and Crest sees it's Nene's Granmoms a few rows over, wearing an armband for Martin Robinson. U sits with her, takes her hands. The other night when he said he was going to be a preacher, Crest

almost fell out his chair. And he'll do it too, Crest could see it
in him. Crest didn't need to come back and say he wanted to
be an artist, that Vanessa had convinced him to go back to
school; U's already working on a scholarship for him.

Onstage, the politicians come out to take their chairs,
and a buzz runs through the crowd. The mayor's there,
Valerie McDonald and some of the other city council mem-
bers, but the one people have come to see is the new congressman from Brushton, Somebody Armstrong, skinny
yellow dude in a big suit and glasses. No one goes to the
podium, they just sit there talking with each other. Behind
them, Sister Turner gets up, and the choir stands. The crowd
goes quiet, then claps along to start.

When they really sing, everyone stands up except
Vanessa, who smiles at him. He claps too, to show it's okay.
Her mother's stopped crying, slipping the tissue in her cuff
so she can sing. He's heard the song a hundred times and
lets his mind rest in the familiar lyrics, thinking how they'll
have to set the grid up, work from the top down. Put Bean
up first. Then how did he have it? He's stuck on the Bellmawr, and what to do with the train tracks they dug up to
build this. The wall's only about twenty feet. Maybe if he
scales down, makes everything a little smaller. Need to leave
room too. Can't freeze out The Champ.

Who really needs to be up?

First, everyone from the block. All the old heads:
Baconman, T-Pop and Marcus. BooBoo. Bean. Nene and
Little Nene. All the ones they lost.

There's more, he just can't think of them with the curtain in the way, like it's hiding the piece it's going to be, the

piece it already is under there, like the plywood in front of Sears turning into the snake or the train. He can almost see the colors burning through the curtain, the faces and names. It's so strong he wants to start now. These people need to remember.

He watches Pops swaying, watching Moms. Can't sing a lick but he tries. Makes Crest think of church a long time ago, U pinching him through his good suit, trying to make him cry. Those hard shoes could put a dent in your shins. He looks over at U singing with Nene's Granmoms and wonders how they all got here, where they're going to go. He sees faces he doesn't know, people he thinks he recognizes just to see. All of East Liberty's here, and some of Homewood too, Lincoln-Larimer, Morningside, even people come up from Oakland and the Hill to say good-bye to Martin Robinson, and looking at the crowd around him in the bright sunlight, Crest wants to do a piece with everyone in it.

The next one, he thinks. He's still got to figure this one out.

The song finishes and everyone sits down and folds their hands. They're ready to hear some speeches, some big-time testifying. They've heard one sermon today, most of them, so whoever gets up there had better flow like Brother Ike, blow heavy or sit their tired ass down. Except the mayor, of course, he doesn't count, being a white boy.

Crest doesn't even listen to them, doesn't have to to know what they're saying. Their voices echo off the concrete. It's what they're *not* saying, who they're *not* talking about that he's thinking of. He's already putting together that second piece, peeking around the crowd at the little kids bouncing on their chairs, making paper airplanes of their programs, the mothers and fathers who came straight from church, who've got to wake up early for work tomorrow. Looks around, doesn't see anyone famous here, no Julian Bonds or Shirley Chisholms, no Paul Robesons, just folks, everyday people.

But that's next. First the dead, then the living. Got to know what you lost to know what you got.

They sing another song, and then Senator Armstrong's the last one up. He takes the longest, and he's weak, reading his speech off a bunch of index cards, zero flow, standing stiff between the flags. The other ones have said everything already, and no one murmurs and nods when he tells anything close to the truth, no church ladies call out, "A-men!" or "Yes, Jesus!" or "Praise God!"

It needs the firehouse, Crest thinks. The old city swimming pool they called the Inkwell.

Sister Payne's little dog.

His own legs.

Someone's balloon flies off to the sky, but he doesn't hear anyone crying. In a minute it's just a dot, then gone.

It's all about Bean—still. Always will be.

"And so it is with great pride," Senator Armstrong says, "that I ask you to join me in dedicating the Martin Robinson Memorial Express Busway."

He lifts his arm as the curtain behind him pulls up on wires, and the choir breaks into "O Happy Day."

Everyone rises except Crest. Everyone cheers. For a second he can't see, only Vanessa beside him with Rashaan, her mother, Pops, U still with Nene's Granmoms. And then he can.

The wall beneath the curtain isn't his piece, a song for everyone they've lost, so true and brilliant that people weep, but bare concrete gray as tablet paper, a shit-ass little brass plaque about halfway up. Pretty much what he expected. He's not disappointed, Crest says to himself. No, it's only now, with the blank wall in front of him, with the crowd around him, that he sees how it's all going to fit.

OUTBOUND

THE BUSWAY'S DOING East Liberty just the way everyone said
it would, keeping people out, keeping business from coming
in. Oh, we've got the Home Depot but none of the real money
from it. Put an apron on you so you can make change, lift the
heavy shit, sweep up before going home. And you know
Nabisco's closed down now. Still no new community center,
no plans for it either. Congressman Armstrong's turning con-
servative on you. Lives in Harrisburg, worries about the fi-
nancial crisis in Thailand. Traffic's nice and light though.

The young people go the way they've been going, most
of them. The old people keep off the streets, think they're
all gone crazy on drugs. Get a shooting or two every month,
fires in the winter, slow emergency-response times. Go to
all the open meetings and protest, but the city says it doesn't
have enough money to tear down the empty buildings.

They didn't have money for Chris's masterpiece either,
but they spend enough trying to make it go away. Sandblast-
ing, steamcleaning. They're down there all the time, and then

the next week it's back up, courtesy of the MDP. Even tried this special Teflon concrete from L.A. The thing grows. People call it The Wall. It's turned into a kind of tourist attraction. Last week there was a TV crew from Germany shooting it. People are hoping all the attention will keep the city from painting it over. Whitewash is the only thing that works. It's turned into a big censorship thing, letters in the *Post-Gazette.*

But that's the whole thing: It's the city against East Liberty, against the people. It's old-style redlining, divide and conquer, nothing new. They'd like you to just shut up, go away, and The Wall says that's not gonna happen. It's a flag waving in their face. You like seeing it, like we're getting over somehow.

Sometimes The Wall glows in the dark. When it rains the colors shine brighter. People say you can see Martin Robinson crying, and at night they say Malcolm bleeds. Folks go down and touch it, leave things, notes and such, pictures of loved ones. It's not enough but it's something. You're never going to get a square deal, not in this city.

The buses come through every morning, full of people with good jobs, homes in the suburbs, country clubs, health insurance—some of them brothers and sisters afraid to look back, thinking how they'll get dragged down. From the busway they can't see the streets, only the walls rising on both sides, just the tip of a steeple. They're blind all the way in, like a lab rat stuck in a maze, glass skyscrapers downtown their big piece of cheese. When they hit East Liberty and see The Wall, you think they even notice?

Maybe, but what do they see? To them it's a curiosity, a little bit of homespun culture. Seen it written up in the paper. Or maybe it's a landmark, a number on a clock, a way to count how much longer to downtown. Better drink up that cup.

But more likely, that time of day they don't see anything, too busy following the stock market. They're thinking about what's on TV, what kind of car they want, how they didn't get enough sleep last night. Pushing sixty, the bus blasts past a blur of color, a jumble of faces they don't know, the letters illegible, different, hieroglyphic, the whole thing in code. And even if they could make out the names and faces, they'd be missing the history behind them, the meaning each of them carries, the price they paid.

None of them waits for it every day, not one out of a thousand turns sideways in their seat to pick out the few celebrities among the dead: Alex Haley—and there, lookit, it's Charlie Parker. None of them can read the names of the other ones, not as famous, in fact almost totally unknown, yet still remembered, honored like the rest. They don't know East Liberty, so the best they could come up with, even if they cared, would be ill-informed stories, pat tragedies in blackface. Maybe some of them—riding in, going home in the rain—see the flash of color flying by outside the window and marvel at the artwork, wonder what's being celebrated here. Maybe for a split second they see what you see, the dreams of a people that will not be denied, the sacrifices made in the name of progress, but that's just easy public-TV jive. No one wants to go beyond their own feel-good bullshit. No one wants to know what it really means. No one sees the three new faces one day and asks: Who is Fats? Who is Smooth? Who is Eugene?